'You can't just forget the past.'

Suddenly Tiffany's throat constricted and she wanted to call back the words, but it was too late.

'It would be better if we could sometimes,' J.D. said, and she knew in a heartbeat that he, too, was fighting unwanted memories; forbidden, painful recollections of something that, if acknowledged, would only cause more hurt. 'It's a tough load. Teenage boy, little girl, part-time job and running this place.'

'Not a problem, J.D. Well, at least not yours.' Tiffany forced a confident smile. No reason for him, or any of the Santini family, for that matter, to know of her troubles.

'It looks like you could use a man around here.'

'Excuse me?' she said. 'A man? Let's get one thing straight, J.D. I *don't* need a man. Not now. Not ever. I—we're—just fine.'

'Are you?'

Dear Reader

Welcome to August's fabulous line-up and what better way to start than with superstar author Nora Roberts! Her famous family **The MacGregors** are back. In *The Winning Hand*, Darcy Wallace goes from being a pauper to a millionaire in an instant—and runs into seductive Robert MacGregor Blade. There's more from this author to look forward to this year—look out for *The MacGregor Grooms*, expected in October!

This month we're also starting a delightful new trilogy, **Prescription: Marriage**, with *From House Calls to Husband*. Three nurses vow *never* to marry doctors—but find it hard to keep their word… And Barbara Bretton brings us a heroine who falls for her pilot after a plane crash!

Tiffany Santini is trying to stop powerful lawyer J.D. from playing 'knight in shining armour' in Lisa Jackson's *A Family Kind of Girl*. And another determined heroine won't let a *Prenuptial Agreement* stand in the way of true love. Finally, catch up with those **Big Apple Babies**, in the last part of the series from Jule McBride.

Happy reading!

The Editors

A Family Kind of Girl

LISA JACKSON

SILHOUETTE

SPECIAL EDITION®

To Mum and Dad
You are the best.

*Silhouette, Silhouette Special Edition and Colophon are
registered trademarks of Harlequin Books S.A., used under licence.*

*First published in Great Britain 1999
Silhouette Books, Eton House, 18-24 Paradise Road,
Richmond, Surrey TW9 1SR*

© Susan Crose 1998

ISBN 0 373 24207 7

23-9908

*Printed and bound in Spain
by Litografia Rosés S.A., Barcelona*

LISA JACKSON

has been writing romance novels for over ten years. With more than thirty Silhouette® novels to her credit, she divides her time between writing on the computer, researching her next novel, keeping in touch with her college-age sons and playing tennis. Many of the fictitious small towns in her books resemble Molalla, Oregon, a small logging community where she and her sister, Silhouette author Natalie Bishop, grew up.

Other novels by Lisa Jackson

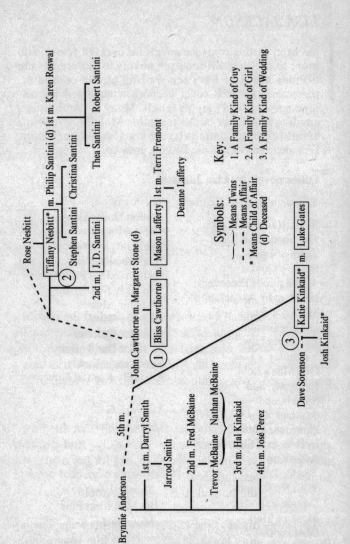

Brynnie Anderson

- - - 5th m.

1st m. Darryl Smith
  Jarrod Smith

2nd m. Fred McBaine
  Trevor McBaine ⎫
  Nathan McBaine ⎭

3rd m. Hal Kinkaid

4th m. José Perez

Rose Nesbitt

Tiffany Nesbitt* m. Philip Santini (d) 1st m. Karen Roswal
  Stephen Santini
  2nd m. J. D. Santini
  Christina Santini
  Thea Santini   Robert Santini

②

John Cawthorne m. Margaret Stone (d)

① Bliss Cawthorne   m.   Mason Lafferty   1st m. Terri Fremont
                                              Deanne Lafferty

Dave Sorenson   Katie Kinkaid*   m.   Luke Gates
  Josh Kinkaid*

③

Key:
1. A Family Kind of Guy
2. A Family Kind of Girl
3. A Family Kind of Wedding

Symbols:
—— Means Twins
- - - Means Affair
* Means Child of Affair
(d) Means Deceased

Chapter One

So this was the place.

With a jaundiced eye, J. D. Santini studied the immense house with its apron of drying lawn and Apartment for Rent sign posted near the street where he'd parked. Gray clapboard accented with bay windows, black trim and a smattering of white gingerbread, this was where Tiffany had run.

Wonderful. Just damned great.

His gut clenched and he told himself that he wasn't throwing her out of her home. Not really. And certainly not right away. What he was doing was for her own good. In her kids' best interests.

Then why did he feel like Benedict Arnold?

"Hell."

Pocketing his keys, he climbed out of his Jeep. The dry heat of southern Oregon in mid-July hit him square in the face.

Bittersweet. A fitting name for the town, he thought; as good a destination as any if a person wanted to turn tail and run. Which is what she'd done.

His jaw clenched when he thought of her. Tiffany Nesbitt Santini. Sister-in-law. Gold digger. *Lover.*

Damn, he hated this.

Get over it, Santini. What did you expect when you took the job with the old man? You dived headfirst into this mess and your eyes were wide-open.

He reached into the back seat of his Jeep Cherokee for his beat-up duffel bag and briefcase.

It was now or never.

Damn, but ''never'' sounded appealing.

His leg still pained him when he walked, but he hitched the strap of his bag over his shoulder and made his way up a brick walk that needed more than its share of new mortar.

He tried not to notice the crumbling caulking around the windows and the trickle of rust that colored the downspouts as he climbed the two steps to the front door.

This house and its sad need of repair are not your problem.

Right, and the Pope wasn't Catholic.

Everything Tiffany did affected him. Whether he wanted it to or not. She was the widow of his brother, mother of his niece and nephew, and the only woman whom he'd never been able to forget.

And trouble. Don't forget the kind of trouble she is.

He jabbed on the bell, heard the chimes peel softly from the interior and waited impatiently. What could he say to her? That, unbeknown to her, he owned part of this old house, because her dead husband, his older brother, had been an inveterate gambler? That he thought it would be better if she sold the place, bought something newer and more modern, that it would be best if the kids were…what? Moved again? Uprooted to live close to the Santini enclave? He snorted at that thought. For years he'd avoided being roped into the tight-knit-to-the-point-of-strangulation clan, but then he was a man. It was different for him, wasn't it? He didn't have kids.

A black cat darted through the shadows of overgrown rhododendrons and azaleas. Footsteps dragged through the house and the door was opened just a crack.

"Yeah?" Suspicious thirteen-year-old eyes peered out at him through the slit.

"Stephen?"

The eyes narrowed. "Who're you?"

J.D. felt a shaft of guilt. The kid didn't even recognize him. That wasn't Stephen's fault so much as it was his. "I'm your uncle."

"Uncle? You mean—?"

"J.D."

"Oh." Stephen's voice cracked and his skin, olive in tone, was instantly suffused with color. A flicker of recognition flashed in his eyes. He opened the door farther, standing aside as J.D. hitched his way into the foyer.

"What happened to your leg?"

"An accident. Motorcycle. The bike won."

"Yeah?" Stephen's eyes gleamed and the hint of a smile slid over his lips. He would be a good-looking kid in a few years, but right now he was a little rough around the edges. Soon his jaw would become more defined and his face would catch up with his nose. The boy reminded J.D. of himself and his own misdirected youth. "You've got a motorcycle?" Stephen asked, obviously awed.

"I did. It's in the shop."

"What kind?"

"A Harley."

"Cool."

He couldn't have impressed the kid more if he'd claimed to be a millionaire. "It doesn't look so cool now. Funny what plowing into a tree does to a bike."

Stephen managed the ghost of a smile. J.D. noted that Stephen's black hair was shaggy, his brown eyes filled with distrust, and his muscles so tense that J.D. half expected him to make a run for it at any moment.

"Is your mother here?"

The kid's gaze fell to the floor and he seemed to be studying the intricate floral patterns of a throw rug at the foot of the stairs. "She's...she's not around right now."

"She's in jail!" a little voice chirped from the landing. A pixieish face, pink-cheeked and surrounded with black curls, was stuck through two balusters.

"What?"

Stephen shot his sister a killing look. "Hush, Chrissie."

Jail? J.D. eyed the boy. "What's she talking about?"

"Nothin', Chrissie doesn't know what she's talkin' about."

"Do too!" the imp retorted indignantly.

Stephen worried his lip for a second, then shrugged, as if he didn't care one way or the other. "Okay. Mom's down at the police station."

"Why?"

"Dunno," he mumbled, obviously lying. "I just got stuck baby-sitting."

"I'm *not* a baby!" Christina dashed down the stairs on her chubby legs. The blue-black curls bounced and her eyes were wide with wonder.

"You're here alone?" he asked.

"Ellie's downstairs." Christina dashed across the hall and through a swinging door leading into the kitchen.

"Who's Ellie?"

"Mrs. Ellingsworth." Stephen shifted uncomfortably from one foot to the other. "She lives in one of the apartments downstairs and when Mom has to work, Ellie looks after Chrissie."

"And you?"

Stephen's spine stiffened. "I don't need a baby-sitter."

This was getting him nowhere fast. J.D. set his bag and briefcase onto the floor. "So...when will your mom be back?" Something was up—something the kid didn't want him to know about.

"Dunno. Soon, I guess." Stephen was prickly, but must have heard the rudeness in his voice because he added, "You can, uh, wait for her here or in the parlor, if ya want...or—"

Christina barreled out of the kitchen and ran to one of the narrow, beveled-glass windows flanking the front door. "Mommy!" she cried with delight. She threw open the door and raced down the steps.

J.D. turned and saw Tiffany climbing out of a sedan she'd parked in the shaded driveway.

Tall and slim, with shoulder-length black hair that framed an oval face, she was more than attractive; she was downright gorgeous, the kind of woman who expected and received more than her share of male attention.

"A male magnet," his mother used to say.

Folding some papers into an oversize bag, she looked up, saw Christina flying across the yard and offered her daughter a smile that froze as her gaze landed directly on J.D. Her eyes, a gold color J.D. had always found disturbing, hardened and the skin stretched taut over her high cheekbones was suddenly suffused with color. "Hi, honey!" she said to her daughter as she scooped the three-year-old up from the ground.

"Lookie who's here."

"I see." She seemed to steel herself in her sleeveless white blouse, still crisply pressed and stark against her tanned skin. She walked toward the front door and the slit in her khaki-colored skirt moved enough to show off her long, well-muscled legs.

Yep. There was a reason his divorced brother had fallen so hard and fast for Tiffany Nesbitt. The same reason that had nearly done J.D. in. Nearly.

From the foyer, Stephen cleared his throat. His voice cracked again. "Mom... Er, Mom, Uncle J.D. is here."

"So I see." She lifted a finely arched brow. White lines of irritation bracketed her lips. "Jay."

"Tiff." His damned pulse elevated a fraction.

"Looks like your timing is impeccable as always," she said with more than a trace of sarcasm.

"What's going on here?" J.D. asked.

Still carrying her daughter, she walked into the house and shut the door. "A misunderstanding."

"With the police?"

"The juvenile authorities," she corrected, her gaze skating to her son for an instant before returning to J.D. She flashed him a look that warned him not to dive too deeply into these murky waters. Whatever was going on, it was serious. Christina wriggled and Tiffany set her daughter on the floor. "You know, J.D., of all the people I expected to run into today, you're the last."

"I should have called."

She lifted a shoulder as if she didn't give a damn, but barely restrained fury snapped in her eyes. "Not your style."

His jaw tightened, but he supposed he deserved the blow. "No."

Stephen glanced up through the shaggy bangs. "I'm takin' off. Me and Sam are goin' fishin' and swimmin'."

"Sam and I," Tiffany corrected as if on automatic pilot. "You're supposed to be grounded."

"I thought we had a deal." Stephen rubbed his nose with the back of his hand. "I did all the chores and my homework."

"Isn't school out for the year?" J.D. asked.

Tiffany shot him another harsh glance. "Summer school."

"Yeah, and it's dumb," Stephen grumbled. "Look, I just want to go swimmin'."

Tiffany glanced at her watch. She looked about to argue with the boy, then thought better of it. Probably because J.D. had shown up. "Okay. But be back by five."

"Ah, Mom. Come on, it's summer—"

"Five or don't go at all," she said firmly.

Stephen obviously wanted to take her on but thought better of it and chewed on the corner of his lip instead.

In J.D.'s opinion, the odds were better than ten to one that the kid wouldn't make curfew. He knew what the boy was thinking; he'd been there.

"And your room is clean?"

"Clean enough."

"Stephen," she reproached gently.

"Clean enough for me and it's my room, okay?" He was already through the front door and grabbing a beat-up skateboard that was propped against the side of the house. The board sported peeling decals of what J.D. assumed were the names of alternative rock bands. "I'll see ya later."

"Five. Remember."

"Yeah, yeah."

Watching him leave, Tiffany worried her lower lip between her teeth. "Teenagers," she said in a tone so low he almost didn't hear the concern in her voice.

J.D. didn't blame her for being apprehensive. Stephen needed to be sat down on, and hard. The kid had an attitude and it wasn't going to get any better over the next couple of years.

Sighing softly, Tiffany shook her head as if she were having a private conversation with herself and losing. Badly.

"Since you're here, I assume you wanted to see me."

He tensed at her choice of words.

"Come into the kitchen," she said curtly. "Christina, you, too." Sandals clicking in agitation, she marched down the hallway, throwing herself through the pair of swinging doors.

J.D. hauled his bags with him and followed, catching one of the doors as it swung back at him. The kitchen was at the back of the house and looked like something out of *Better Homes and Gardens*. Sunlight spilled through the windows, giving the room a warm, golden glow. Shining pots and pans hung from the ceiling over a center island while bundles of fragrant herbs, suspended from hooks, scented the air. The refrigerator was adorned with a three-year-old's artwork, notes about repairs that needed to be done to the house, and emergency phone numbers.

Homey.

Charming.

And as phony as a three-dollar bill.

Tiffany reached into the windowsill for a bottle of aspirin and shook two white tablets into her hand.

"Headache?"

"At least." She turned on the tap, grabbed a glass from a nearby cabinet, filled it and tossed the pills and a huge gulp of water down her throat. "Now, what is it you want, Jay?"

J.D. set his bags on the floor and leaned a hip against

one of the cupboards. A needle of guilt pricked his conscience as he thought about the deed to this house tucked into a pocket of his duffel bag. As much as he disliked Tiffany Nesbitt Santini, he didn't relish adding to her problems.

"There must be something. You didn't drive all the way down here from Portland just to say hello."

"No, but I did come to see you."

He noticed the slight catch of her breath, the widening of her eyes, but the look of anticipation was quickly masked. "Why do I have a feeling this isn't going to be something I want to hear?"

An older woman wearing oversize coveralls, a straw hat and gardening gloves appeared at the back door. Sunglasses covered her eyes and in one hand she held clippers and a bouquet of roses.

"I thought I heard voices," she said as she shouldered open the screen door. She stopped short at the sight of J.D. "Oh, I didn't know you had company."

"Roberta Ellingsworth, this is my brother-in-law, J.D. Santini."

"Pleased to meet you." J.D. offered his hand.

The woman chuckled as she, still holding the roses, extended her gloved fingers.

"You, too. Call me Ellie. Everyone does."

"Ellie, then," J.D. replied.

"I brought these in for you," she said to Tiffany as she released J.D.'s hand.

Tiffany was already reaching for a vase. "Thanks. They're lovely."

"I helped pick them!" Christina announced.

"That you did, honey," Ellie acknowledged, handing Tiffany the roses and winking at the little girl. "You were a big help."

"So were you," Tiffany said, sniffing the fragrant blooms. "Thanks for pinch-hitting with the kids."

"Any time, honey, any time."

"Would you like something to drink? I've got iced tea or coffee—"

"Oh, not right now, but I'll take a rain check," the older woman said, wiping her brow and lifting her sunglasses as if to peer at the strange man in Tiffany's kitchen more closely. "It's about time for my program." Her eyebrows rose a fraction as she looked at J.D. "I try not to miss my soap."

Tiffany grinned and her eyes sparkled with sudden merriment. "Don't tell me—Derek's evil twin has kidnapped him and is going to marry Samantha in his place."

Ellie laughed. "Close enough, honey, close enough. On 'This Life Is Mine' you never know what can happen. I'll see you later." She was peeling off her gardening gloves. "Nice meeting you," she said to J.D. before leaving.

"My pleasure." J.D. watched her slowly descend the steps, then round the corner to disappear from sight.

"Ellie watches the kids for me when I'm at work, and believe me, she's an absolute godsend," Tiffany said, her smile fading a bit, and then, as if she'd belatedly realized that she'd been a little blunt earlier, she added, "So how about you? I've got coffee or iced tea."

He shook his head.

"Something stronger?"

"Later, maybe."

"Later?" she asked, her gaze moving to his duffel bag and her eyes narrowing enough that he noticed the curl of her eyelashes. "Don't tell me you're planning on staying?"

"For a while."

She tensed. "How long a while?"

"Till I accomplish what I set out to do."

"Don't talk to me in riddles, okay?" She arranged the roses in the vase, added water and set the bouquet in the center of the old table. Christina hovered near the back door. "Can I do drawing?" she asked.

"Great idea," her mother replied, wiping her hands on a kitchen towel. She reached for a pack of crayons on the counter, only to have her daughter turn up her little pug nose.

"I want to draw outside!"

"Outside?"

"With the chalk."

"Why not?" Tiffany scrounged in a drawer filled with cards, pencils, keys, batteries—anything a person could imagine—until she came up with a box of colored chalk.

Beaming, Christina snagged the prize from her mother's outstretched hand and scurried out the back door. The screen slammed behind her as she rushed to plant herself on the cracked concrete patio, upon which she began to doodle in pink, yellow, green and blue.

Tiffany watched her daughter until she was engrossed in her task, then turned to face J.D. "So, *brother-in-law,* to what or to whom do we owe the honor of your presence?" she demanded, then shook her head at the question. "No—" she held out her hand as if to ward off his words "—let me guess. You're here on a mission. Just checking up on your brother's widow. Trying to figure out if she really is the right kind of mother to raise Philip's kids."

She'd always been smart. Calculating. He leaned a hip against the center island. "I'm here on business." That wasn't a lie. Well, not much of one.

"Sure. That's why you're standing in my kitchen. With your bag. Come on, Jay, you can do better than that." She closed the short distance between them and a hint of her perfume teased his nostrils. It was the same fragrance she'd worn the last time he'd seen her. Touched her. He gritted his teeth and decided it was time to take the offensive.

"Before we get into all that, why don't you explain what you were doing with the juvenile authorities."

"I don't really think it's any of your business."

"Isn't it?"

"I can handle my children," she said with a cold smile. "No matter what the rest of the Santini family thinks." With a quick glance through the screen door to assure herself that her daughter was safely out of earshot, she lowered her voice. "I *know* what your father thought of me when I met Philip. I *know* he tried to convince Philip that I was a no-good, gold-digging woman who was barely an adult, one who looked at Philip as a...a father figure," she said, pain sweeping through her eyes.

You don't know the half of it, he thought with another stab of guilt.

"And I heard that you tried to talk Philip out of marrying me."

The muscles in J.D.'s shoulders tensed. "Careful, Tiff," he said. "I had my reasons."

She flushed and her eyes sparked with anger. For a second he thought she might slap him. "None of them good, Jay," she said through lips that barely moved. "None of them good."

"Good, no. Valid, yes."

"Philip and I had a...a strong marriage." Her chin inched up a notch as if she dared him to challenge her.

"If it worked for you."

"It did."

He bit back a sharp retort and stared down at her. His gaze lingered on her lips for a second before lowering to the neckline of her blouse, where her skin was flushed with anger, her pulse leaping at the base of her throat. His bad knee throbbed, his stupid crotch was suddenly tight and he realized that he still wanted her. As he always had. Hell, what a mess.

"Mind if I sit down?" he asked, then didn't wait for an answer, but slid into one of the tall ladder-back chairs that flanked an old claw-footed table.

"Suit yourself." She ran stiff fingers through her hair, then seemed to realize she was being too defensive. Waving with one hand, as if to disperse the cloud of fury surrounding her, she said, "Come on, Jay. Why don't you tell me what you're doing down here? If it isn't to spy on me, there must be a reason. The last I heard, you hated all things that had to do with me or this town."

"Hate's a pretty strong word." But she was right. He didn't trust her and as far as Bittersweet, Oregon, went, he had plenty of reasons to despise this small town filled with small-minded citizens.

Folding her arms over her chest she lifted one delicately arched eyebrow, silently urging him on.

"As I said, I'm here on business."

"In Bittersweet?" She shoved a lock of blue-black hair from her eyes. "Don't tell me you chased an ambulance all the way from Portland down here."

That stung. "I left the firm."

"No way." She cocked her head as if she hadn't heard him correctly. "But I thought you were a partner."

"I was. Sold out."

"So," she encouraged, suddenly wary, "why?"

"Dad offered me a job with his company."

She laughed without a drop of mirth. "Come on. Don't give me that worn-out line about an offer you 'couldn't refuse,' Jay." She rolled her eyes. "Oh, this is rich. You with Santini Brothers. I never thought I'd see the day."

"Neither did I." He stretched his bad leg and rubbed at the pain in his knee through his jeans. "Since I was down here on business anyway, I thought I'd check up on you and the kids."

"Ah. As I suspected." Her shoulders slumped a bit and she looked at her nails. "Since when do you care?" she asked in a voice barely above a whisper.

She always had been forthright. Nearly to the point of being rude. Well, two could play that game. "I've always cared."

Her eyes darkened for a second. A shadow flickered in their whiskey-colored depths and the pulse in the hollow of her throat, above the deep V of her blouse, beat a fraction more rapidly. Hell, she was beautiful. No wonder his brother hadn't been able to resist her. Neither had he.

"So how have you and the kids been doing?"

"I already told you. We're fine."

"No problems?"

Her jaw tensed a bit. "None that we can't deal with, Jay," she said and wished he'd just disappear. She glanced out the window and spied Christina drawing stick figures on the walk. "You can tell your dad that we're doing fine. No, change that." She waved expansively. "Tell him we're great. Not a care in the world." She'd never gotten along with Philip's father, Carlo, nor with his mother, for that matter. As his second wife, so many years younger than her husband, Tiffany had been looked upon as a bimbo, a fraud, a little girl who didn't know her own mind and worst of all, as someone who was after all the Santini family's wealth. Considering the circumstances, all those thoughts were nothing but a cruel, ironic joke.

And what did J.D. care? When had he ever? Her heart pumped a little at the sight of him and she silently called herself an idiot. He was just as ruggedly male as she re-

membered him, with his long, jeans-clad legs, black hair
in need of a trim and penetrating silver-gray eyes.

"What about the juvenile authorities?"

Her fingers tightened into fists. "Don't worry about it."

His smile was cynical and downright sexy. If a woman
noticed. Tiffany told herself she didn't. She'd known
J.D.—James Dean Santini—too many years to trust him.
She'd let down her guard a couple of times and in both
instances she'd gotten herself into trouble—the worst kind
of jeopardy. It wouldn't happen again. Too much was at
stake.

"You know, Tiff, you're still a member of the family."

"Since when?" she retorted, skewering him with a look
that, she was certain, could kill. She pointed a long finger
at him. "I've *never* been considered a part of the family.
Over fourteen years of marriage and neither one of your
parents accepted me." *Nor did you,* she silently seethed,
but held her tongue. There had been enough pain borne
on both sides. She had always longed to be part of a real
family, one with a father and mother and siblings, unlike
her own small group of relatives. Shivering inwardly, she
pushed those thoughts aside and stubbornly refused to
think of them even though, at the end of this very week,
her father—her biological father, for that was all he really
was, a man who had donated his share of genes to her
DNA—was marrying his longtime mistress.

Wrapping her arms around her middle, she walked to
the window that overlooked the backyard. A smile teased
her lips as she watched her daughter.

Right now, the little girl was chasing after the cat, Charcoal, as he darted between the shrubs.

"What kind of trouble is Stephen getting himself into?"
J.D. persisted. She'd forgotten how determined and mad-
deningly single-minded her brother-in-law could be.

"Nothing that serious."

"Just serious enough that you had to talk with the authorities."

Silently counting to ten, she rotated her neck and worked out the kinks. "You know, J.D., the last thing I need right now is to be grilled or given some kind of lecture by you. I don't know why you've decided to come to visit right now, but I'm sure it wasn't just to harass me."

He snorted. "Just a simple question."

"Don't give me that. Nothing you've ever done is simple or without a purpose."

"And you're dodging the issue."

"Because it's none of your business, *counselor*."

"The kid's my nephew."

She whirled on him. "And you've never given a damn."

"I'm giving one now." His expression was hard and demanding, just as she remembered, his eyes relentless and piercing. He hadn't changed much except for the fact that she'd never before seen him seated in one position for so long. He'd been too restless, too filled with nervous energy. But now he was waiting.

"He got caught with alcohol about a month ago," she admitted as if it wasn't the big deal she knew it was.

"At thirteen?"

"Yes, at thirteen. He was with an older boy, the brother of one of his friends, who was throwing a party. Anyway, the neighbors complained, the police showed up, everyone ran, but Stephen and a couple of other kids were caught. Even though Stephen hadn't been drinking, he got himself into some hot water. A juvenile counselor was assigned to his case and just a few minutes ago I was speaking with her."

J.D.'s eyebrows slammed together. "And you don't think this is serious."

"Serious enough," she admitted, though she wasn't going to let her bachelor brother-in-law, a man who'd never had any kids, know just how worried she was. It was too easy for him to criticize. "Stephen will be all right."

"If you say so."

"He's a teenager—"

"Barely."

Tiffany bristled. She stepped closer to him and tried vainly to keep her temper in check. "Don't start passing judgment, J.D. You remember how much trouble you can get into during those years, don't you? According to Philip, your adolescent exploits were practically legendary."

His jaw hardened and he climbed to his feet. He winced, then hitched himself across the room to stare out the window over the sink.

"What happened?" she asked, angry with herself for being concerned. J.D. Santini was the last man she should care about. "Did you hurt yourself?"

"Tore a couple of tendons. It's not a big deal."

"When?"

"A few months ago. Motorcycle accident."

"Oh." So there was still a bit of the rebel in him. Good. For some reason she didn't want to examine too closely, she found that bit of information comforting, but she couldn't dwell on it. Wouldn't. "No one told me."

"Why would they?"

"Because, dammit, I am still part of the family."

"I was laid up for a few days. No big deal. Believe me, if it had been life-threatening, you would have been notified."

"Before or after the funeral?"

His jaw tightened. "You act as if you're ostracized. The way I remember it, you came down here and cut the ties, so to speak, because you wanted to."

That much was true. She'd run fast and hard to get away from the suffocating grip of the Santini family.

"Let's not get into all that," she suggested. "It's water under the bridge, anyway. Why don't you tell me why, if you're working for the company, you're in Bittersweet?"

"Dad's interested in buying some land around here someplace. Potential winery."

"And you're the expert?" This wasn't making a lot of sense.

"Looks like."

She didn't remember him being so evasive. In fact, the J.D. she'd known had been blunt and direct, a man who could make you squirm with his intense, no-nonsense gaze, thin-lipped mouth that rarely smiled and somewhat harsh demeanor. With raven-black hair, thick eyebrows and sculpted features, he never gave an inch and was known to call them as he saw them. And never had he worked for his father. The way Philip had told it, J.D. the renegade, eleven years his junior, was forever at odds with his old man. But then who could get along with Carlo Santini, patriarch with the iron fist and closed mind?

Something wasn't right. She sensed it and began to perspire. She cracked open the windows in the kitchen nook. "You know, Jay, you're the last person, the very last, I expected to cave in and join the family business."

"Life has a way of not turning out the way you expect it, Tiffany. Haven't you learned that by now?" His lips barely moved, his eyes caught hers in a breathtaking hold that she hated, and she felt the first trickle of sweat slide between her shoulder blades. Her stomach did a slow, sensual roll, reminding her of just how easy it was to fall prey to his charm.

But not now. Not again. Never.

She swallowed hard and avoided his eyes. Suddenly the kitchen was much too small. Too close. She needed a reason to break up this unexpected atmosphere of intimacy with J.D.

"Oh, gosh, it's almost three," she said, staring pointedly at her watch. "Christina," she called, looking through the window and spying her daughter drawing on the side of the garage with a piece of yellow chalk. "Time for your nap."

"No nap!" The little girl dropped the chalk.

"Excuse me," Tiffany said, hurrying out the back door and feeling the much-needed breath of a breeze touch her face and bare arms. It had been a long, strained week capped by a hellish day speaking with Stephen's counselor. On top of it all, she'd learned that her father—John Cawthorne—actually expected her to show up at his wedding after thirty-three years of pretending she didn't exist. Fat chance!

Charcoal, who had been rolling over in a spot of sunlight, scrambled to his feet and dashed under the porch. "Come on, sweetheart," Tiffany cajoled her daughter as she picked up broken bits of chalk and stuffed them into the tattered pack.

"I not tired."

"Sure you are."

"No, I not!" Christina's lower lip protruded and she folded her chubby arms across her chest.

"Well, Bub and Louie are tired and they're waiting upstairs in bed for you. It'll just be for a little while." She hoisted her daughter into her arms and Christina, still pouting, didn't protest.

Unfortunately J.D. had watched the entire display from the kitchen window. Tiffany wished he'd just go away. She didn't need any member of the Santini family, especially not J.D., intruding into her life right now—or ever, for that matter. She knew they all thought she hadn't been good enough for Philip while he was alive, so they could all just go and take the proverbial leap.

She carried Christina into the back of the house, mouthed, "I'll be back in a few minutes" to her erstwhile guest, then lugged the tired three-year-old through the hallway and up the stairs to her room.

This part of the house, aside from the addition of the bathroom, was as it had been for nearly a hundred years and Christina's room was a small alcove that overlooked the fruit trees in the backyard. The bedroom next door belonged to Stephen, and Tiffany's was across the hall. There were two occupied apartments in the basement and a third one—an empty studio—on the top floor. The ground floor of the carriage house that flanked the backyard was rented, while the upper level was, at the moment, standing empty.

"There you go," she said, as she tucked Christina under a hand-pieced quilt her grandmother had made. She arranged Bub, a floppy-eared stuffed rabbit missing one eye, and Louie, a black-masked toy raccoon, beside her daughter.

"Just a little while," Christina insisted.

"That's right." Tiffany leaned over and planted a soft kiss on the little girl's forehead. Christina, whom Tiffany had dubbed the "miracle" baby, had been an unexpected blessing three years ago, long after she and Philip had decided that one child—Stephen—was enough. Philip had two nearly-grown children from his previous marriage and he hadn't thought it was necessary to "overpopulate the world," especially when he'd already been "paying a fortune" in child support.

Gazing down at her daughter now, Tiffany was thankful that God had seen otherwise, and that despite the use of birth control and Philip's lack of interest, Christina had been conceived. "Destiny," she'd told her husband upon learning the news.

"Or a curse," Philip had replied with a scowl. "How many kids do you think I can afford?"

"It's just one more."

"That you planned," he stated flatly, insisting that she'd intentionally tricked him by not using her diaphragm. The fight had simmered for days, with Philip brooding and spending more time at the office. Philip had slept in the den for nearly two weeks, acting as if she wasn't even in the same house with him until she'd confronted him and flown into a rage.

"I want this baby!" she'd told him. "Stephen needs a sister or brother."

"He's got one of each."

"Half siblings who don't live with him." She'd advanced upon him as he'd sat in his chair, holding the newspaper firmly in white-knuckled fists, his jaw set, his nostrils flared in a seething, silent rage. "I didn't plan to have this baby, but now that it's coming, I consider it a gift and you should, too."

"I'm too old to be a father again."

"But I'm not too old to be a mother. It'll be all right," she'd said, aching inside. She wanted this baby so badly. "I'll make it right."

His snort of derision and snap of the sports page had been the end of the argument.

Tiffany had been crushed by Philip's attitude but determined to bear this child and bring it into a loving world.

Eventually, after brooding and pouting for a week or two, Philip had come to terms with the prospect of diapers, formula and interrupted sleep. He'd come home with a bouquet of spring flowers and told her that another baby, though not in his plan for the future, might be the best thing that had ever happened to him—to them and their marriage. "It'll either keep me young or make me old real fast," he'd said.

Tiffany felt a pang of remorse for a man she'd thought she loved, then stepped out of the room as Christina yawned and sighed softly, her eyelids slowly lowering.

J.D. was waiting for her, his hips resting against the balustrade, arms folded across his chest, jaw set with determination. As she closed the door gently behind her, he cocked a thumb at the open door to the third floor. "You've got an empty room upstairs."

Obviously, he'd already checked it out.

"That's right. I'm hoping to rent it soon."

His grin was slow-spreading and positively wicked. "Well, Ms. Santini, I guess this is your lucky day."

No! She steeled herself. Surely he wasn't suggesting...

"That's right, Tiff," he said, as if reading her expression. "It just so happens I need a place to stay while I'm in town."

No way. She couldn't have him this close. He was too intrusive, too damned sexy. But then, he always had been.

"Sorry, Jay, but I don't rent week to week, or, uh, month to month for that matter. I, uh, always insist upon a six-month lease, first and last month's rent, and both a cleaning deposit and a security deposit."

"Do you?" One dark eyebrow lifted in mocking disbelief.

"Always."

"Fine," he said, his eyes gleaming as if he loved calling her bluff. "Just show me where to sign."

Chapter Two

"This is crazy," Tiffany muttered under her breath as she climbed the curved stairs to the top floor. J.D. followed after her, his steps uneven as he hauled his damned duffel bag and briefcase with him. As if he really intended to rent the place.

There was no way! He was the last man on earth, the *last* person to whom she would hand over a key to her house.

"A little crazy," he conceded as he reached the top and tossed his bag onto the stripped mattress of the antique brass bed. She saw the white lines around the corners of his mouth and watched as he limped slightly to the French doors that opened onto a small balcony overlooking the backyard then set his battered briefcase on the floor.

"You should try to find something on the ground level."

"Should I?" he mocked, then tossed his hair out of his eyes. "Don't worry about it, Tiff."

"Why do you need a place in Bittersweet, anyway?"

"I told you, the winery—"

"I know, but why here? Why not in California? Sonoma or Napa."

"Dad likes to do business in Oregon."

"There are lots of vineyards in the Willamette Valley, closer to Portland." Her mind was spinning. What would it mean to have the Santinis here, in her hometown, her place of refuge? She'd thought when she'd moved here, to this house that Philip had bought as an investment, that she would have the time and distance she needed to start over, to keep from thinking about the pain, about the guilt.

"He thinks the climate is better here for what he wants to do. He's already got a couple of wineries up north."

"I know," she interjected, remembering all too well the rolling hills of Santini Brothers' vineyards, the place she'd met her future brother-in-law.

J.D. lifted a shoulder as if it made no difference to him. "As I said, I'm just checking out some possibilities."

"And in the meantime you thought you might stop by and look in on me, see if I'm being the model mother I'm supposed to be," she snapped angrily. For as long as she could remember, Carlo Santini hadn't trusted her. He had thought she wanted his son in order to get a chunk of the Santini money. What the Santini family hadn't understood was that when she'd met Philip, it wasn't his family's wealth that had attracted her, but his aura of sophistication, his charm, his way of making her feel loved for the first time in her life. She'd been young, naive and impetuous. Well…no longer.

And as for Philip's money, that had become a moot point: there wasn't much.

"No one's ever accused you of being a poor mother," J.D. said, turning the crank to open one of the windows. A breeze, fresh with the scents of cut grass and roses, whispered into the slope-ceilinged room.

"Just a lousy wife."

He didn't respond.

"I know what they thought, J.D.," she said, unable to leave the subject alone. "I heard them say that I was looking for a father figure, that I needed an older man because I didn't grow up knowing my dad."

"And what do you think?"

"I think I loved your brother. End of story. Not that it's anyone's business."

His jaw tightened.

"Just because I was raised by a single mother didn't mean I was insecure or needed an older man to take care of me." She swiped a speck of dust from the coffee table and hoped she didn't show her true emotions. Inwardly she cringed at the accusation. Especially this week, the subject of her own parentage was difficult enough to consider when she was alone with her thoughts. When anyone else brought up the taboo topic, she saw red.

"No reason to get so defensive."

"No?" she challenged, crossing the short space separating them. "Then what's the real reason you're in Bittersweet, Jay? And don't give me any garbage about the winery, okay? There are dozens of little towns down here around the border. Some in Oregon and more in California. It's more than just bad luck that you're here."

His eyes, gray as the dawn, held hers and she braced herself. What was it about J.D. that seemed to bring out the worst in her? Whenever she was around him, her usually smoothed feathers ruffled easily. One disbelieving look from his suspicious eyes and she was itching for a fight, more than ready to defend herself and her children.

"Look, do you really want to rent this place?" She waved widely, taking in all four-hundred square feet of living space. It was sparse, with only room for a bed, bureau, table, love seat and television. The kitchen consisted of a small stove, refrigerator and sink tucked into an alcove. The bathroom was confining and bare bones with its narrow stall shower, toilet and sink.

"It'll do," he allowed in that drawl she found so irritating.

"But you won't be down here long, so why bother?"

He studied his fingers for a second, then looked at her again. "Maybe you're right, Tiff. Maybe I just want to be close to you." He eyed her carefully and her breath caught in her throat.

"For all the wrong reasons," she said, then regretted the words.

"Are there any right ones?"

"No!" she said so quickly that she blushed. "Of...of course there aren't." Clearing her throat, she added, "Well, if that's the way you want it—"

"I do."

He was too close. Perspiration broke out along her spine. This wasn't going to work. "Then I guess there's nothing more to say but make yourself at home."

"I will."

Why she found those last words so damning, she didn't know, but as she hurried down the stairs she was struck by the feeling that her tightly woven little world was unraveling by the minute. First, as a widow and single mother, she had to deal with an adolescent boy who was on the verge of trouble. Possibly big trouble. Next, she'd suddenly been faced with her biological father—a man she'd been told throughout most of her growing-up years was dead. Now that man, John Cawthorne, was trying to become part of her life. And he didn't walk alone. No, the man carried baggage and lots of it in the form of two other daughters—Tiffany's half sisters, whom she didn't know and wasn't sure she cared to. And lastly, J.D. and the Santini family. Too much. It was all too much.

"Wonderful," she muttered in the second-floor hallway, where she peeked in on a napping Christina before continuing downstairs. "Just great."

Why right now, when everything in her life was spinning out of control, did she have to face J.D. again? The mercurial and volatile nature of her emotions concerning her brother-in-law had been the bane of her existence ever since she'd married into the Santini family. Nothing would change now that J.D. had moved in. In fact, she was certain that things would only get worse.

"I just don't get it," Stephen said as he tucked his skateboard into a corner of the back porch. The board was battered and scratched, the decals for Nirvana and Metallica nearly worn off, the wheels not quite as round as they'd once been. He yanked open the screen door and walked into the kitchen where Tiffany was trying and failing to balance her checkbook while cooking dinner. "Why's *he* here?" Stephen didn't bother hiding the sneer in his voice or his dislike of his uncle, a man he thought was intruding into his life.

"Business."

"Yeah, monkey business if ya ask me." Stephen wiped his hands down the front of his jeans and tossed his too-long hair from his eyes. "I don't like this."

Neither do I, Tiffany was tempted to say, but held her tongue. Her feelings for J.D. were far more complicated than simple like or dislike. Too complicated to examine very closely. "He won't be around that much," she said as daylight was beginning to give way to dusk. She snapped her checkbook closed and put the statement back into its envelope until she had more time to go through it. It wasn't that she couldn't make the figures add up, it was that it seemed impossible to stretch her salary and the rent she collected far enough to cover all her expenses.

"Good," Stephen grunted, eyeing the barbecue sauce that was simmering on the stove.

The temperature still hovered near eighty and a hummingbird was flitting near the open blossoms of the clematis that draped over the eaves of the back porch. Bees droned while a woodpecker drilled loudly in a nearby oak tree and the muted sound of traffic reached her ears.

"Is he eatin' with us?" Stephen asked.

"I don't think so."

"Good."

"He *is* your uncle," she reminded him gently. *And he's your brother-in-law, whether you like it or not,* she told herself. J.D. had signed his six-month lease, given her a check and started carting his few belongings up the stairs. His limp was noticeable, but just barely, and she wondered if his brush with death had been the cause for his reconciliation with his father. Or had it been because Carlo had lost his eldest son?

Her heart squeezed at the thought of the accident that had taken Philip's life. Guilt, ever her companion, encroached upon her, wrapping its fingers around her heart. She had loved Philip once, but it had been such a long time ago.

"So why did you have to see the counselor today?" Stephen asked for the first time. He rubbed one elbow with the fingers of the opposite hand, a nervous trait he'd developed from the time he was four years old.

"She just wanted to talk to me."

The cat cried at the back door.

"Come on in, you," Tiffany said with a smile, then noticed as she held open the screen door that the small tear in the mesh was getting larger. Sooner or later it would have to be fixed. Charcoal streaked inside.

"I *know* she wanted to talk to you. But why?" Deftly plucking a bunch of grapes from a bowl on the table, Stephen leaned insolently against the doorframe and began plopping the juicy bits of fruit into his mouth.

This was the opportunity she'd been waiting for, because deep down, though she would never admit it, she was scared. Scared to death.

"Well, she started out by asking about you—you know, just checking on how things were going."

"She just saw me the other day."

"I know, but she had a few more questions. She's worried about you, Stephen, and frankly, so am I."

"I'm fine, Mom."

If only she could believe it. Oh, Lord, how she wanted to trust her boy. "She had a few questions about your relationship with Mr. Wells."

He froze for a second, then spat the seed from his grape into the sink. "I worked for him. Big deal."

"What do you know about him? They think *you* know something about why he disappeared," she said, finally admitting what the juvenile officer had implied. It was ridiculous, of course. It had to be. Isaac Wells had disappeared over a month ago, vanished without a trace. Whether it was foul play or by his own intention, no one knew what had happened to the elderly man. It was the biggest mystery Bittersweet had seen in years. Though Tiffany believed without a doubt that her son was innocent of any wrongdoing, she wanted to hear it from Stephen himself.

"I don't know nothin'."

"That's what I said, but now someone, and I don't know who, has come forward and said that he...well, or she, for that matter, saw you out at the Wells place on the day that Isaac disappeared."

Stephen blanched and Tiffany's heart seemed to fall through the floor. "Someone saw me?"

"That's what she said."

"Then they're lyin'. I wasn't near the place."

"You're sure?"

"Don't you believe me?" he cried, licking his lips nervously, his eyes round with an unnamed fear.

She ached to trust him. "Of course I do, but—"

"But what?" Stephen interrupted.

"But it's your word against this other person's."

"Whose?"

She turned her palms to the ceiling and wished her love was as blind as it had been a few seconds before. "I don't know, really," she said. "But you've had a fascination with that ranch for a long time."

"Yeah. I liked old Isaac's cars. That's all. Come on, Mom, you don't really think I had something to do with him up and leaving—or maybe even being killed?" Stephen asked, clearly astounded by her apparent lack of trust.

"Of course not. But I know you were there before."

"For cryin' out loud, Mom, I drove his old Chevy once. Yeah, I admit it, I did. But that's all. It wasn't like I was going to steal it or anything. I would never do anything like *that.*" His face was as pale as death. He swallowed so hard, his Adam's apple bobbed. "I...mean, I didn't— Oh, gosh, what're you saying?"

"I know you didn't hurt Mr. Wells, Stephen," she said, instantly filled with remorse. "Oh, honey, I know you didn't have anything to do with him disappearing, believe me." She took hold of his arm only to have it ripped from her overly protective fingers. "But..." He was staring at her with the eyes she'd loved from the minute he was born and her heart hurt that she would have to broach such an awful topic. "Look, Stephen, I trust you and I love you, but I do want to know what you were doing there that day—the time you were caught by Mr. Wells. Then I want to know why you lied about it."

There. It was finally in the open.

Stormy eyes glowered from beneath dark brows. "I didn't—"

"Uh-uh-uh," she warned. "Come on, honey."

His jaw worked and he looked out the window, pretending interest in the white trail of a jet that was slicing across the sky. His broadening shoulders slumped as if from an invisible weight. "The day that I took the Chevy—it was just because I was bored. Well, and because I was dared, I guess."

"Dared?"

"By Miles Dean, don't you remember?"

How could she forget? Miles Dean, a couple of years older than Stephen, was a bad influence on her son. "I didn't lie about it. Wells caught me, made me do some extra chores that he didn't pay me for and that was it. You know all this."

"Go on." Nerves strung tight, she walked to the stove and stirred the tangy sauce with a wooden spoon. Though it was warm in the kitchen, her fingers felt like ice. "What about the day that Isaac was last seen?" she asked and watched her son swallow hard, as if the lump in his throat was as big as a cantaloupe.

"Okay, okay. The next time, the *last* time I was there," he said, nudging the edge of the carpet with his toe, "it was another dare, okay?"

"Oh, Stephen, no."

"It's true." He shoved both fists into the front pockets of his baggy jeans. "Some of the kids knew I'd worked for the old guy and that I knew where he kept his keys to his vintage cars, since I'd spent a few days working for him, so…I…" He hesitated, as if he was afraid to say what was on his mind.

"So you what?" she prodded, surprised at his candor. This was a secret he'd managed to keep.

"Miles Dean, he dared me to swipe the keys." Stephen bit his lower lip.

"Again? Why?"

"I—I don't know." He looked genuinely filled with regret. "Maybe he was gonna drive one of 'em. He liked that old Buick, but anyway it was the day the old man split."

Her throat was as dry as a desert wind, her pulse pounding out, No, no, no, in her ears. *Don't ask it, Tiffany. You don't want to know.* But she couldn't stop the question from forming on her lips. "And did you?"

"Take the keys?" He shook his head vigorously. "Heck, no! I climbed the fence and was going to sneak into the barn but I just had this…this weird feeling. I can't really explain it. I looked over my shoulder at the house and there was Mr. Wells, sittin' in his rocker, a rifle on his lap, starin' at me." Stephen took in a deep breath. "It was weird, Mom. *Really* weird. So, so I—I took off." He looked at the floor and blushed. "I was scared and I ran and Miles was really mad and…he threatened to beat the—er, tar out of me."

"And that's why you couldn't admit that you were there?" she asked.

He nodded mutely, tears of mortification causing his eyes to glisten.

"Oh, honey—" She wanted to enfold him in her arms, but didn't dare. The look he shot her warned her to keep her maternal instincts under wraps.

"And you never saw him again?"

Stephen shrugged. "I don't think anybody did," he whispered in a voice that was barely audible over the hum of the refrigerator, the bubble of the simmering sauce and the stutter of the woodpecker tapping at the oak tree outside the window.

"Why didn't you tell the police?"

"I said, I was scared."

"So am I," she admitted, tapping the wooden spoon on the edge of the saucepan. She believed her son, but wished he'd come clean earlier; that he'd trusted her enough to confide in her. The timer chimed, reminding her to check the coals she'd lighted in the barbecue.

"Mommy?" Christina's voice filtered through the doorway just as the little girl, dragging her blanket behind her, toddled into the kitchen.

"Well, look who woke up." With a smile, Tiffany picked up her daughter and placed a kiss on her crown. "Are you still a sleepyhead?"

"No!" Christina snorted out the word and rested her head on her mother's shoulder.

"Yeah, right," Stephen muttered under his breath as he plucked another grape from the cluster in the bowl and tossed it into the air before catching it in his mouth. "Grumpy Gus."

"I'm not a Grumpy Gus!" Christina grouched.

"Shh! Of course you're not, sweetheart." Tiffany sent

her son a look that would cut through steel. "Your brother was only teasing you."

"He's a big…big…dumbhead."

"Oh, wow, like that's a problem," Stephen mocked. "A dumbhead, Chrissie? Is that what I am?"

"Enough!" Tiffany said. "Come on, sweetie, you can have some grapes while I put the chicken on the grill."

"I *hate* grapes."

Tiffany set Christina into a chair at the table and Stephen, on the other side, had the audacity to cross his eyes.

"Lookie what he's doing. I *hate* you, too, dumbhead."

"Christina, don't call your brother any bad names and you, Stephen, should know better than to bother her when she's still sleepy. You weren't all that sunny-side up when you used to wake up from your nap."

"Make him take one now!" Christina said in the bossy tone she'd adopted since turning three.

"I'm too old for naps."

"But not to set the table," Tiffany said as Stephen, grumbling under his breath about "women's work," got to his feet and searched in a drawer for place mats.

"So how come we're not going to the wedding?" he asked as he slid three woven mats onto the top of the table, then reached into a cupboard for glasses. She heard the sound of footsteps on the back porch and turned to see J.D. through the screen door. Instantly she tensed. Living in the same house with him was sure to be torture.

"The wedding?" she repeated.

"You know. Grandpa's." He scowled as he said the word, as if it tasted foul.

She opened the door and J.D. strode in. "Wedding? What're you talking about? Your grandparents have been married for over fifty years."

"He's not talking about the Santinis," Tiffany said,

wishing she could drop the subject, but J.D. was going to find out sooner or later. In a town the size of Bittersweet, gossip spread like a windswept wildfire. "My father's getting married on Sunday."

"*Your* father?" He scowled slightly, his eyes narrowing. "But I thought— Well, I always had the impression that he was either dead or out of the picture."

"He seems to be back in. Big time." She pulled a pan of chicken from the refrigerator and carried it outside, then forked the meat onto the grill. The chicken sizzled on the hot rack. "Stephen, bring out the pan of sauce on the stove—and the wooden spoon."

J.D. came through the door with the items in question. "Tell me about your father."

She hesitated, took the pan from his outstretched hand and began drizzling barbecue sauce over the chicken. She didn't really want to discuss the wedding with her brother-in-law, but she had no choice. "It's a long story, but it seems my biological father is really John Cawthorne. I found out years ago, but it was easier to keep up the lie my mother had started when I was a little kid—that my dad was dead."

"Easier?"

"Than thinking he just didn't give a damn," she said in a voice barely audible because her kids were still arguing at the table on the other side of the screen door.

"Cawthorne?" he repeated as if the name was vaguely familiar.

"Yeah, a cowboy-turned-developer-and-businessman. Married. One daughter. Well, one legiti—" She held her tongue as both her children had turned their heads in her direction. "Uh, would you, uh, like to eat with us?" she asked as much to change the subject as anything else. She set the lid onto the barbecue. J. D. Santini was the last person she wanted to spend time with and in the corner of her peripheral vision she caught a glimpse of her son rolling his eyes theatrically.

J.D. hesitated, then shook his head. "Thanks, but another time. I just wanted to work a deal with you."

"A deal?" She was instantly wary.

"I'll need a phone until mine's connected."

"No problem." She let out the breath she hadn't realized she'd been holding. The man made her so damned nervous. She picked up the empty saucepan and spoon and told herself not to let down her guard for a minute. J.D., she reminded herself for the fiftieth time, was a man to avoid. If possible. "There's the wall phone in the kitchen."

"Seen it."

"And an extension in my bedroom on the second floor."

"The kitchen will do."

He started up the two steps leading to the back porch and Tiffany felt a wash of color flood her cheeks. "Fine."

"When the bill comes, I'll take care of the extra charges." He hesitated. "Thanks."

"No problem." But it was. Everything about him seemed to be a complication in her life. "I was serious about dinner," she added, knowing she was making a big mistake, but unable to stop herself. She was going to live in the house with him for the next few months. If life was going to be tolerable, they had to get along. "Look, it's not a big deal, but I thought we should try and…and…"

"And what, Tiffany?" he asked, his eyes as dark as slate.

What was it about one of his looks that could make her feel like a fool? "Never mind. I was just being polite."

He looked over his shoulder to the well-used barbecue

and the smoke escaping from a hole in the lid. Furrows etched his brow and suspicion tightened the muscles of his shoulders. "I think we're past being polite."

"Then we should go back a step or two, don't you think?"

He shoved his hands into the back pockets of his jeans. "What is it they say? Something about never going back."

"Then they're wrong." She stepped closer to him, close enough to notice the few flecks of gray at his temples. "You barged in here. Asked all sorts of questions about me and the kids. Demanded to live here. So I think—no, I *insist* that we be civil and, yes, at times even polite to each other. If we don't, I can guarantee our new living arrangements aren't gonna be worth a single red cent."

He glanced toward the house and the kitchen, where her kids were lurking near the open door. He nodded. "Thanks for the offer," he said. "Another time, maybe. Thanks." Then he went through the screen door and Tiffany didn't know whether to be relieved that he was gone or insulted that he hadn't accepted her invitation. It had been her way of offering an olive branch, a way to bridge the gap that had been forever between them.

Not forever, she reminded herself. There had been a time when she'd been close to her brother-in-law. Too close. She swallowed hard and let out her breath as she watched him walk through the kitchen and press a shoulder against the swinging door to the hallway. She wondered if his limp was permanent but decided it didn't matter. Any way you looked at it, J. D. Santini was a very sexy man. Just the kind of man she didn't need around here.

"J.D.'s a jerk," Stephen said as she returned to the house and set the empty saucepan in the sink.

"Let's not tell him, okay?" Tiffany flipped on the faucet and rinsed the small pot.

"Why not?"

"'Cause it's not nice," Christina said with a knowing nod that caused her curls to bounce precociously.

"Big deal. I thought we were always supposed to tell the truth."

Tiffany placed a bowl of pasta salad on the table, zapped some leftover garlic bread in the microwave and decided to ignore her son's need to vent some of his anger. How could she defend J.D.? The man was an enigma and someone she was certain would only cause her trouble.

She poured the kids each a glass of milk and hesitated, thinking she might have a small glass of wine, then discarded the idea. As long as J.D. was living here, she would need a clear head.

Who knew really why he was in Bittersweet? Judging from past experience, she realized she couldn't trust him.

J.D. was and always had been dangerous. If she were smart, she'd stay as far away from him as possible.

Even if he was living in her house.

The kid was already in trouble with the law.

"Hell." J.D. sat on the edge of his new bed and ignored the mental image that leveled a guilty finger in his direction. It wasn't his fault that Stephen had decided to rebel. What thirteen-year-old wouldn't? Stephen had lost his father, been uprooted and moved to a new town, and become the man of the family all in one fell swoop.

It was too much for any boy. No wonder the kid was full of piss and vinegar.

What a mess. And J.D. wasn't going to make it any better. He rifled through his duffel bag until he found a crisp manila envelope. Inside the packet was the deed, bill of sale and proof that this house—Tiffany's home since the accident that had taken Philip's life—belonged to the

Santini family. Well, at least most of it. A portion—one-fourth, to be exact—was still hers; the rest had been signed away to pay off Philip's gambling debts.

"Great," J.D. said, tossing the envelope onto the foot of the bed and wishing he hadn't agreed to step into Philip's shoes in the first place. He'd never wanted to work for his father, had avoided anything to do with Santini Brothers Enterprises for years, but then, after Philip's death, he'd felt obligated. His parents had been devastated by the loss of their eldest, and his father had hoped to "step down," or so he'd claimed. At the same time J.D. had become jaded with the law, tired of the constant court-room battles and legal arguments he'd once thrived upon, sickened that settlements and awards were always more important than justice.

His motorcycle accident had been his own personal epiphany. When a colleague had suggested he sue the manufacturer of the bike, or the highway department, or the parents of the kid he'd swerved to avoid, he'd decided to chuck it. J.D. had been pushing the speed limit, the accident had been his fault; he'd nearly lost his life and he wasn't going to blame anyone or anything but himself.

But the accident had made him take a good long look at himself and what he did for a living.

When his father had offered him the job, he'd accepted, as long as they both understood it was temporary. He wasn't going to be sucked permanently into the fold.

For the time being he took the job that Philip, in dying, had vacated. Carlo kept talking about retiring and had tried to lure J.D. into becoming more involved—about someday running the multifaceted company—but deep in his heart, J.D. didn't believe his old man would ever voluntarily give up the reins of an operation he'd started nearly fifty years earlier with his own brother, who had retired five years ago. Not so Carlo; the day Carlo Santini quit work was the day he gave up on life.

One of the first duties of J.D.'s employment was to deal with Tiffany. The family wanted to be certain that she and the children were dealt with fairly, but Carlo had never liked his second daughter-in-law, nor had he forgiven his son for divorcing his first wife. Whether he admitted it or not, Carlo blamed Tiffany for the marriage breakup, though she hadn't even met Philip until after his divorce was final.

Or had she?

J.D. really didn't give a damn. He only had to do his job down here, find the right piece of land for the new winery, then make tracks. He'd check on the kids, make sure the widow Santini was handling things okay, inform her about the ownership of the house, then return to Portland.

He couldn't wait.

He tucked the legal papers inside his bag again and stuffed the duffel into a drawer. Walking stiffly across the room he sat on the edge of the windowsill and looked into the backyard where Tiffany, in the gathering dusk, was watering some of the planters near the carriage house. She was humming to herself, seemingly at peace with the world, but J.D. sensed it was all an act. The woman was restless; disturbed about something. Ten to one it had to do with her little foray down to the police department today. She set down her watering can and glanced up toward the window.

He didn't move.

Through the glass their gazes met. J.D.'s stomach tightened. His pulse raced. As he stared into those amber eyes, something inside him broke free. Memories he'd locked away emerged and turned his throat to dust. He remembered touching her, kissing her, feeling her sweet, forbidden surrender. God, she was beautiful.

She licked her lips and his knees went weak at the silent, innocent provocation.

Or was it innocent?

Damn it all to hell. Sweat tickled the back of his neck. Desire crept through his blood.

She looked away first, as if her thoughts, too, had traveled a sensual and taboo course. She turned her attention back to the planter boxes and J.D. snapped the blinds closed. This couldn't be happening. Not again. Not ever.

His fascination for his deceased brother's wife was his personal curse, one he'd borne from the moment he'd first laid eyes on her.

Chapter Three

"**D**id you hear that we're getting a new neighbor?" Doris, the owner of the small insurance agency where Tiffany worked, asked the next day. Tiffany was just settling into her chair, balancing her coffee cup in one hand while reaching for the stack of mail sitting on the corner of her desk.

"Who is it this time?" Tiffany took a swallow of coffee and snagged her letter opener from the top drawer. In the small cottage converted into offices there had been everything from acupuncturists to a toy store, a bead shop and a phone-card business. All had failed.

"An architect," Doris said with a wry smile.

Tiffany froze. "You don't mean—?"

"Yep. Bliss Cawthorne's going to be right next door."

"Great." Tiffany sliced open the top envelope as if her life depended upon it. She didn't need to be reminded of her half sister, her *legitimate* half sister. Not this week.

"Thought you'd be pleased." Doris's eyes gleamed from behind thick, fashionable frames. Near sixty and divorced, she had the energy and stamina of a woman half her age. "She already stopped by this morning, asking about tenant's insurance, spied your nameplate, and after half a beat, said she'd be back later."

"To see me."

"I guess." Doris lifted a shoulder and rolled her chair back as the fax machine whirred to life. "Uh-oh, looks like someone found us. Probably from the main office." Adjusting her reading glasses, she walked to the fax machine and waited for the paper it spewed forth. "Another memo about Isaac Wells, wouldn't you know," she said, clucking her tongue and shaking her short blond curls. "Aren't we lucky to have policies out on him. I wonder what happened to that old guy."

"You and everyone else in town," Tiffany said uneasily. Any talk of Isaac's disappearance reminded her that the police thought Stephen knew more than he was telling. She shivered. Impossible. Not her boy. He was only thirteen.

Doris snapped up the page of information.

"When is Bliss moving in?" Tiffany asked in an effort to change the course of the conversation. How would she deal with seeing her half sister every working day? Bliss Cawthorne, "the princess." John's indulged and adored daughter. The only one of his three offspring allowed to bear his name. *Get over it,* she told herself as she settled into her morning routine, opening letters and invoices and scanning each with a practiced eye. It wasn't Bliss's fault that their father was an A number-one jerk, a man who'd ignored both of his other daughters for years. Until it was convenient for him.

Now, after his brush with death, he wanted to make

everything nice-nice. As if the past thirty-odd painful years could be swept away. Just because he'd had himself a heart attack, he wanted to start over. Well, in Tiffany's estimation, facing one's mortality didn't do a whole lot toward changing the past.

Give it a rest, she told herself and, taking her own advice, buried herself in her work. Several policyholders came into the office to pay their bills or fill out claim reports.

Tiffany worked through lunch, balanced the previous day's invoices, made her daily trip to the bank, and had found time to chat with Doris about the kids and Doris's planned trip to Mexico while eating a container of strawberry yogurt at her desk.

It was nearly quitting time when the bell over the door tinkled and Tiffany glanced up. Her insides tightened a bit as she recognized Bliss, her face flushed, striding to the front counter.

Wonderful. Tiffany's good mood disappeared.

With cheekbones a model would kill for and eyes as bright as a June morning, Bliss Cawthorne looked like a woman who had everything going for her. Slim and blond, she exuded the confidence of a person who knew her own mind and had never wanted for anything. She wore a white skirt, denim shirt, wide belt and sandals. Upon the ring finger of her left hand she sported a single pear-shaped diamond, compliments of her fiancé, Mason Lafferty, a local boy who, despite his poor roots, had returned to Bittersweet a wealthy, successful man.

Bliss practically glowed, she seemed so happy, and Tiffany had to stanch the ugly stream of resentment that flowed whenever she was face-to-face with her half sister. Fortunately, their meetings had been few and far between. Until now.

"Hi," Bliss said with a smile.

Tiffany forced a grin. "Hello."

"Did you sign the lease?" Doris asked and Bliss, her steady gaze never leaving Tiffany, nodded.

"Looks like for the next year at least, I'll be your neighbor."

"Welcome aboard," Doris said, walking around her desk to shake Bliss's hand. Her bracelets jangled in the process and she grinned widely enough to show off the gold caps on her back teeth. "It'll be nice to have another woman around here, won't it?" she asked, cocking her head in Tiffany's direction.

"Absolutely."

"It's just us and Randy around back. He organizes guided tours into the wilderness—canoeing, backpacking, trail riding, whatever." She fluttered her fingers by the side of her head, as if dismissing Randy's occupation. "Seth was in the office you're renting. Semiretired accountant, but he had a cancer scare last winter and decided to sell his business."

There was nothing that Doris liked more than gossip and she didn't get as many opportunities as she wanted, so she was anxious to bend any ear she could.

"I hear you're marrying that Lafferty boy."

Bliss's grin widened. "Next month."

"Pretty soon after your father's big to-do," Doris observed.

"I guess it is." Bliss was a little noncommittal, and Tiffany realized that her half sister had her own reservations about their father's impending nuptials. Not that Tiffany blamed her. It seemed that the old man had kept Brynnie, his bride-to-be, as his mistress off and on during most of the duration of his first marriage to Bliss's mother, Margaret. The guy was a creep. A slime. *And you've got his blood running through your veins whether you like it or not.*

"I've decided to take out the renter's policy," Bliss said, as if the subject of her father's wedding was a little touchy. "I've listed all the assets—computers, fax machine, copier and furniture." She and Doris began discussing the policy as Tiffany printed invoices. She heard Doris giving Bliss her best sales pitch for life, auto and liability insurance while slipping her a business card.

"We could take care of all your insurance needs and we'd be right down the hall," Doris was saying as Tiffany pulled the billings off the printer.

"I'll think about it."

"And talk to your dad. We could help him out, too." Doris nodded toward Tiffany. "I've asked Tiffany to call him and show him how we could help out, but she—"

"Doris!" Tiffany reproached, shaking her head. That was the trouble with her boss. Doris didn't understand the word *soft* when it was applied to sell. "You don't have to talk to John," she said to Bliss. "Doris can call him herself."

"I suppose," Doris said with a theatrical sigh. "But I should wait until after the wedding."

"Good idea."

"You can't blame a girl for trying, now, can you?" Doris slipped a thick bundle of papers into an envelope and handed the packet to Bliss.

"Wouldn't dream of it," Bliss replied, tucking the envelope into her leather bag. "I, uh, was hoping that you and I," she said to Tiffany, "could have lunch or coffee or something. You know, get to know each other."

"As long as it's what you want and not John's idea."

"Tiffany!" It was Doris's turn to appear aghast.

"Bliss understands," Tiffany said. "Ever since John

came back to Bittersweet, he's been trying to steamroller me into doing things I'm not comfortable with."

"That's between you and Dad," Bliss said.

"So you're not going to try and pressure me into attending his wedding?"

"Wouldn't dream of it." Bliss sounded sincere. "But it's up to you. This whole concept of a new family—stepmother, half sisters and the like—hasn't been easy for me to swallow, either. But I'm trying. And I'd like to start by having coffee or…a glass of wine…or whatever with you. But it's your choice." She glanced back at Doris, who was assessing the situation between the two half-siblings with surprised eyes. "Thanks." To Tiffany, she added, "I'll give you a call."

"Any time."

Bliss left and Doris stared after her. "You could have been more friendly, you know."

"Just because she bought a policy—"

"That has nothing to do with it. You should be friendly because she's your damned sister, Tiffany."

"Half sister."

"Whatever." Doris straightened the papers on her desk. Her lips were pursed into a perturbed pout, little lines appearing between her plucked eyebrows. "You're lucky, you know. A sister—even a half sister—is a special person. More than a friend." She cleared her throat. "There isn't a day goes by that I don't think of mine."

Tiffany cringed and felt like an insensitive oaf. Doris's sister had died less than a year ago from heart disease. "I suppose you're right."

"There's no 'supposing' about it. I am right. It's not Bliss's fault that her father's a jerk who never claimed his other kids. The way I look at it, Tiffany, you have a chance to have a family now. Your father, well, you can take him or leave him. Your choice. But your sisters, they're gifts. Now, let's go over these casualty reports, then you can tell me about your love life.''

"There isn't much to tell," Tiffany said.

"A situation that needs to be remedied and I just happen to know a divorced father of four, forty years old, six-foot-three with gorgeous blue eyes and a smile to die for.''

"I'm not in the market."

"He has a great job, nifty sense of humor and—''

"And I'm still not in the market."

"You can't mourn forever, honey," Doris said, her eyebrows lifting over the tops of her glasses.

"I'm not mourning—not really."

"Then why not go out, kick up your heels a little?"

"When the time is right."

Doris walked to the coffeepot and poured its last dregs into her mug that seemed permanently stained with her favorite shade of coral lipstick. "You've got to make it right, Tiffany."

"I will."

"When?"

"Soon," she promised but knew she was lying. She wasn't interested in men right now. There was a chance she never would be. *So what about J.D.?* that horrid voice in her head nagged, and Tiffany did what she did best: she ignored it.

"You've come to the right place," the Realtor, an egg-shaped man with freckles sprinkled over every square inch of his exposed skin insisted as he drove J.D. along the winding, hilly roads outside Bittersweet. The grass was bleached dry and wildflowers bloomed in profusion along the fencerows while Max Crenshaw blabbered on and on about the merits of one farm over another.

"I don't know much about growing grapes down here and I'll admit it right up front. But there're several wineries around Ashland and Medford, up the road a bit. They seem to do a bumper business, and the soil here grows about anything."

J.D. was barely listening. He gazed through the dusty windshield at the small herds of cattle and the occasional thicket of oak trees that dotted the fields flashing by. Nondescript music wafted from the speakers of the older Cadillac and was barely audible over the rush of cool air from the air conditioner and the drone of Crenshaw's voice.

"Been here all my life, let me tell you, and I've seen cattle farms turned into llama and ostrich ranches.... You know times change, so I'm sure we'll find the right place...."

J.D. tried to pay attention, but his mind strayed. To Tiffany and her kids. There was more trouble in that house than she was willing to admit. Stephen was well on the path to becoming a juvenile delinquent. J.D. could read the signs—the same signs that he'd displayed as a youth. As for Christina, the imp had woken up in the middle of the night wailing and sobbing. Through the floorboards J.D. had heard Tiffany's hurried footsteps and soft voice as she'd run to her daughter's room and whispered words of comfort.

Yep, she had her problems at the old apartment house. There were four tenants besides himself. Mrs. Ellingsworth, whom he'd already met, occupied one basement unit, an art student lived in the other, and a recently married couple resided on the main floor of the carriage house. The upper story was empty, recently vacated by a man named Lafferty.

He'd learned all this from Max Crenshaw as they'd

driven from one place to the next. The Realtor seemed to know everything that happened in Bittersweet.

"Now, I'm gonna show you something that I don't have listed yet—well, no one does, but it's part of our latest local mystery and since we're driving by anyway…" Crenshaw braked at a run-down old ranch with a small cabin near the front of the property, a couple of sheds and an imposing barn at the back. Vast, untended acres stretched behind the house.

"Weird deal, this," Max said as he nosed the Cadillac into the drive, shoved the gearshift into Park and let the car idle. "You mind?" he asked as he rummaged in his breast pocket and came up with a crumpled pack of cigarettes.

"No."

"Good. I'm tryin' to cut back, but, hell, you know how it is." He shook out a cigarette, offered one to J.D. and punched in the lighter.

"No, thanks."

"Ever smoke?"

"Years ago."

"Wish I could quit. Anyway, this place belongs—or belonged, depending upon what you want to believe—to a guy by the name of Isaac Wells."

"Did it?" J.D. was suddenly more interested in the dilapidated cabin and desolate acres.

"Yep. Old Isaac lived here all by himself. Never married. Had a sister who died a long while ago and some brothers who have scattered to the winds, but, oh, a month or two ago, Isaac just up and disappeared." The lighter popped and Max, after rolling down his window, lit up. "Weird as hell, if ya ask me. No one's heard anything from him. You'd think if he died or was killed, someone would've found his body by now. If he was kidnapped, he would have been ransomed, though what for I can't imagine. Some of the people in town think he had money locked in a deposit box in one of the banks or buried in tin cans around the ranch, but that's all just hearsay as much as I can tell.'' He smoked in silence for a few minutes. ''You know, if he just took off on his own, someone he knew would have heard from him, wouldn't they?'' He shook his head and jabbed his cigarette out in the ashtray. ''Anyway, this place could be on the market—I'm sure as hell looking into it. Then again, it might stay just as it is forever.''

J.D. studied the abandoned acres through the windshield. The house was small, in need of paint, with a couple of windows that were cracked. The barn, built of cedar planks that had weathered gray, was huge and sprawling; the other outbuildings looked worn and neglected. The entire spread seemed lonely. Desolate.

''He was an odd one, old Isaac, but didn't have any enemies that I knew of. Like I say, it's a mystery.''

''Without any clues?''

''If they've got 'em, the cops aren't saying.'' He shifted the car into Reverse. ''Let's mosey on down the road a piece. I've got a couple more ideas. The first place—the Stowell spread—is listed with a Realtor in Medford. It's about a hundred acres, well-kept and the owners are anxious to sell, would even agree to terms—not that your company would need them—but let's take a look-see just in case.''

He backed the Cadillac out of the drive and J.D. watched Isaac Wells's place disappear from sight in the sideview mirror.

Max prattled on. The boring music continued to play. The miles rolled beneath the wheels of the old car and J.D. itched to be anywhere else on earth. With each passing minute, he felt that he'd made this biggest mistake of his life by showing up in Bittersweet.

Juggling two sacks of groceries, Tiffany managed to unlock the front door. "I'm home," she called out, but knew before no one answered that she was alone. On a chair in the parlor, Charcoal lifted his head, then arched his back and stretched lazily. "Anybody here?" she said to the house in general, then sighed. "I guess it's just you and me, eh?" The cat yawned and padded after her to the kitchen.

A note in Mrs. Ellingsworth's chicken scratch told her that she had taken Christina to the park. Stephen was still at his grandmother's house doing yardwork. She set the sacks on the kitchen counter and started unpacking the groceries only to notice that the wedding invitation she'd tucked away was on the counter, lying open, seeming to mock her.

"Great," she muttered, fingering the smooth paper.

While she was growing up John Cawthorne had never been around. She'd never even met him until a few months ago, and for years—*years*—she'd believed him dead. So it seemed unbelievable to her that now, when she was thirty-three years old, a widowed mother of two, she should be expected to forgive and forget. Just like that. Well, guess again.

For the dozenth time in as many days she read the embossed invitation.

Mr. John Andrew Cawthorne and Ms. Brynnie Perez
Request the Honor of Your Presence
at the Celebration of Their Marriage
on Sunday, August 7th
at 7:00 p.m.

at the Chapel of the Rogue
Reception Following
at Cawthorne Acres
R.S.V.P.

"Fat chance," she whispered to herself.

As far as Tiffany was concerned, John Cawthorne's upcoming marriage was a sham. She wanted no part of it and had refused to attend the nuptials. Even though John had called over, even though she'd felt a ridiculous needle of guilt pierce her brain for not accepting the olive branch he'd held out to her, she'd held firm.

Scowling against a potential headache, she retrieved a handwritten note that was still tucked inside the envelope. In a bold scrawl, good old John had tried to breach a gap he'd created when he'd turned his back on her mother thirty-three years ago.

Dear Tiffany,
I know I don't deserve your support, but I'm asking for it anyway. Believe me when I say I've turned over a new leaf and more than anything I want you and your sisters to be part of my family.

God knows, I've made more than my share of mistakes. No doubt I'll make more before I see the pearly gates, but, please find it in your heart to forgive an old man who just wants to make his peace before it's time to face his Maker. In my own way, Tiffany, I love you. Always have. Always will. You're my first-born. I hope you will join me and your sisters at the wedding.

Your father,
John Cawthorne

Father. There was that painful word again. Where had he been when her mother was working two jobs trying to raise an illegitimate daughter? Where had this wonderful "father" been during her growing-up years when she'd needed someone—anyone—to explain the complexities of the male of the species? Where had he been when she'd gotten married and had no one to give her away at the small wedding? What had he thought when she'd had children—his grandchildren?

John Cawthorne didn't know the meaning of the word *father.* She doubted that he ever would. She curled the letter in her fist, felt the edge of one sheet cut into her finger and tossed the crumpled pages into a wastebasket near the back door. Why was she even thinking of the man?

Because in a few days it will be his wedding day.

So what? So he was finally marrying the woman he'd professed to love after all these years—a woman who had collected more husbands than most women had pairs of earrings.

As for her "sisters," she wasn't sure she had anything in common with either of them. Bliss was a few years younger than she. Just as she'd appeared today in the agency, Bliss seemed always to be a cool, sophisticated woman who had been born with the proverbial silver spoon firmly lodged between her teeth. She had always had John Cawthorne's name; had never experienced the feelings of loneliness and despair at being poor or different from other kids who, even if their parents had divorced, knew who their father was. Tiffany was fairly certain she wouldn't get along with Bliss Cawthorne.

As for her other half-sibling, Katie Kinkaid—well, Katie was a dynamo, a woman who was naive enough to think she could change the world by sheer willpower.

Tiffany had nothing in common with either of them. Not that she cared. She went upstairs, changed into jeans and a sleeveless blouse, scraped her hair back into a functional ponytail, then returned to the kitchen where she started unpacking the groceries. She was just about finished when she heard the sound of voices in the backyard. Folding the grocery sacks and placing them under the sink, she glanced through the window and spied Mrs. Ellingsworth carrying Christina toward the porch.

"Mommy!" the three-year-old cried as Tiffany opened the screen door. Christina scrambled out of the older woman's arms and ran up the back steps.

"She's plumb tuckered out," Ellie said.

"Am not." Christina yawned nonetheless and the corners of her mouth turned down.

"Well, I am. I wish I had half that kid's energy." Ellie mopped her brow as Tiffany held the door open and leaned down. Christina flew into her arms.

"We swinged and got on the merry-go-round," she announced, her cheeks flushed.

"Did you?"

Ellie laughed as she stepped into the kitchen. "A few times."

"Bunches and bunches of times," Christina said, then struggled out of her mother's arms and chased Charcoal outside.

"She's a goer, that one," Ellie said, chuckling and watching through the mesh as Christina found an old tin pie plate on the back porch and toddled down the yard. "She'll be tired tonight."

"Good." Maybe then she would sleep through without the nightmares that had plagued her since Philip's death. "Taking her to the park was above and beyond the call of duty."

"Any time. She's a joy, that one." Then, as if realizing they were alone for the first time, Ellie asked, "Isn't Stephen back yet?" Before Tiffany could answer, she added, "That's odd. Octavia called and asked him to come over to mow the lawn. Said it would only take an hour. That was, when?" She checked her watch again. "Nearly three hours ago."

"Figures," Tiffany said. "I didn't find any note from him, but this was lying open." She pointed to the invitation on the counter.

"Was it?" Ellie's face puckered thoughtfully. "I didn't see it."

"Stephen must have found it and left it here." Tiffany checked for another note, found none, and told herself not to worry, that Stephen was probably just with his friends fishing or swimming or hanging out.... But where? "Well, I suppose I'll hear from him before too long," she said. "Now, how about a glass of iced tea or lemonade?"

Ellie reached for a tissue from the box on the counter and dabbed at her forehead. "I could use a drink, believe me. A vodka collins sounds nice, but it's a little early. Besides I've got a date."

"A date?" Tiffany repeated, surprised. "Who's the lucky guy?"

The older woman positively beamed. "Stan Brinkman. Retired. Once owned a roofing company that he sold to his sons. He's widowed, too, and spends his summers up here and drives a fifth wheeler down to Arizona each winter."

This was news to Tiffany. "How long have you known him?"

"Long enough." Ellie gave an exaggerated wink and walked to the door. "I'll tell you all about it later." With a wave she was out the door, pausing long enough to say a few words to Christina who was feverishly plucking blades of grass and dropping them into the pie tin.

The phone rang. Tiffany grabbed the receiver on the second ring and still watching her daughter through the screen, said, "Hello?"

"Mom?" Stephen's voice cracked.

"Oh, hi, kid." She rested her hip against the counter. "All done with Grandma's lawn?"

"Uh…a long time ago."

There was an edginess in his voice and she realized something was wrong. Very wrong. She froze. "So where are you?" she asked.

He hesitated.

"Stephen?"

"I'm at the police station, Mom, and…and someone wants to talk to you."

Chapter Four

"*You're where?*" Tiffany sagged against the kitchen wall for support. Dear God, this couldn't be happening.

"I said I'm down at the—"

"I know what you said, but how did you get there? Are you all right? What happened?" A jillion thoughts raced through her mind, none of them good, when she considered her thirteen-year-old son and his recent knack for getting into trouble.

"Yeah. I'm okay."

"You're sure?" She wasn't convinced.

"Yeah. The officer wants to talk to you."

"Wait, Stephen, should I come get you—"

"Mrs. Santini?" an older male voice inquired. "I'm Sergeant Pearson."

Tiffany's throat was dry, her heart a beating drum. "What's going on? Is my son okay?"

"Aside from a shiner and a sore jaw, I think he'll be

fine.'' The sergeant's voice was kind but did little to soothe her jangled nerves.

"What happened?''

"He and another kid, Miles Dean, got into a scuffle down at the Mini Mart.''

"A scuffle?'' she repeated, anxious sweat causing the back of her blouse to cling to her skin. The older boy's father, Ray Dean, had been in and out of jail and it looked like Miles was following in his old man's footsteps. What in the world was Stephen doing with him this time?

"The boys got into a quarrel. One thing led to another and a couple of punches were thrown. The clerk gave us a call and we picked 'em up. All in all, your boy's fine.''

Relief caused her shoulders to droop but she rubbed at the headache pounding in her forehead. "And Miles?''

The officer hesitated and Tiffany felt a niggle of dread. "Miles always manages to get himself out of trouble.''

Nervously she twisted the telephone cord in her fingers. "Are there any charges filed against Stephen?'' she asked. Despite a breeze gently lifting the curtains as it slipped in through the open window over the sink, the temperature in the kitchen seemed to have elevated to over a hundred degrees.

Tiffany stretched the cord and looked outside to see that her daughter was still busily making mud pies in the dirt.

"None against your son.''

"And Miles?''

"That remains to be seen.''

"Can I come and get him now?''

"Actually, an officer will bring him home. They should be there in about ten minutes.''

"I don't have to sign anything?''

"No—but just a minute.'' Pearson's voice was muffled

as he spoke to someone else. "Yeah, she's waiting for him. Now listen, Steve, no more horsing around, right?"

"I won't," her son mumbled as if from a great distance.

"I mean it. The next time it could be real trouble. And I'm gonna have to report this to your juvenile counselor."

There was another muffled response that Tiffany couldn't discern. A second later Sergeant Pearson was on the phone again. "Okay, he's on his way."

"Good." Or was it?

"Look, Mrs. Santini, this incident at the Mini Mart, well, it doesn't amount to much more than a couple of kids getting into a difference of opinion and taking a swing or two on a hot afternoon. However, the way things are today, we tend to worry. If either of the boys had pulled a weapon—a gun or a knife—this could have turned out bad."

Her thoughts exactly. A chill slid through her despite the heat. Guns. Knives. Weapons. She had moved to the small town of Bittersweet to get away from the gangs and violence of the city, but it seemed that no community was immune. Not even a little burg in southern Oregon. In this part of rural America, boys were given hunting knives and rifles routinely about the time they hit the age of ten or twelve, as if the owning of a weapon was a rite of passage from childhood to becoming a man. "I'll talk to Stephen."

"Do that," Pearson advised. "I think a ride in the squad car and having to come down to the station probably gave him a scare."

"Let's hope so."

She was ready to hang up, to wait for Stephen and see that he was okay, then read him the riot act if necessary, but Sergeant Pearson wasn't finished.

"There is something more, Mrs. Santini," he said, and there was a solemnity in his voice she hadn't heard before.

She was instantly wary, her fingers tightening around the receiver.

"Yes?"

"As I said, the boys were fighting about something—who knows what, maybe even a girl. At least that's what the clerk at the Mini Mart thought she heard, but there was some discussion about Isaac Wells."

Tiffany froze. "Pardon me?"

"The man who disappeared. Owned a place on the county road just out of town."

"I know who he is," she said, trying to keep the irritation and, well, the fear, from her voice. Deep inside she began to tremble. "I just don't see what he has to do with Stephen."

"Probably nothing. But when we emptied your son's pockets—just part of procedure, you know—he had a set of keys on him."

"Keys?" she repeated, having trouble finding her voice. "To my house," she said, but knew she was only hoping against hope. Stephen had one key. Only one. No set.

The sergeant hesitated. "Maybe. But the chain is unique and engraved." She closed her eyes because she knew what was coming. "Initials I.X.W. I'm thinkin' it could be for Isaac Xavier Wells."

"I see."

"Talk to your boy."

"I will," she promised as she hung up and felt as if the weight of the world had just been dumped upon her shoulders. None of this was making any sense. Why was Stephen still hanging out with Miles Dean? What was he doing with that set of keys? What was the fight about? And, what could Stephen have to do with the old man whom he'd worked for, the man who'd disappeared?

She walked to the back door and noticed John Cawthorne's wedding invitation on the counter. By the end of the week her father—well, if that's what you could call the snake-in-the-grass John Cawthorne—would be getting married. But Tiffany couldn't think of that now. Suddenly she had more important things to consider.

"Mommy!" Christina shouted from the backyard.

Tiffany managed a tight smile as she opened the window over the sink. "What's up kiddo?"

All smudges and bright eyes, Christina, standing beneath a shade tree, proudly showed off her latest creation of mud and grass piled high in the tinfoil plate that had once held a chicken pot pie. A clump of pansies had been thrown onto the top for color. "Lookie!"

"It's beautiful," Tiffany said as Charcoal mewed loudly at the back door.

"You want a bite?"

"You bet," she lied, trying to push her worries about her son far to the back of her mind. She'd deal with Stephen when he arrived home. "A big bite." She pushed open the screen door. Charcoal slunk into the kitchen.

Christina, holding out her prize, started to run up the back steps.

"Watch out!"

Too late. With a shriek Christina stumbled over one of Stephen's in-line skates and pitched headlong onto the porch. Tin pie plate, grass and clumps of mud flew into the air.

Tiffany was through the door in a second, picking up her daughter just as Christina took in a huge breath and let out another wail guaranteed to wake the dead in the entire Rogue River Valley. Tears streamed and blood began to trickle from a raspberry-like scratch on Christina's knee.

"Mom-meeee!" Christina sobbed as Tiffany held her.

"Shh, baby, you'll be fine." Tiffany hauled her daughter into the house to the small bathroom off the kitchen.

"It hurts!"

"I know, I know, but Mommy will fix it."

In the medicine cabinet she found antiseptic and a clean washcloth. As Christina, seated on the edge of the counter, wriggled and sucked in her breath, Tiffany washed each scratch and cut on her knee and chin.

The doorbell rang.

Probably the officer with Stephen in tow. "I'll be right there!" she called out over Christina's whispers. Balancing her daughter, she reached into the medicine cabinet for a package of bandages.

The bell chimed sharply again.

"Just hold your horses," Tiffany muttered, placing a bandage over the biggest area of Christina's wounds. "Come on, sweetie, we'd better answer the door." She tossed the washcloth into the sink, picked up her sniffling daughter and carried her to the front door. Expecting to have to apologize to a police officer and Stephen, she yanked on the knob and found herself face-to-face with J.D.

"You were going to get me a key," he reminded her.

"Right." His key had been the last thing on her mind. He shot a look at Christina and his brows drew into a single, condemning line. "I didn't think about it. The back door was unlocked." She shuffled her daughter from one hip to the other while Christina blinked back tears.

"What happened here?" J.D. asked.

"I falled down!" Christina said with more than a little pride. All of a sudden she was like a soldier home from battle, showing off her war wounds.

"That you did." Tiffany pressed her lips to Christina's curly crown. "Well, come on in—" She waved to the back of the house and then stopped short as she looked over his shoulder toward the street. "Oh, no."

J.D. turned in time to see a police cruiser easing up to the curb. His gut clenched, an automatic reaction from too many conflicts with the law when he was a kid. In the house, Tiffany paled and J.D. realized that for a beautiful woman, she looked like hell. Her normally cool facade had slipped, her hair was falling out of a makeshift ponytail, and her clothes—faded jeans and a sleeveless blouse— wrinkled and smudged with dirt were a far cry from her usually neat and tidy, no-nonsense appearance.

"Excuse me." Like a brushfire devouring dry grass, she was past him in an instant. Holding her daughter to her, she dashed down the two steps of the porch to the edge of the lawn, where shade trees lined the narrow street.

J.D. followed, his eyes narrowing as the rear door of the police car opened and Stephen sheepishly crawled out. All of J.D.'s worst fears congealed right then and there, and he wondered if Tiffany was at the end of her rope as far as the kids were concerned.

Christina was dirty and bleeding, like a refugee from a war zone. Stephen didn't look much better. Most of his usual bravado had evaporated and his face was bruised, one eye nearly swollen shut. Scarcely a teenager and yet, it seemed, on the brink of big trouble with the law.

Not good. Not good at all.

But then J.D. had suspected as much.

"Mrs. Santini?" The officer who had driven the car, a short man with thick, wavy brown hair and wire-rimmed glasses, approached.

"Yes."

"Officer Talbot, Bittersweet Police."

"Hi."

He glanced at J.D. "Mr. Santini?"

"Yes, but I'm not the boy's father."

Brown eyebrows sprang upward, over the tops of the policeman's glasses. J.D. thrust out his hand. "J.D.," he said. "I'm Stephen's uncle."

Stephen shot J.D. a suspicious glance that spoke volumes, then reached into the back seat of the patrol car for his battered skateboard.

"You might want to have his eye looked at," the officer said to Tiffany. "Helluva shiner, if you ask me."

"I will," Tiffany promised as Christina buried her face into the crook of her mother's neck, smearing blood and dirt on the long column of Tiffany's throat.

"I'm okay," Stephen mumbled, a hank of black hair tumbling over his forehead and partially hiding the eye in question.

"I still think it should be checked," Tiffany said, her nervous gaze skating over Stephen's injuries. Then she asked, "How's the other boy?"

"Looks about like this one here." The officer touched Stephen on the shoulder. "Let's hope this is the last of it."

Sullenly Stephen studied the ground.

"It will be," Tiffany promised as Talbot offered a patient smile, then turned back to his car just as the interior radio crackled to life. Talbot's pace increased and he climbed behind the wheel of the cruiser. He snapped up the handset of the radio.

"What happened?" J.D. asked Stephen. The cruiser took off.

"Nothin'."

"Black eyes like that don't appear by themselves."

With a disinterested lift of his shoulder, Stephen carried his skateboard and sauntered toward the house.

"Wait," Tiffany commanded. "I think we should have your eye checked at the clinic or the emergency room."

"I already told you it's okay."

Christina, as if sensing all of the attention was focused on her brother, sniffed loudly. "My chin hurts."

"I know it does, honey." Tenderly Tiffany placed a kiss upon her daughter's temple. "We'll fix it while we take care of your brother," she assured her daughter.

Stephen snorted. "I don't need you to take care of me."

"Sure you do," she quipped back and followed him inside. J.D. didn't hesitate but walked past a fading Apartment for Rent sign and up the two steps to the front porch.

"Gosh, Mom, just get off my case, okay?" He rolled his one good eye and with as much attitude as he could manage, he dashed up the stairs. An instant later a door on the second floor slammed and within seconds the sound of angry guitar chords filtered down the stairway.

Tiffany hesitated as if she wanted to chase after him, but finally shook her head. "I'll just be a minute," she said to J.D. and he noticed the worry in her amber eyes, as if some of the fight had left her.

His heart twisted stupidly. "You need some help?"

She looked at him straight on, those intense gold eyes holding his for a second. He saw the beat of her pulse at the base of her throat and some of his suspicion melted. Maybe she was just an overworked single parent. "Thanks, but I can manage," she said coolly as she carried Christina to the little bathroom tucked beneath the stairs. "I have the extra key, if you just give me a minute I'll get it for you. It's in my purse, in the kitchen. Why don't you wait for me there—have some iced tea or…whatever in the refrigerator."

"Fair enough." The scent of her perfume teased his nostrils as she closed the door behind her and his groin tightened at a sharp, poignant and oh-so-sensual memory. *Don't go there, Santini.* Silently he called himself a blind fool, then strode to the kitchen. He nearly banged his head on one of the pots suspended over the cooking island and resisted temptation upon spying a plate of home-baked cookies that rested on the edge of the counter.

Christina let out a yelp. "Stop it, Mommy!" she cried, then he heard Tiffany's voice, hushed and soothing, though he couldn't make out the words.

Gritting his teeth, he opened the refrigerator, found a couple of bottles of beer tucked inside the door and pulled one of them out. What the hell was going on here? One kid was banged up and the other beaten to a pulp before being escorted home by the police. Despite all her intentions, good or not, Tiffany seemed to be sliding in the motherhood department.

He twisted off the cap and tossed it into the wastebasket under the sink.

"Owww, Mommy, that hurts!" Christina was admonishing, her voice trembling.

"Shh, honey, it'll just sting for a minute." Tiffany's voice faded again. Disturbed, J.D. walked out the back door into the hot afternoon. The covered porch opened onto a wide backyard. A swing and two rocking chairs were pushed against the worn siding and planters filled with blossoming petunias, marigolds and some other flower he didn't recognize, splashed color against the porch rail. A small foil pie plate had landed upside down on the top step and a spray of mud, flower petals and grass littered the walk.

J.D. eased past the mess and stepped onto the sun-dried lawn. Philip had bought this place—an investment of sorts, as their father was interested in expanding to this part of the state—just a year before his death. All the buildings—

house, garage and carriage house—were painted a soothing dove gray and trimmed with black shutters and doors. The white gingerbread trim and steeply pitched roofs added a touch of Victorian élan that, he supposed, appealed to nostalgic types who felt more comfortable in a rambling old manor than in a modern, utilitarian apartment house. Those renters would gladly forgo the convenience of a dishwasher for the gloss of original handcrafted woodwork.

He took a long sip from his bottle and felt the cold beer slide down his throat. Philip had never intended that his small, second family would move down here, but then Philip hadn't planned on dying suddenly at forty-eight. Scowling, J.D. took another cool swallow. A hornet buzzed past his head while a neighbor's dog began to bark incessantly, only to be scolded by a woman's sharp voice.

"Cody, you hush!"

The dog ignored her and kept yapping.

A wail from a discordant guitar screamed down from the open window on the second floor of the main house. Squinting, J.D. looked up and saw his nephew standing in the middle of his bedroom. Biting his lower lip, Stephen bobbed his head, a hank of dark hair falling over his eyes while he banged on the strings. As if he sensed he was being watched, Stephen glanced through the window and the guitar immediately fell silent. He disappeared from view.

J.D. wondered about the kid. Would he make it? Stephen seemed about to embrace the wild side of being a teenager. Just as he himself had done. J.D. had had a broken nose, stitches running up one leg from an automobile wreck and a juvenile record that fortunately had been cleared before he reached adulthood. Stephen seemed about to embark on the same dangerous path away from the straight and narrow—a path that included drinking underage, joyriding in "borrowed" cars, shooting BB guns at mailboxes and generally raising Cain.

"Hell," J.D. muttered under his breath as Tiffany, with Christina in her arms, stepped outside.

The little girl had a bandage on her chin as well as her knee, but she was clean again, face scrubbed, with no trace of the tears or dirt that had tracked over her round cheeks.

Tiffany, too, had taken the time to release her ponytail and apply lipstick. Her glossy black hair framed her face which, aside from the touch of lipstick, was devoid of makeup. Nonetheless she was a striking woman. No doubt about it. With high cheekbones, pointed chin, straight nose and those golden eyes accentuated with thick, curling lashes, she had a way of making a man notice her. Add to the already fine features eyebrows that arched so perfectly they appeared arrogant and the image was complete.

"Are you Daddy's brother?" Christina asked. Her eyes rounded as if she'd just made the connection.

"That's right."

"Daddy's in heaven," the imp said so matter-of-factly it was almost chilling.

"I know." J.D.'s jaw tightened.

"He's not coming back."

He exchanged glances with Tiffany and her eyes warned him to be careful. "I know that, too."

"Are you staying in a 'partment?"

"For a while," he said and felt more than a trace of guilt.

"How come?"

Good question. He noticed Tiffany stiffen, the tremulous smile on her lips freezing. "Uncle Jay is here on business—for his work—and…he decided to visit us."

"That's right," J.D. said, mentally noting that it really wasn't a lie. "But I'll be in town awhile."

Tiffany's mouth tightened a little.

Bored with the conversation, Christina wriggled and Tiffany set her on the ground. "You know, Jay, I still can't picture you working for your dad. You were always... well...you know."

"The black sheep, the son who swore he'd never work for his old man, the guy who did everything he could to keep his distance from anything remotely associated with Santini Brothers Enterprises."

His off-center smile was a little self-deprecating and his eyes, gray as evening clouds, darkened as if a summer storm were gathering in his soul. Tiffany tried not to notice. She'd been caught in the web of those eyes before and wouldn't make that mistake again. She couldn't. He tipped his bottle back and drained it. "As I said before, the prodigal had a change of heart because his older brother died." The grin fell from his face.

She folded her arms over her chest and sighed. "Life has changed for us all."

"Hasn't it, though?" His gaze touched hers so intimately she shivered, then looked away.

"So what's going on with Stephen?"

If only I knew. "He's nearly fourteen."

"And already in trouble with the law."

"Nothing serious," she countered, ready to defend her son against anyone and anything, including his uncle if need be. Rather than meet the questions in his gaze, she went to the back porch, grabbed a broom and swept up the remnants of Christina's mud pie.

"Looks serious to me." J.D. followed her and rolled his bottle between his palms.

"You should know about being a rebellious youth."

He hesitated, then set his empty bottle on the rail. "That was a long time ago, Tiffany." The way he said her name sent a stupid little thrill down her spine and an unwanted memory started to rise to the surface of her consciousness, a memory that she'd sworn to bury so deep it would never appear again. But there it was, in her mind's eye. Clear as the day it had happened: J.D. stripped to the waist, drips of sweat sliding down the finely honed muscles of his chest and abdomen.

"You can't just forget the past, pretend it didn't happen." Her throat constricted and she wanted to call back the words, but it was too late.

"It would be better if we could sometimes," he said, and she knew in a heartbeat that he, too, was fighting unwanted memories; forbidden, painful recollections of something that, if acknowledged, would only cause more damage.

This conversation with its intimate overtones was getting her nowhere in a big hurry. She swept the last of the drying pansy petals into the shrubs and noticed that Christina was busy plucking blades of grass and tossing them into the air. "Don't worry about Stephen," she said a little too sharply. "I can handle him."

"It's a tough load. Teenage boy, little girl, part-time job, and running this place."

"Not a problem, J.D. Well, at least not yours." She forced a confident smile and wiped her hands on her jeans. No reason for him or any of the Santini family, for that matter, to know any of her troubles.

"It looks like you could use a man around here."

"Excuse me?" she said, nearly stammering at his gall. "A man? Is that what you said, that I could use a man?" She let out a puff of disbelief. "Let's get one thing straight, Jay. I *don't* need a man. Not now. Not ever. I— we're—just fine."

"Are you?" He hooked his thumbs in the belt loops of

his jeans and she was suddenly aware of his bronzed fore-arms, all muscle and sinew, where his sleeves had been rolled up. His fingers framed his fly and she looked up sharply to see an amused smile slash across his face. Set defiantly, his jaw showed the first shadow of a dark beard and his teeth flashed white as he spoke. "Let me tell you the way I see it," he said, moving closer. Too close.

Tiffany's heartbeat quickened.

"Your daughter is only three, probably doesn't really understand what happened to her daddy, your son is on his way to becoming a major delinquent, this house is fall-ing down around you, and you're dead on your feet."

"Is that what you see?"

"On top of all that, you're trying to deal with being a widow and single parent."

"Not that it's any of your business."

"These kids are my brother's."

She rolled her eyes and fought a surge of anger. "Come on, J.D., you haven't shown much interest in them until now. Why all of a sudden? Don't tell me that just because you had a motorcycle accident you've had some kind of epiphany, because I won't believe it. It's not your style."

"And you know what my 'style,' as you call it, is?" His voice was low. Way too sexy. It brought back all those old, ridiculous emotions that she'd fought for much too long a time.

"Unfortunately, yes. I think I already mentioned that you're too independent, irreverent and self-serving to work for your father."

His eyes glinted with male challenge. "No doubt he'd agree with you, but he didn't have much choice because he seems to think blood is thicker than water."

"Is it?" There was no use continuing this conversation. "Time will tell." She turned toward her little girl. "Chrissie, I'm going into the house and check on Stephen. Stay in the backyard.''

The imp, squatting and watching a butterfly flit from one dandelion head to another, didn't reply.

''I'll watch her,'' J.D. offered.

''The gate's locked, she'll be all right,'' Tiffany retorted. ''You don't have to—''

''I said I'll watch her.''

Fine. What did she care? ''I'll just be inside,'' Tiffany said rather than argue with the man. She stalked through the house and up the stairs, telling herself that she only had a few weeks with J.D. so close at hand, several months at the most. She could handle it.

She had no choice.

A Do Not Enter sign was posted on the doorknob of Stephen's room. Tiffany ignored it, tapped lightly on the door and opened it herself.

Stephen was half lying on his unmade bed, staring up at pictures of models and rock bands and fast cars that he'd taped to the ceiling. His guitar lay across his abdomen and his injured eye was nearly swollen shut. He rolled it toward her as she approached. ''I want you to come with me to the emergency clinic and I don't want to hear anything else about it,'' Tiffany said.

''Forget it.''

''We're going, and right now. I can't take a chance with your eye. So come on and get into the car. On the way there you can tell me why you and Miles got into it.''

''It wasn't a big deal.''

''Of course it was, Stephen. Otherwise you wouldn't have landed at the police station sporting the biggest shiner I've ever seen.'' She stepped over CDs and video games to stop at the window. Christina had climbed into the old tire swing and had conned J.D. into pushing her. Tossing her black curls over her shoulder, the three-year-old clung to the ropes suspending the swing from a branch of the old apple tree and laughed delightedly. Tiffany sighed. When was the last time Christina had laughed—really laughed? When had Philip pushed her in a swing, or helped her onto a slide, or sat on the other end of a teeter-totter? Never. He'd never had the time, and here was J.D.—with most of his weight resting on his good leg as he shoved on the worn black rubber—sending Christina into a slowly spinning circle in the shade of the leafy tree.

Muttering under his breath, Stephen set his guitar aside and climbed to his feet.

"The officer said there was talk about a girl."

Stephen snorted. "It wasn't about a girl."

"Then what? Isaac Wells?"

Stephen's muscles tensed. Suspicion slitted his good eye. "I already told you that I don't know nothin' about him taking off."

"I know, but the officer on the phone said you were found with keys that might belong to Mr. Wells."

Stephen paled to the color of chalk.

"No way."

"They have the keys down at the station. With Mr. Wells's initials on them." She paused at the door and her son, chewing nervously on the corner of his lip, nearly ran into her. "You want to explain?"

"They weren't mine."

"Then whose?"

His jaw worked in agitation. "I—I don't know."

"Stephen—"

"I mean it, Mom. I found 'em. In, in, the park when I was in-line skating."

"And you didn't tell me or turn them in to the police?"

Oh, how she wanted to believe him, but this was way too much of a coincidence.

"No."

"You know that the police are going to take those keys out to Mr. Wells's place. If any of them fit in the locks of his house or his cars, they'll have a lot more questions for you. A lot."

Stephen's lips clamped together and Tiffany realized it was useless to argue with him at this moment. She'd give him a little time to think things over, but then she intended to get to the bottom of whatever it was that was bothering him.

"Wait for me in the car," she told her son, and stopped at the back porch where Christina, her small hand fitted snugly in J.D.'s large one, was skipping toward the house.

"Unca Jay says we can get ice cream," she announced.

"Does he?"

"After dinner."

"That'll be a while, honey. I've got to run Stephen to the clinic. Come along."

She reached for Christina's hand, but her strong-willed daughter thrust out her little bandaged chin. "Ice cream," she ordered.

"In a while."

"Now."

"Come on, Christina," Tiffany said, exasperated. Who was J.D. to try and interfere? *Give it a rest,* she reminded herself. He was just trying to help.

Or was he? She didn't trust her brother-in-law's motives. This sudden change of heart about his brother's family had to be phony or, at the very least, exaggerated. Nervous sweat broke out between her shoulders.

"I'll come with you," J.D. offered.

"You don't have to—"

"Come! Come!" Christina cried merrily as she tugged at J.D.'s arm.

"I want to," he said, his eyes serious as his gaze caught her. "I'll watch Christina while you get Stephen stitched up."

"You don't have to take care of us, you know," she retorted, feeling cornered. "This... We...aren't your duty. Don't you have work or something better to do?"

"Than look after my brother's kids?"

"They don't need looking after. They have a mother."

"But not a father."

"Oh." She laughed without a hint of mirth as a horn began to blast impatiently. Stephen. She started for the car. "So now you're applying for the job. Substitute dad? Give me a break."

With lightning speed, he grabbed her arm with his free hand and spun her around to face him. "Give *me* one, Tiffany," he said, his face suddenly stern. "From the moment I set foot here you've been baiting me and fighting me."

"Maybe it's because I don't trust you."

His jaw slid to the side and he dropped her wrist.

"Come *on*," Christina insisted, pulling on his other hand. He waited. The car horn blared again.

"Fine, fine! Come with us!" Tiffany said as she marched across the dry grass and fished inside her purse for her keys. Christina sprinted ahead and crawled into the back seat.

J.D.'s voice, calm and so in command that it irritated her, chased after her. "You know, Tiffany, we don't have to fight."

She stopped short and her temper flared. "Of course we do, Jay. It's what we've always done."

"Not always," he reminded her and she, remembering

too vividly how intimate they'd been, how she'd let down her guard before, felt fire climb up her cheeks.

"There are some things better left forgotten," she warned before opening the door of her car and motioning Stephen to climb into the back seat. Grumbling, he did as he was bid and J.D. slid into his recently vacated spot. He winced a little as he dragged his bad leg into the warm interior. Sweat dripped down the side of Tiffany's face as she inserted the ignition key.

Just get me through this, she silently prayed and flicked her wrist. The engine caught on the first try. If only the rest of the evening would go so well. But what were the chances, now that she was trapped with J.D. for the next hour or so? Slim and none leaped readily to mind, along with several wanton, and unwanted, illicit memories.

J.D. slipped a pair of sunglasses onto the bridge of his nose and Tiffany slid a glance in his direction. Wearing the aviator glasses he reminded her of the first time she'd seen him, and she willed that memory to fade.

She didn't have time to dwell on the past. Not now, not ever. They drove to the clinic in silence.

Only much later, after Stephen had been stitched up and they had returned home to a late dinner, had she, after spending hours with J.D. and her children, finally unwound.

Alone in the bathtub, with cool water surrounding her and the lights dimmed, she remembered, in vibrant Technicolor, the first time she'd come face-to-face with J. D. Santini.

She closed her eyes, sighed, and finally let all her old emotions come to the surface. It had been nearly fifteen years ago, she'd been eighteen at the time and more naive than any girl should have been.

She could almost hear the sound of champagne bottles

popping over the strains of "The Anniversary Waltz" played by a pianist seated at a baby grand so many years ago. She'd been much too young, had thought what she'd felt was love for an older man and had never expected to run into the likes of James Dean Santini.

But she had, and she remembered the first time she'd seen him as clearly as if it had been only this afternoon....

Chapter Five

Tiffany rested in the bathtub and remembered that evening so long ago....

"Look at that rock!" Mary Beth Owens, a friend who had graduated with Tiffany this past spring, reached for Tiffany's hand and eyed the diamond sparkling on her ring finger. "Wow," she breathed, her eyes as bright as the stone.

Blushing, Tiffany pulled her hand away and concentrated on lighting the candles that would warm the serving trays for the wedding reception she and Mary Beth were catering at the Santini winery in McMinnville.

"I would *die* for a ring like that. Philip must be loaded," Mary Beth gushed as she placed napkins with the name of the bride and groom onto a long cloth-covered table already laden with hors d'oeuvres and empty champagne glasses. A silver fountain was flowing with sparkling wine, the pianist was warming up and the guests, arriving from the church, filtered among the folding chairs in the huge tent that was the center of the reception. Under its own separate awning stood a round table crowned with the tiered wedding cake; to the right was another table laden with gifts. Near the entrance to the main tent, an ice sculpture of two entwined hearts was starting to drip. "So what's he worth? Do you know?" Mary Beth asked.

Tiffany only smiled. The truth of the matter was that she didn't know and really didn't care. Money wasn't her reason for planning to marry Philip.

Mary Beth, ever the gossip, pushed a little further. "The way I hear it, Philip's in line to inherit all of this." She gestured widely, her fluttering fingers encompassing the acres of vineyards, stately old brick manor, the winery buildings and the natural amphitheater tucked into the hills where the reception was being held. Vast and well-kept, the Santini winery was one of the most well-known in the region, but Tiffany wasn't interested in the profit-and-loss statements of the company. Philip's potential inheritance wasn't on the list of reasons she'd fallen in love with him.

"You know," Mary Beth confided in a hushed whisper, "there are two brothers, but Philip's the good one. The other—" She rolled her eyes. "Big, big trouble. Always has his father in knots or court or worse."

"Is that right?" Tiffany wasn't interested.

Mary Beth nodded, her head bobbing rapidly. "Good-looking as all get-out and just plain bad news. Always in trouble with the cops. My mom says that J. D. Santini is all piss, vinegar and bad attitude."

"Sounds like a real winner." Tiffany hadn't heard much about him, didn't really care. All she knew was that Philip's brother was quite a bit younger than he and had no interest in the family business. Whenever she'd asked about him, Philip had just shaken his head and sighed.

"James is just James. I can't explain him. Wouldn't want to try." Truth to tell, Tiffany wasn't all that interested in the guy.

She lighted the final candle beneath a silver chafing dish and nearly burned her fingers on the match.

"Are you and Philip gonna have a spread like this?" Mary Beth asked, clearly awed.

"No." Tiffany shook her head. "He was married before, so we agreed that we'd just have a private ceremony."

"Bummer. You should at least have a gown and bridesmaids and— Oh, look, here's the limo."

Sure enough, a white stretch limousine rounded a bend in the winery's private drive to park near the manor. The bride, a willowy blonde in a beaded gown, emerged still holding hands with her groom, a short, balding, wealthy dentist who had been married four times previously.

"Being married before didn't stop Dr. Ingles from having a big to-do."

That much was true, but the good dentist's fifth wife, the pampered daughter of a local television celebrity, had wanted a lavish wedding since this was her first and, as she'd been quoted as saying, her groom's "last." Tiffany didn't care about the ceremony; the less pomp and circumstance, the better, as far as she was concerned. She couldn't imagine a huge church wedding without the support of a father to give her away. Besides, as the bride she insisted upon paying for the event herself and her budget was limited. "Where's the punch bowl for the kids?" she asked, turning the subject away from her own situation.

"All set up. Over there. André handled it." Mary Beth motioned toward yet another table, then turned her attention to her job and Tiffany was relieved that she didn't have to make any more small talk. She smiled to herself as she spied Philip, tall, dark-haired and in command. She'd met him three months earlier at another event where she'd worked. He'd stayed late and offered to drive her home. She'd declined, refused to give him her number, but he'd persisted and within two weeks they were dating. Sure, he was older than she—fifteen years older—but it didn't matter, she kept telling herself.

Before meeting Philip, she had planned to start college in the fall, intending to take business courses at Portland State University while working two part-time jobs.

But then Philip had asked her to marry him and she'd said yes. He was everything she wanted in a husband. Stable. Smart. Educated. Successful.

The age factor didn't bother her. His ex-wife and he were cordial if not friendly, and his kids—a boy and a girl—were twelve and ten and weren't a worry. She, as an only child with a single mother, wanted to embrace a large family. She would love Philip's children as if they were her own as well as have her own children someday.

But things weren't perfect. Philip's parents, devout Catholics, had never approved of his divorce and didn't want him to remarry. And her own mother, who had struggled in raising Tiffany alone, had warned her to wait.

"You're only eighteen," Rose Nesbitt had said, shaking her head as she'd dusted the piano bench where countless youngsters had sat as Rose had spent hours trying to teach them what had come so naturally to her. "Give yourself some time, Tiffany."

"Philip doesn't want to wait. He's thirty-three, Mom."

"And too old for you."

"We love each other."

"He thought he loved someone else once."

"I know, but—"

"But it didn't last." Her mother had tossed her dusting

rag into a plastic bucket that held cleaning supplies. ''Just give it time.'' She had sighed and rubbed the kinks from the back of her neck. ''Real love isn't impatient.''

''Why wait?''

''Why rush in?''

''Because Philip wants to,'' she'd argued.

''This shouldn't be all his decision, honey. You're talking about marriage. Two people. Give and take. I know I'm not one to talk because I've never walked down the aisle, but I just think you should slow down a little. Date boys your own age.''

That was the trouble. They were boys. Tiffany had never felt comfortable with them. They were too young, too immature, too stupid. Philip was none of those things and as she watched him now, walking briskly between the rows of beribboned chairs, his hair starting to gray at the temples, his smile fixed and professional, she felt an inward satisfaction that this man loved her.

Unlike the father who had abandoned her and her mother before she'd been born.

''Hi,'' she said as Philip stopped at the table on his way to the bar where Santini wines were being served.

''Hi.''

''Everything set?''

''Looks like.'' She smiled up at him and Philip winked at her.

''Good job, kiddo. I'll see you later.'' He disappeared into the throng of guests that were arriving as if in a fleet. Valets parked cars, the pianist played, she and Mary Beth served and the best Chardonnay, Chablis, and claret the Santini Brothers Winery offered flowed like water. Guests in designer gowns and expensive suits talked, drank and nibbled at the appetizers.

The bride and groom cut the cake, sipped from crystal

glasses, smiled and glowed, then started the dancing on a platform set near a waterfall and fishpond.

The scene was romantic and Tiffany told herself to be practical; she didn't need this kind of expensive wedding and reception. She wasn't interested in limos and a designer wedding dress and all the show. She just wanted to marry Philip.

She was standing at her post, nearly forgotten as the guests had gathered around the bar and dance floor, when she caught her first glimpse of the stranger.

Tall, lean, hard as nails, this was a man who obviously didn't belong with the others.

In faded jeans and a matching jacket tossed over a white T-shirt, he stalked toward her tent. Tinted glasses covered his eyes and yet she could feel him staring at her with such intensity she wanted to run away. She didn't. Instead she managed a frosty smile. "May I help you?"

"You tell me."

"You're with the Ingles party?"

"If this is the Ingles party."

Should she call security? No. Just because he wasn't wearing a suit and tie didn't mean he wasn't invited. Every family had its rebel. "We have lobster thermidor or beef Wellington or—"

"You're Tiffany Nesbitt?"

Who was this guy? "Yes."

He reached across the table, grabbed her left hand and held it up to the light. Her ring caught one of the last rays of the setting sun, glittering brightly on her finger.

The man's jaw tightened, his already harsh features grew more taut. She yanked back her hand somehow and suddenly felt the ring she loved was ostentatious and obscene. "And you're...?"

"J.D."

Her stomach dropped. Her throat turned to sand. She was staring into the hard expression of the hellion.

"Philip's brother."

"I...I recognize the name."

"Good." His smile was as cold as death. "Looks like we're going to be related."

She couldn't hide her dismay. While Philip was refined and polished, this guy was as rough and edgy as a cowboy fresh from a two-week cattle drive. She tried to retrieve her rapidly escaping manners. "Pleased to meet you, James."

"No one calls me that."

"But Philip—"

"Is a snob. The name's J.D. or Jay." He reached into the breast pocket of his T-shirt for a pack of cigarettes. "Let's keep it simple."

"Fine," she said, feeling a general sense of irritation. What was James—oh, excuse me, *J.D.*—doing crashing the party in disreputable jeans and tattered jacket? He lit up, surveyed the crowd from behind his tinted lenses and rested a hip against the table. Tiffany tried to ignore him as she helped another couple of guests. But he never left her side. Standing in the shade of the tent, arms folded across his chest, lips razor thin and compressed, he smoked, then crushed the cigarette beneath the worn heel of his boot.

Tiffany hoped that Philip would return, that he would rescue her from having to make small talk with this guy; but her fiancé was busy, moving from one cluster of guests to the next, doing what he did best as vice president in charge of local sales for the winery.

She sensed rather than saw J.D. observing her, knew that he was watching her every move. She felt like a horse at an auction and was nervous, wary, her muscles tense.

"So what is it you do?" she finally asked, tired of the uncomfortable silence that stretched between them.

He slid his sunglasses from his nose and eyed her with a gaze that was as gray and cold as the barrel of a gun. "What do I do?" he repeated. "Depends upon who you ask, I guess."

"Pardon me?"

"My father thinks I'm a borderline criminal, my mother thinks I can walk on water and my brother sees me as a big pain in the ass. Take your pick."

"What do you think?"

One side of his mouth lifted in a smile that couldn't decide whether to be boyishly charming or wickedly sexy. "I'm definitely not an angel."

Goodness, was he flirting with her? Her silly heart raced at the thought. "I believe that."

"Smart girl."

Night was falling, shadows deepening across the grass. Candles and torches were lit, adding warm illumination to the luster of a new moon and the light from a sprinkling of stars. The piano player was into waltzes and love songs and Tiffany longed to be with Philip and away from his brother. Whereas Philip was strong and silent, a man whose patience and understanding added to his allure, this man was all pent-up steam and energy, a man who would have trouble finding satisfaction in life.

"So when's the big day?" J.D. asked. He fished into his breast pocket for his cigarettes again. Shaking the last one out, he crumpled the empty pack in one hand.

"Excuse me?" She began to pick up empty plates and cups since it was time to shut down the tent.

"Your wedding day. When is it?"

"We haven't decided."

He clicked a lighter to the end of his filter tip. "Doesn't

sound like Philip. He has his life planned down to the last minute. He's probably already picked out his cemetery plot.''

She cringed inside. That much was true. Philip balanced his checkbook to the penny, filled his gas tank when the needle hit the one-quarter mark, wore his suits by the days of the week and, as far as she could tell, his only vice was that he liked to gamble a little. But just a little.

''Philip would like to get married before Christmas,'' she said, then instantly regretted the words as J.D. surveyed her with eyes that called her a dozen kinds of fool.

''For tax purposes?'' He sucked in a lungful of smoke.

Because we're in love, she wanted to cry out. The tent was too dark, too close, and Philip's younger brother too…male—the kind of male a smart girl avoided like the plague. ''It makes sense.''

''Does it?'' He gave her a last once-over and tipped his head. ''Good luck. I think you're gonna need it.''

''I doubt it.''

''You haven't lived with my brother yet. I grew up with him.'' He sauntered away and spent some time talking to the bartender while, disdaining his family, he got himself a bottle of beer rather than the traditional Santini glass of wine.

She watched as he found a tree to lean his shoulders against, then smoked and slowly sipped his drink as night fell.

What did J.D. know about Philip? They were eleven years apart in age and light-years apart in maturity. *Don't let him rattle you, Tiffany,* she told herself as she blew out the candles under the warming trays and chafing dishes. She knew the entire Santini clan was against her marriage to Philip. J.D. was just up-front about it.

She saw J.D. off and on that summer. Their conversations were brief, cordial and detached. He didn't bother hiding his disapproval of her engagement, and she bit her tongue whenever she was around him, which, thankfully, wasn't often. He dated several women, all sophisticated, rich and brittle, none of whom he spent enough time with to justify introductions to the family.

J.D. made Tiffany nervous and fidgety, too aware of herself and his all-too-virile presence. She'd found out through snippets of conversation that he'd finished college and was thinking of applying to law school, though Philip found it ironic that his brother, who had come as close to becoming a criminal as anyone in the family, would want to practice law.

"But there are all kind of attorneys, I suppose," Philip had confided to Tiffany. "Some who believe in the system, others who try to use it to their advantage. I'm afraid James is going to be one who bends the law to fit his own skewed perception."

Tiffany wasn't so sure, because for all his faults—and there were more than she wanted to count—J.D. possessed an underlying strength. He had his own code of ethics, it seemed. Still, the less she was around him, the better she felt.

She made it through that summer and into fall, dealing with J.D. from a distance, talking with him as little as possible when they were forced together, and generally avoiding not only him, but the entire Santini family. Carlo had made it abundantly clear he thought his eldest son should, for the sake of the family and his children, wait to get married. J.D. thought his brother should forget about walking down the aisle altogether and Frances, Philip's mother, didn't like the fact that Tiffany was fifteen years her son's junior. "She'll get used to the idea," Philip assured Tiffany, but his mother barely tolerated her.

"You can still back out," her own mother said only two weeks before the wedding. It was early October and Indian summer was in full force. The days clear and warm, the nights crisp and bright.

Tiffany was feeling the first twinges of cold feet. She knew she wanted to marry Philip, to be his wife and the mother of his children, but everyone else seemed to be pulling them apart.

The occasion was a dinner at his house, ostensibly to celebrate the upcoming nuptials, but Carlo had drunk too much of his own wine and become surly, Frances had repeatedly touched Philip's arm and brought up his ex-wife and children, and J.D., seated across from Tiffany, had caught her eye time and time again. His gaze wasn't openly hostile, nor was it friendly; just intense. He managed a smile or two during the meal but clearly felt as uncomfortable with his own overbearing family as she was.

Philip, Carlo and Mario, Carlo's brother, were leaving for a convention that night in Las Vegas. Upon Philip's return, he and Tiffany were to be married. She only had to get through this dinner and the next week, then she'd become Mrs. Philip Santini. Sweat broke out on her forehead as she tried to concentrate on the conversation while picking at her rack of lamb and seasoned potatoes. To make the meal even more uncomfortable, every once in a while Mario and his wife would lapse into Italian and everyone at the table, aside from Tiffany, understood the conversation. She sensed that she was being spoken about, but never heard her name and silently prayed that the ordeal would be over soon.

God, it seemed, had other plans.

The family lingered over coffee and sherry as the clock in the front hallway of the old brick house chimed eight.

"Don't you have a nine-thirty flight?" Frances asked, startled as she counted the chimes. They were over an hour away from the airport.

Philip glanced at his watch. "It is getting late. We'd better get a move on, Dad." He looked across the table. "You wouldn't mind giving Tiffany a lift home, would you, James?"

Tiffany froze. The thought of being alone with J.D.— truly alone—was terrifying. "I thought you were going to drop me off," she said, trying to pretend that she didn't really care one way or the other.

"Change of plan. We're running late, so you'll need a ride." Philip winked at her and for the first time, Tiffany wondered if he was being a bit condescending.

"But—" She looked across the table at J.D. and caught the amusement in his gaze.

"Don't worry. I'll be good," he said. "Trust me."

Her words caught in her throat and she swallowed hard. She wanted to argue, but couldn't risk making a scene in front of Philip's parents. They already had reservations about her and she couldn't let them think she was a spoiled, insecure little girl. "Fine," she agreed with a smile that felt as phony as it probably looked. She'd foreseen something like this happening with Philip's schedule so tight, and she'd offered to drive herself to his father's house, but Philip had been adamant about their arriving together.

Now, it seemed, she was stuck with J.D.

She had no option but to make the best of a very bad situation. Philip and his father left, Tiffany offered to help with the dishes, but her prospective mother-in-law waved off her attempts and told her the servants would take care of the mess. Within half an hour she was riding on the bench seat of J.D.'s pickup, clutching the strap of her purse as if her life depended on it and trying to make small talk. He was, after all, going to be her brother-in-law. It was ridiculous for her to be on edge every time she was near him.

"Tell me," he said as they drove along the narrow country road cutting through the hills surrounding Portland, "what is it you see in Philip?"

"Excuse me?" What did he care? Storm clouds brewed in the night sky, obliterating the moon and hiding the stars. Fat drops of rain began to splatter onto the windshield.

"I mean, let's face it. He's nearly twice your age."

She bristled. "So I've heard."

"I'll bet." Shifting down, he took a corner a little too fast. The storm began in earnest. Rain peppered the windshield, drizzling down the dusty glass.

"Are you going to try and talk me out of it?"

"Could I?" He slid a glance in her direction and her pulse jumped.

"No."

"Didn't think so."

Headlights from an oncoming car illuminated the inside of the pickup with harsh, white light, instantly casting J.D.'s face in relief. Tiffany looked away from his strong profile. His hard, thin lips, tense jaw, eyes squinting as he drove, were far too sensual, far too male. The oncoming car passed them and the interior was dark again.

He poked the lighter. "Well, I guess it's your funeral."

"Wedding. You mean it's my wedding."

"Whatever." The lights of Portland came into view and Tiffany felt a sense of relief as J.D. lit a cigarette from the pack on the dash. She just needed to get out of the truck and away from Philip's disdainful brother. What did it matter what he thought or what anyone thought? All that was important was the one simple fact that she and Philip loved each other.

"You know, you could just try and accept the situation," she said finally as he cracked a window. The smell of fresh rain mingled with smoke. "You don't have to be antagonistic."

"Is that what I am?"

"At least."

"You'd rather I be what? Friendlier?" He snorted, smoke shooting from his nostrils.

"That would be a start."

"Would it?" He let out a huff of derision as he cranked the wheel around a corner. "How much friendlier would you like?"

Bristling, she quietly counted to ten. "Look, J.D., you don't have to try and bait me, okay? I just think we should be civil."

"Why?"

"Because we're going to be family."

The look he sent her could have cut through granite. "I've got more than my share of family." He eased into the lane for the Sellwood Bridge and as they crossed the inky Willamette River, he tossed his cigarette out the window. The ember died in flight.

"Just tell me what it is that you don't like about me," she said as he angled the car through the city streets. It was time to deal with all this pent-up and ill-directed hostility.

"It's not you," J.D. said.

"Liar.

"Turn here," she prompted when he nearly missed her street. "If it's not me, then what's the problem?"

"You really want to know?" Tires skidded on the wet pavement.

"Yep. That one, third house on the right."

He parked at the curb directly under a streetlight and cut the engine. Rain pounded on the car roof. "Philip already made one mistake when he got married the first time."

"And now you think he's making another."

He gazed at her with eyes as dark as coal. "Definitely."

"Well, excuse me if I seem offended," she said as his gaze shifted to her throat and the smoky air in the cab was suddenly stifling. She cranked down her window. "But I am. Philip and I are in love and we want to— Oh!"

He reached for her so suddenly, she didn't have a chance to react. His arms were around her, his mouth claiming hers with a wild abandon that stole her breath. She tried to push away, but he only tightened his embrace, his arms like steel bands surrounding her as his lips moved sensually over hers.

Her heart thudded, her pulse hit a fever pitch and the small soft moan that escaped her throat sounded like a plea.

He shifted, drawing her closer, his tongue sliding easily between her lips.

Closing her eyes she sagged against him, wanting more—only to realize what she was doing. *This was wrong. So very wrong.* She stiffened and pushed him away, half expecting a fight. Instead he let her go and his smile in the darkness was silently mocking.

"That's why you shouldn't marry Philip," he said, and she wiped her lips with the back of her hand.

"Go to hell."

He laughed as she scrabbled for the door and shot out of the truck as if she'd been propelled from a cannon. Her skin tingled with a wash of hot, deep color and she stumbled up the steps of the walk to her house. What kind of a fool was she? Why had she let him kiss her, touch her, create a whirlpool of want deep inside? She fumbled with her keys, unlocked the door and slid into the dark interior.

Oh, God, oh, God. Despair flooded her. What had she done? Slamming the door, she threw the dead bolt, as if the twist of an old metal lock could keep her safe from the horror of her own actions.

It was only a kiss, she told herself. A kiss. Big deal. Philip probably wouldn't even care.

Then why was her heart still pounding, her lips tingling, her insides quivering? There were names for women who did what she'd done.

Tease.

Flirt.

Two-timer.

Those were the good ones. The harsher, cruel names that she wouldn't even think about nibbled at the edge of her conscience and made her shake with shame.

She covered her face with her hands. It was only a kiss. One he forced upon her. She hadn't expected it. But she'd reacted, dammit.

Sagging against the inside of the door, she heard the tires of J.D.'s truck squeal and its engine roar, as he drove away.

Thank God.

"Don't come back," she whispered, clutching her throat and trying to still her heart. "You damned bastard, don't ever come back!"

But come back he had. Years later. And now, like it or not, he was living in the same house with her. Worse yet, that same ridiculous sexual hunger that she hadn't felt for years had resurfaced.

And this time she was free.

Chapter Six

Thank God it's Saturday, Tiffany thought as she wrote out a list of weekend jobs. She was already on her second load of laundry, waffles were warming in the oven and she'd pulled out her basket of cleaning supplies. Stephen could mow the lawn and wash the car while she tackled the floors and windows. As for her nemesis and newest tenant, he'd left early this morning. Before she'd gotten up, she'd heard J.D.'s Jeep fire up and roll down the drive. She was grateful that, for the next few hours, she didn't have to face him.

Ever since he'd rented the room upstairs, she hadn't been able to quit thinking about him. "Stupid woman," she grumbled, as she heard Christina stirring in her room.

"Mommy?" her daughter called from the upper hallway.

"Down here, sweetheart." She smiled as she heard footsteps running toward the stairs.

"Someone's here."

"What?" she asked just as the doorbell chimed.

Thinking she had a prospective new tenant, Tiffany smoothed her hair and headed for the foyer. Christina was standing on the bottom step and holding on to a corner of her tattered blanket. She was staring unabashedly out one of the narrow windows flanking the door. A tall, thin man with blue eyes and a nervous smile peered through. All Tiffany's muscles tightened as she recognized the bold features of John Cawthorne, the lying, cheating jerk who had the audacity to call himself her father. He literally held his hat in his hands, his big-jointed fingers worrying the brim of a dusty Stetson.

"I don't believe this," she muttered under her breath.

"Believe what?" her daughter asked guilelessly.

"Oh, nothing. Come here, honey," she said to Christina.

"Who's he?" The little girl stared straight at the stranger who had spawned her mother.

Tiffany's throat tightened. "My... Your... Uh, Mr. Cawthorne." Lifting Christina and balancing her on one hip, she braced herself, then opened the door.

"I thought we should talk," he said without so much as a "Hello." His eyes brightened when his gaze landed on Christina and for a fleeting instant Tiffany wondered if he could care for his granddaughter at all. Was blood really thicker than water? If so, why had it taken him over thirty years to figure it out?

"Now?"

"Before the wedding."

Her voice nearly failed her. "Well, then, I guess it better be now, because we're running out of time, aren't we?" Telling herself she was every kind of idiot on the planet, she added, "There's really not a whole lot to discuss, but come on in."

You're asking for trouble, she silently thought as she led him into the kitchen and tried to come up with an excuse to get rid of him. So what if he was the man who had sired her? Where had he been when she'd needed a father, when her mother had needed a husband, or at the very least, a lover she could depend upon?

Tiffany let Christina slide to the floor while John, damn him, eyed the refrigerator with its artwork, grades and personal notes to the family.

"I've got waffles in the oven," she said to her daughter and wished Cawthorne would disappear. She had nothing to say to him. Nothing.

"Not hungry," Christina said, winding a ringlet of her dark hair and eyeing the stranger suspiciously.

John turned and smiled, his eyes actually warming as he met his granddaughter's curious gaze for the first time. "So you're little Christina." Tiffany's heartstrings tugged ludicrously. This was *not* the way a family was supposed to be. Despite her own upbringing, she foolishly believed in the traditional family—of parents, grandparents, aunts, uncles, cousins. Holidays spent together. Vacations. Memories.

Fool.

"Christina, say hello to Mr. Cawthorne," she said.

"She can call me—"

"Mr. Cawthorne." Tiffany sliced her father a glare that dared him to argue.

His jaw worked for a second. "You can call me John," he replied and Tiffany nodded as she found a pot holder and pulled the plate of warm waffles from the oven.

Christina climbed into her chair and as Tiffany forked a waffle onto her plate, she lost interest in the stranger and her mother's reaction to him. "I want syrup," she ordered.

"I'd like some syrup, *please,*" Tiffany corrected as she

opened a bottle of maple syrup and doused the waffles to Christina's satisfaction.

"Where's Stephen?" John asked.

"Still sleeping." Automatically she cut her daughter's breakfast into bite-size pieces, then poured a small glass of cranberry juice.

"I'd like to see him."

She couldn't believe her ears. After thirteen years, suddenly it was important that her estranged father connected with them. "Let's go into the parlor and talk." Without asking, she poured them each a cup of coffee from the glass pot warming in the coffeemaker, then handed him a mug. "If you want sugar or cream—"

"Black is fine," he assured her.

"Good. Chrissie, we'll be in the parlor."

"'Kay."

Why she was even being civil to the man, Tiffany didn't understand. Gritting her teeth, she led him through an arched doorway and into the small, formal room at the foot of the stairs. For a man with as much wealth as John Cawthorne, the room with its re-covered camelback couch and secondhand floral rug tossed over floors that needed refinishing probably seemed simple and unrefined, she thought, then changed her mind. Wasn't he marrying Brynnie Anderson Smith McBaine Kinkaid Perez? There was a simple woman with far-from-refined tastes. Perhaps this room done in peach and forest green with its hardwood floors and lace curtains wasn't as quaint as she'd first thought. And so what if it didn't suit John Cawthorne's tastes, whatever they were? She loved it. The parlor was light, airy and filled with pictures of Tiffany's family. Her mother, Rose, and grandmother, Octavia, smiled from portraits hung on the walls. Stephen's baby pictures and school photos were displayed on several shelves of a built-in bookcase. Christina's toddler shots were mounted on one wall and a framed portrait of Philip and Tiffany on their wedding day stood on the mantel, but nowhere was there even a snapshot of John Cawthorne or anyone remotely connected with him.

And that wasn't going to change.

"Have a seat," Tiffany offered and John shook his head.

"I'd rather stand."

"Suit yourself." She settled into an antique wing chair and tried to relax. Impossible. This man, frail though he appeared, had humiliated her mother and abandoned her. She couldn't forget that fact. Ever. She could be civil, but that was all.

He set his hat on the rounded arm of the couch and sipped from his cup. "This is good."

"You didn't come all the way over here to check out whether or not I could brew coffee."

He winced. "Nope."

"Didn't think so." She waited and he studied the dark liquid in his cup as if he couldn't find the right words to say what was on his mind. As if she didn't know.

"You know I'm getting married Sunday."

"I'd have to be a hermit not to know."

"You got the invitation?"

"Yes."

He shifted from one foot to the other and she noticed how old he looked. Tired and worn. Like a scuffed, sagging cowboy boot whose heel had worn to nothing. *Don't do this, Tiffany. Don't feel sorry for him. He left you for thirty-three years. All of your life. Until now. When he wants something.*

"I was hoping you and the kids would attend," he said in a voice that was barely audible.

"I, uh, I don't think I can do that."

He swallowed hard and closed his eyes for a second. "I don't blame you. I know I've been a pitiful excuse for a father to you, but—"

"No father, John," she said as her throat began to close and tears threatened. "You've been no father to me." This was ridiculous; she couldn't be crying for this man who had done nothing in all his life for her or her children.

"All that's gonna change."

"It is?" She couldn't believe her ears. "Just like that?" She snapped her fingers.

"If you'd just give me a chance."

"Oh, please—"

His lips compressed. "Look, Tiffany, this isn't easy for me," he said, his voice firmer. "I'm not the kind of man who likes to admit to his mistakes. Hell, I know I fouled up with your ma. With you. I don't blame you for hating me, but I'm here because deep down, whether you want to admit it or not, we're family."

"Family isn't about blood ties," she retorted, standing as she blinked against the hot tears filling her eyes. "It's about love, sharing, commitment. It's about being around when you're needed, about sharing the good and the bad, helping bear the pain. Family isn't just about being together at weddings and births and funerals, it's about supporting each other every day of your life."

She stared at him and he managed to look ashamed for a second. "What can I say?" he asked, staring into his cup again and shaking his head. "I've changed. I nearly died after that last heart attack and I realized, then, what's important in life." Clearing his throat he looked at her and she bit her lip to keep from crying. "You are, Tiffany. You and your children. I won't lie to you and say that I loved your ma. Lord knows, we were never meant to be together. But you and the grandkids, that's a different story.''

There was a snort from the vicinity of the stairs and Tiffany glanced over her shoulder to find Stephen, his black hair rumpled and sticking out at odd angles, his good eye still a slit, his injured one swollen shut, standing on the landing.

"Oh. Stephen. Uh, you know John Cawthorne."

"Yeah." Stephen straightened a bit and walked down the remaining steps. "Grandpa." He spat the word as if it tasted bitter.

"Yes. He's your grandfather."

John managed a tight smile and extended his hand. "How're ya, boy? What happened there?" He nodded to Stephen's black eye as the boy crossed the foyer, shook his hand for a mere instant and shrugged.

"A fight."

"Did ya win?" One of John's gray eyebrows rose expectantly.

"No one wins in a fistfight," Tiffany interjected.

"Sure they do."

Sullenly Stephen lifted a shoulder again. "I did okay."

The room was tense, suddenly devoid of air. "There's breakfast in the oven. Waffles." At that moment Christina barreled into the room. Syrup was smeared over her lips and across the scrapes on her chin. A few strands of her hair were stuck to her cheek.

"I see you're busy," John said as he set his cup on a table. "Just remember I'd love to see all of you at the wedding tomorrow."

"You mean that?" Stephen asked.

"Absolutely."

The boy looked at his mother. "We goin'?"

"No." She wasn't going to change her mind.

"Give it some thought," John countered and for a ridiculous second, Tiffany felt sorry for him.

"I can't imagine I'd change my mind."

If possible, Stephen's eyes narrowed more suspiciously. Christina asked, "What wedding? You mean with brides?"

John grabbed his beat-up hat and bent down on one knee. "That's right, but only one bride. Her name's Brynnie and she would think it was just great if you were there," he said to Chrissie, then straightened. "If all of you were there."

Stephen's head tipped to one side as he eyed the stranger who was his grandfather.

"Don't count on it," Tiffany said, but the ice in her voice had melted and she felt a ridiculous stab of guilt for being so cold. "We're busy."

"Sure." He smiled sadly but didn't accuse her of the lie. "I'll be seein' ya."

With that he squared his hat on his head and was out the door in a minute.

"Weird guy," Stephen said as he walked to the window and stared outside. Through the glass Tiffany saw the man who had sired and abandoned her climb into a shiny silver truck—so new it still sported temporary plates. "He's rich, right?"

"Rumored to be."

"Maybe you should be nice to him, you know. Go to that wedding."

"So that I'm in the will?" she said and rolled her eyes. "I don't think so, Stephen. Money isn't everything."

"But he is your dad."

"That depends on what you think a father is," she said. "Now, let me get Christina dressed and you go in and have breakfast. Then you and I had better talk."

"About what?"

She picked up her daughter and started for the stairs. "We'll start with Miles Dean and end up with Isaac Wells."

"I told you everything I know."

"So I forgot. You can tell me again. Come on, Chrissie, time for a bath."

"I don't want a bath."

"Too bad." Tiffany chuckled as she climbed the stairs and touched the tip of her daughter's nose. "You need one. Big time."

"J. D. Santini." J.D. extended his hand to the lanky man on the other side of the desk in the small office. The building was quiet; the other businesses on the second floor had shut down for the weekend. "I appreciate you coming in to meet me. I hear this is a busy weekend for your family."

Jarrod Smith lifted a shoulder. "I come from a big family. There's always something going on." A sardonic smile sliced his square jaw. "Mom's getting married and yeah, it's a big deal, but it's not the first time or the second. Have a seat." Jarrod waved toward one of the two empty chairs facing his old metal desk. J.D. settled into a plastic cushion that protested against his weight.

"I'll get straight to the point. I heard that you're running your own personal investigation into Isaac Wells's disappearance."

Jarrod nodded. His eyes bored into J.D.'s. This man was intense.

"Well, the police are sniffing around my nephew, I think, and I want to find out why." J.D. sketched out his relationship to Tiffany and her children and his concerns for Stephen.

"Rumor has it the kid mixed it up with Miles Dean yesterday," Jarrod said.

"Ended up with a shiner that won't quit."

"And the police found a set of keys on him. Keys they think belong to Isaac Wells."

"The boy didn't do anything to the old man."

"No one's proved anything was done to him. Isaac might have just up and taken off on his own," Jarrod reminded J.D. as he picked up a pencil and turned it thoughtfully between his fingers. "But I agree with you. Ever since Tiffany Santini moved down here, her boy's had more than his share of scrapes with the law. Until now they've been minor. Nothing like the Wells mess."

J.D. relaxed a little. Smith seemed to be on his wavelength. "So what happened to Isaac?"

"That's the million-dollar question," Jarrod admitted. "People usually don't just disappear without a trace. Sooner or later he'll turn up."

"Alive?"

"We can only hope."

J.D.'s stomach clenched. What had Stephen gotten himself into? He reached into his back pocket and slid out his checkbook. The pain in his leg twinged a bit. "What kind of a retainer do you want to prove that the kid's innocent?"

Jarrod snorted. "I'm already working on the case."

"I know, but everyone needs incentive." He snagged a pen from a cup on the desk.

With a smile that bordered on evil, the investigator shook his head. "Believe me, I've got plenty." He stood and thrust out his hand again. "I'll keep you posted."

J.D. had no choice but to take the man's hand. "I'd feel better if we had some kind of agreement."

"You've got my word. That's good enough," Smith

insisted. "Trust me, I'm going to find out what happened to Isaac, come hell or high water."

"Okay, kiddo, I want the entire story. Beginning to end," Tiffany insisted as she nosed her car into traffic. Mrs. Ellingsworth was watching Christina and she and Stephen were alone, on their way to do some errands. He hadn't wanted to accompany her, not with so many questions hanging in the air, but she had forced the issue and won.

"'Bout what?"

"Let's start with yesterday," she said as they drove along the tree-lined street. Joggers and dogs ran on the sidewalks, dodging mothers with strollers near the park. "Do the keys the police found on you belong to Isaac Wells?"

Staring out the passenger window, Stephen lifted a shoulder.

"Do they? And don't give me any song and dance about you finding them in the park. That's not what happened and we both know it."

"Okay," he said, rebellion flaring in his eyes. "They were his."

Her heart plummeted. "Oh, Stephen."

"You wanted to know."

"I need to know the truth." Her hands began to sweat. "Let's hear it."

He sighed as if pained. "It's not a big deal."

"Wrong. It's a very big deal. The man is missing. No one knows where he is or even if he's dead or alive. And you lied to me."

"It was nothing, okay?" Frowning, he flipped his hair out of his eyes. He rubbed his elbow with the hand of his other arm. "I told you that Miles Dean had dared me to take 'em."

"Right, but you said that you didn't. That you saw Mr. Wells on the porch and changed your mind."

Stephen worried his lower lip with his teeth. "I did see Mr. Wells. On the porch, just like I said. But that was after I'd swiped the keys. He didn't say nothin' to me, just stared me down, and I took off."

Her insides twisted. "You have to tell the police the truth."

"I know." He stared out the passenger window and his shoulders slumped in resignation.

"Why didn't you before?"

His Adam's apple bobbed nervously. "Because... because Miles told me if I so much as breathed a word of it, he'd kill us."

"You gave him the keys?"

"No." He was emphatic as he shook his head. "I don't know why, but I didn't feel right about it, so I hid 'em in a box in my room. Then I thought I'd sneak 'em out to the ranch and put 'em back, but...I never got around to it. There was all that yellow tape around the house, sayin' it was a crime scene and..." He shrugged. "I thought I'd wipe 'em clean of any fingerprints and toss 'em into the creek. I was gonna do it when I ran into Miles at the Mini Mart."

Calm down, Tiffany, she told herself as her fingers held on to the steering wheel in a death grip and she felt sweat dampen her spine. *Don't judge, don't yell, just listen.* "Okay. What did Miles want with the keys?"

"Don't know." Stephen was as pale as death, but he appeared to be telling the truth.

"Is he planning on stealing one of Mr. Wells's cars?"

"Who knows? It doesn't matter. I never gave him the keys."

"Thank God." She braked at the hardware store where she had planned to pick up some supplies, but thought better of it. "Let's go down to the police station. You can tell Sergeant Pearson what you just told me."

"No way."

"Yes, way." She wasn't going to take no for an answer. Slowing at the intersection, she waited for the red light to change, then took a right. The police station was in the older part of town, not far from the park.

Stephen squirmed uncomfortably in his seat. "Mom, please, don't make me do this."

"You don't have a choice, Stephen."

"But Miles will kill me."

"I doubt it," she said, though she knew the older boy's reputation for violence. Miles was a tough kid who was angry at the world. "I'll handle Miles."

Stephen snorted as the courthouse came into view. Old brown brick, the building was three stories and housed the circuit court, the parks-and-recreation department, the mayor's office, library and, of course, the police station. "I hate this place," Stephen grumbled as she glided into a parking spot beneath the spreading branches of a maple tree.

"Good. Then let's avoid it. All you have to do is stay out of trouble." She cut the engine, pulled her cell phone from her purse and called Ellie so that the older woman wouldn't worry if they were gone longer than expected. "We'll come home as soon as we're done here," Tiffany promised her.

"Oh, good gracious." Ellie, who believed Stephen was an angel, was worried. "Don't let them bully him into saying anything he doesn't want to."

"I won't."

"Well, I'll be here with Christina. Now, don't you worry about us."

"I won't." She hung up, flipped the telephone closed and stuffed it into her purse. "Okay, kid, you're on," she said to her son as she opened the car door. Mumbling under his breath, Stephen reluctantly climbed out of the car. She started for the building, then stopped dead in her tracks as she spied Katie Kinkaid, her younger half sister, striding across the hot asphalt.

"Oh, great."

"What?" Stephen asked, his attention drawn to the red-headed woman fast approaching. "Uh-oh."

"Tiffany!" Katie waved one hand frantically in the air. Wearing a pair of khaki slacks, a white scoop-neck T-shirt and tan jacket, she headed toward them, the heels of her sandals slapping against the pavement. In her right hand she hauled an oversize leather briefcase.

"This is the one who's your half sister, right?" Stephen whispered.

"One of them."

"The other one's 'the princess.'"

"We shouldn't call Bliss that."

"*You* named her."

"I know, I know. Shh." She pasted a plastic smile on her lips. "Hi, Katie."

"Hi." Katie's wide smile was bright and infectious. Her green eyes sparkled, reflecting the afternoon sunlight. "Oh, gee, what happened to you?" she asked, cocking her head for a better view of Stephen's injuries.

"Nothin'."

"Doesn't look like 'nothin'' to me," Katie said, her face suddenly a mask of worry.

"A disagreement down at the Mini Mart," Tiffany clarified and Katie's eyes rounded.

"That was *you?* Gosh, I get to write about it, you know. Along with the obits and gardening news, I type up the police reports and while I was getting the info, I heard there was a scuffle down at the Mini Mart yesterday, but I didn't know who was involved." She touched Stephen's temple and he jerked away. "Of course, if I'd really wanted to know, all I would have had to do was have coffee down at Millie's, I guess."

"It'll be in the paper?" Stephen was horrified.

"Nope. Because you weren't cited. Looks like you lucked out this time.... Well, maybe not, judging from the size of that shiner. I'll bet it hurts."

"A little." Stephen was noncommittal.

"Well, be careful, would you? You've got a dynamite face and I'd hate to see it all banged up before you were twenty." Adjusting the strap of her briefcase, she faced Tiffany. "I heard John came to see you this morning."

Tiffany nodded and steeled herself for the onslaught she felt was coming. "He showed up around nine, I think."

"I told him it was a mistake."

"Did you?"

"Hey, we all have to handle this the way we think is best. I'm going to the wedding, of course, even though I'm not sure I totally approve. But it is both my mother and father, and if they can find some happiness together... Well—" she turned her free palm skyward "—so be it."

"If that's the way you feel." Tiffany wished her own emotions were so easily defined. Ever since seeing her father this morning, she'd been in knots, second-guessing herself.

"It is. I'd like to see Mom happy."

"Will this do it?" Tiffany asked, trying not to sound as skeptical as she felt.

"Time will tell, but I can't see any reason to rain on their parade. Sure, John was a jerk—" She slid a glance at Stephen, but Tiffany waved her concern aside.

"Stephen knows the story."

"Then he realizes that his grandfather made some mistakes in his life. Major mistakes. But now he's trying to rectify them. I figure why not give the guy a chance."

"I can think of a few reasons."

"Yeah, I suppose, but I figure it's time to let bygones be bygones."

"I don't think I can," Tiffany admitted, though she felt a tiny twinge of guilt.

"Hey, whatever you want to do is your business. But the wedding could be fun. At least the reception out at Cawthorne Acres will be. If you don't have anything better to do, why don't you and the kids show up? Josh, my son—you probably know him from school, Stephen. He's some kind of cousin to you and he'd love it if another boy around his age came."

Tiffany couldn't find a way to say no without getting into another argument. "I—I'll think about it."

"Do." Katie checked her watch and sucked some air between her teeth. "Oops. I'm late already. See ya." Half jogging to an ancient convertible, she climbed inside. With a clank, pop and cloud of black smoke, the car started. Waving, Katie wheeled out of the lot.

"Wow," Stephen said, watching Katie, her red hair flying, disappear around a corner.

"She's a real go-getter." Squinting against the midday sun, Tiffany added, "I didn't know we were related until we moved down here."

"You always said you wished you had a sister or a

brother," Stephen reminded her. "Every time Chrissie bugs me and I tell her to get lost, you tell me how bad it was for you growing up without any other kids."

"I do, don't I?" Tiffany said, touched by the irony of her predicament. Throughout her childhood and awkward teenage years, she'd felt so alone growing up with only her mother and a grandmother as family—three women who depended solely upon each other. Every night on her knees by her twin bed, she'd prayed for a sister or a brother.

Or a father.

Old, forgotten loneliness crawled into her heart—the same painful feeling of being alone in the world she'd hoped would disappear when she married. She'd bound herself to an older man, from an established family, with two kids of his own, and had hoped to raise three or four children of her own and become part of a huge, chaotic and happy family. Philip had come up with his own plans. More children hadn't been a part of them.

Clearing her throat, she turned toward the police station. "Come on, kiddo. We'd better get this over with."

Stephen looked as if he'd just as soon drop dead, but they walked past parked cars and spindly trees until they came to the wide double doors of the century-old building.

"This is a waste of time," Stephen grumbled.

"I don't think so." She pushed the door open. "Come on."

Inside the police station there was no air-conditioning and the few windows that were open were barred or screened, reminding Tiffany of where they were. The offices were now smoke free, but the walls and ceilings were stained by years of cigarette smoke that had hung cloudlike in the corridors and rooms. Stephen's feet seemed to drag on the industrial carpet, but they made their way through a maze of hallways to Sergeant Pearson's battle-scarred desk. Papers, memos, photographs and books were piled high. Three near-empty coffee cups were placed strategically around a computer screen.

A thick-set man with a crew cut that didn't much hide the fact that he was going bald, Pearson sat at his desk. He cradled the earpiece of his phone between a meaty shoulder and his squat neck, and managed to scribble notes on a legal pad covered with doodles.

"Uh-huh… And what time was that…? About eight last night? That's when the dog started barking?" He held up one finger, indicating that he was about through with his call, then waved them into the two molded-plastic chairs tucked between his desk and a partition separating his space from the next cubicle. "Don't worry. We'll look into it," he promised the person on the phone, then hung up and shuffled his papers to one side of the desk. "Stephen. Ms. Santini. What can I do for you?" he asked. He leaned back in his chair.

"Stephen has something he wants to tell you."

"Is that right?" Ted Pearson's smile wasn't the least bit friendly. "Good. Since the keys we found on Stephen yesterday fit into the ignitions of several of Isaac Wells's cars, I think it's time we had a chat." He raised his voice. "Jack, you want to come hear this?" he asked and a tall rangy man appeared from behind the partition. "This is Detective Ramsey. He's been working on the Wells case."

"Call me Jack." He shook hands with Tiffany and Stephen.

"Mrs. Santini, and her son, Stephen."

"Tiffany." She shook hands with the tall man and wished her palms hadn't begun to sweat.

His smile seemed sincere. He swung a leg over the corner of Pearson's mess of a desk and said, "Okay, Stephen, let's hear it. Shoot."

"Wait a minute."

J.D.'s voice rang through the offices.

Tiffany froze. Now what? Glancing over her shoulder, she watched as J.D., his limp hardly noticeable, made his way along the short hallway until he was standing beside her. "I'm the boy's uncle. What's going on here?"

"Who invited you?" the detective asked.

J.D.'s smile was cold and there was a spark of challenge in his gray eyes. "I invited myself. J. D. Santini." He thrust out his hand. "And I guess I should mention, I'm an attorney."

Jack eyed him warily. "A criminal attorney? The boy doesn't need representation."

"Good." J.D. stood right behind Stephen as if to shield him from an attack to his backside. "As I said, I'm Stephen's uncle and his attorney if he needs one. So." He rubbed his hands together and pinned both officers with his harsh gaze. "Now, what's this all about?"

Chapter Seven

"**Y**ou are *not* a criminal attorney," Tiffany said under her breath as J.D., in his new role of concerned uncle, escorted them outside the courthouse. A hot summer breeze blew through the streets, causing dust to swirl and rustling in the leaves of the maple trees.

"They don't know that."

"The police aren't the enemy, J.D." They crossed the parking lot and she wanted to throttle him. Who was he to play the role of concerned father? "Besides, you have no right—" she stopped at her car and whirled, thrusting a finger into his chest "—*no right,* to come barging in there."

"I thought you might need a little help and all I did was to encourage him to tell the truth without falling into any traps. Stephen did fine." His eyes when they found hers stopped her cold. An awareness of something dangerous and primal slid through her and she had trouble finding her tongue.

"I think I already told you that I...we...are doing fine on our own."

"Are you?" He gestured to Stephen as the boy slid into the passenger seat of her car. "He looks like he just came out of a war zone and he's getting into more than his share of trouble."

"I'm working on it, Jay."

"Then what about Christina? I've heard her scream in the middle of the night."

"I don't think this is the time or place," she said. The conversation was twisting in directions that she couldn't control.

"When?"

"What?"

"When would be the time and place?" he asked. "Whether you know it or not, we need to talk."

She shot a glance at Stephen and saw him staring at her with wary eyes. "Later."

"How much later?"

"I don't know—"

"Tonight," he said.

"No, the kids—"

"They can stay alone for a couple of hours."

He waved to Stephen as he made his way across the parking lot to his rig. Stephen lifted his hand halfheartedly and J.D. nodded. Without a backward glance he climbed into his Jeep and drove away, leaving Tiffany to simmer and stew. Angry and confused, she slid into the sun-baked interior of her car and quickly started it.

"What was that all about?" Stephen demanded. He fiddled with the buttons of the radio, changing from station to station.

"Who knows?" Checking her rearview mirror, she backed out of the parking lot.

"I don't remember him hanging out with Dad a lot."

"He didn't."

"So why's he here now?" Stephen settled on a station that Tiffany didn't recognize, then slumped in his seat and stared glumly through the window.

"I don't know. He's just concerned, I guess."

"Is he really a lawyer?" Stephen asked, chewing on his lower lip and rubbing his elbow nervously.

"Yes." She felt a needle of fear prick her scalp. "Why?"

"Just wonderin'," Stephen said, but Tiffany read more into the question and her heart sank. "Stephen," she said softly. "Do you need an attorney?"

"No," he answered quickly. Too quickly.

Careful, Tiffany, she cautioned herself. *Tread lightly.* "You're sure?"

"I was just curious, okay? It's not a crime." He stopped short at his own words, blushed and punched another button on the dash. Settling back in his seat, he chewed on a fingernail and closed his eyes as a song Tiffany recognized from one of his Nine Inch Nails CDs thrummed through the speakers.

Leave it alone, she told herself. *This isn't the time.* She drove through town and tried not to worry. Everything was going to be all right. Stephen had his share of troubles, but he wasn't a criminal, for goodness' sake. He was just a thirteen-year-old boy who was confused by his father's death and his recent move. For the first time she wondered if uprooting him had been a good idea. There was a chance he would have felt more secure in Portland with his old friends.

Now he was scared.

And so was she.

J.D. couldn't concentrate. Seated at the small table in his apartment, he shuffled the papers he'd received from the real-estate agent—information about the half-dozen properties that would work for his father's latest idea for expansion into a new winery and vineyards, but the words blurred.

He unscrewed the cap of his thermos and poured hours-old coffee into his cup. Frowning at the bitter taste, he added a splash of bourbon he'd bought for just that purpose.

For all of his life, he'd never had a problem keeping his thoughts on track. In high school, despite the fact that he'd spent more time rebelling than studying, he'd breezed through his classes. College hadn't been tough and he'd managed to work full-time and attend law school.

When he'd finally started working for a large firm in Seattle, he'd been able to spend hour after hour in the law library, or at his desk, poring over old cases, reviewing and researching, and generally working eighteen-hour days. He could get by on four hours' sleep and kept in shape by running the hills of the city while honing his thoughts on whatever case he was working on at the time.

He had chased ambulances—or, as he preferred to call it, he'd been a "personal injury" lawyer. That was where the money had been; that was where he could help individuals fight corporations, insurance companies, hospitals or whoever had wronged them.

He'd never been one to lose sight of his goals. Never been unprepared. Never been distracted. Well, almost never. The women he'd dated, slept with, or nearly loved, hadn't been interesting enough to deter him.

Except for his brother's wife.

Tiffany Nesbitt Santini had been the exception—and, he was afraid, his undoing.

Swearing under his breath, he took a long swallow from his cup and felt the coffee and alcohol hit his stomach in a warm, welcome flood.

Tiffany had gotten to him from the start.

Maybe it was because J.D. had always been competitive to the point of being considered cutthroat. Maybe it was because he'd always vied with his brother for his family's attention. Maybe he just hadn't liked being second-born. The fact that Philip had been a screw-up made it worse.

When Philip had dumped his first wife and kids, J.D. had been furious. He'd nearly beaten the living tar out of Philip, for all the good it had done. In J.D.'s opinion, Philip had failed his wife and kids by getting involved with another woman, and then he'd started to gamble more than he should. It was as if he'd given up all sense of responsibility and jumped feetfirst into a raging mid-life crisis. As soon as his divorce was final, Philip had moved on from that woman and zeroed in on Tiffany, who, in J.D.'s opinion, was far too young and naive for his older brother.

His family considered her a gold digger, and maybe she had been, but she'd stuck by Philip, given him another couple of kids, and, to J.D.'s knowledge, had never run around on his brother.

And J.D. had wanted her.

From the get-go.

Badly.

"Forget it," he snorted, as he heard Stephen tuning up his guitar. Discordant music rose from the room below. Tapping the edges of his real-estate reports on the table, J.D. stuffed them into his briefcase where he spied the deed to the house. Now, there was a problem. One he couldn't solve. His father owned most of the place. It was

J.D.'s unenviable job to determine if the apartment house Tiffany ran and called home was worth the time and effort of keeping it. The old man didn't necessarily want to cut the mother of his grandchildren out of what was rightfully hers, he just wanted to know if the property was a viable investment. It was Carlo's contention that Tiffany and the kids could live closer to the family in a more comfortable home. As Carlo was estranged from the grandchildren from Philip's first marriage and it didn't seem that J.D. would ever have children, the old man was deeply interested in Stephen and Christina.

But he didn't give a damn about Tiffany. He'd made that clear on more than one occasion.

Rubbing the area of his thigh that still bothered him, J.D. decided to call it a night. It was after ten and he was beat. He gulped the last of his coffee and wiped his mouth with the back of his hand. The thrum of guitar chords had stopped and the house was quiet. He went to the window and stared through the clear panes.

Past the leafy branches of the trees in the backyard, he spied a few stars that were bright enough to defy the lights of the town. Low in the sky was the moon, or half of it. He stretched and glanced down to the lawn where Tiffany was watering a few potted plants.

Her gauzy white dress caught in a breeze that teased at the hem, giving him a few glimpses of her bare legs. Unaware that she was being observed, she bent over each terra-cotta container and sprinkled the showy petunias, pansies and geraniums placed strategically around the drying grass. Her slinky cat wound about her bare feet, rubbing against her calves.

God, she was beautiful. Her black hair was wound into a knot pinned to the back of her head, but strands of hair had escaped to frame her face and nape. Thoughtfully she bit her lower lip, showing off a hint of pearly teeth as she plucked dead blossoms from the plants.

He couldn't resist. Knowing he was about to step over an invisible but very definite line that he might not ever be able to recross, he set his papers and coffee cup aside and grabbed the neck of a bottle of wine he'd bought earlier in the day. The Cabernet was local and J.D. had decided to check out the competition. Quickly he headed downstairs.

The steps creaked a little but the second level was quiet with only a nightlight in the bathroom offering partial illumination. He hurried down the final staircase to the first floor. A radio was playing softly in the kitchen but the only light was a glass-encased candle flickering on the table.

Quietly he opened several cupboards before finding the glassware, then plucked two wineglasses from a shelf and didn't bother to question his motives. The corkscrew was in a drawer with odds and ends of kitchen utensils.

He slipped noiselessly through the screen door and stood on the porch for a second. Tiffany was near the carriage house, refilling her plastic sprinkler at a faucet and he watched as she watered the planter boxes of impatiens.

Only when she'd turned and faced him, did he step out of the shadows of the porch.

"Oh." She froze, then recognized him. "For the love of Pete, Jay, you scared me." Wiping drips of water from her hands, she approached and he tried not to notice the way her dress hugged her breasts or the slight bit of cleavage that was visible at the neckline. Nor did he concentrate on the way her hips moved beneath the thin fabric.

He lifted up the bottle. "I brought this as a peace offering."

She stopped only inches from him and lifted a dark, suspicious brow. "Because—"

"Of our disagreement."

She shook her head and laughed. The sound was musical and vital. "If you buy a bottle of wine every time we disagree, you're going to go broke fast."

"You think?"

"No, I know."

"Then," he said, placing the glasses on the rail of the porch and beginning to slice the foil surrounding the cork with the tip of the corkscrew, "maybe we should just call a truce."

"You think that's possible?"

He skewered her with a look that made her swallow hard. "Anything's possible, Tiffany. You know that."

She looked quickly away as he placed the bottle between his knees and pulled the cork.

"It's late."

"Yeah, but where're you going?"

"Upstairs. To bed."

He left that line alone and poured them each a glass. "You can spare a few minutes."

She looked like she wanted to bolt, but took the glass and together they sat on a bench beneath a willow tree in the backyard.

"How about a toast?" he asked.

"To what?"

"Better days?"

She smiled sadly and he was undone. For an unreasonable second he wanted to enfold her in his arms and tell her everything would be all right. Instead he studied the ruby-dark depths of his glass. She squared her shoulders and nodded. "Better days," she agreed, touching the rim of her glass to his. "Lots of them."

"Amen."

They both took a sip and the night seemed to hold them closer. Faint light fell from the windows of the nook where the candle burned and somewhere down the street a dog gave a soft "Woof." Crickets chirped from hidden crevices and the rumble of traffic, slow-moving and sparse, was barely audible.

"So," she finally said as if the silence between them was unbearable. "How did you just happen to show up at the police station today?"

"When I got back here, I heard what was going on from Mrs. Ellingsworth."

"Ah," she said, taking a swallow. He tried not to watch the motion of her throat, but it was impossible. "Discretion isn't one of Ellie's strong points."

"No?"

She frowned at her glass. "No. But she's honest, kind, loving, fun, and she adores my children." With a half smile, she added, "I guess I can live with her need to gossip."

"She's just lonely. Wants someone to talk to."

Tiffany nodded and twisted the stem of her glass between her fingers. "So how's the search coming?" she asked. "Have you found a place for the winery?"

"I'm narrowing it down."

"To—?"

"A couple of places. One of which is the Wells ranch."

Tiffany sighed. "It seems we never can get away from that place, can we?"

"I told you I'd help," he said.

"And I told you I don't need any." She took another long swallow from her glass and he drained his.

"You're a lousy liar, Tiffany."

"What?"

"You heard me. You need a lot of help. You've got a house that's falling down around you and a job that takes a lot of your time. On top of that you're worried about your son and I don't blame you. Right now Stephen's rebelling all over the place. Maybe it has to do with Philip's death, but maybe it runs deeper. No one knows, but the simple fact is that he looks like he's been in a prison fight and he's probably still in some trouble with the police. Whether you admit it or not, you're afraid that he's somehow connected with Isaac Wells's disappearance."

"He's just a boy!" she protested.

"A boy who might know too much. He's running with a rough crowd, getting into fights and you don't know how much else, but the fact of the matter is he ended up with Isaac Wells's keys."

"It was a dare."

"One he shouldn't have taken," J.D. said, seeing her face whiten in the night.

"Then there's your daughter."

She gasped. "Christina's fine."

"Is she? Why the nightmares every night?"

Tiffany bristled and set her drink on the ground. What was J.D.'s game? What did he want? "What do you expect, Jay? She was barely three when she watched her father die, for God's sake. Of course that's going to cause some trauma. But it's normal. She's been to a child psychologist." Tiffany crossed her arms under her breasts and glared at him. What did he know about raising kids? About becoming a single parent? About dealing with a truckload of guilt because your husband died in an automobile accident while you survived? About facing yourself every morning knowing that you were at the wheel of the car when it slid out of control? Her stomach twisted into painful knots and she cleared her throat.

"I'm just concerned," he said so quietly that for a split second, she believed him.

"Why all of a sudden? Most of Stephen's life you haven't been around."

"I had my reasons," he said.

"Which were?"

He leveled her with a gaze that caused her heart to knock. "You don't want to know."

"Of course I do."

He lowered his glass to the ground and grabbed her bare shoulders in his big, callused hands. She started to shrink from him, but held her ground and inched her chin up a notch. "If you want to know the truth—"

"I do." Or did she?

"Most of my reasons for staying away had to do with you, Tiffany."

"With me?" she whispered, then stared into his eyes. Dark with the night they made promises of slow seduction, of a forbidden desire that no amount of time could erase. Memories cascaded through her mind, erotic images that tumbled, one after another, of the one night, just after Philip's death, when she'd given in to him, of the few desperate hours when she'd clung to him in her tormented and anguished grief. "You're right," she said, swallowing hard and trying with all her heart to forget those painful-yet-bittersweet memories. "I don't want to know."

"Too late." His fingers tightened, he lowered his head and his mouth slanted over hers as familiarly as if they'd been lovers just last night.

A small sound filled her throat—not the note of protest she'd intended, but a soft plea. His arms surrounded her and she knew she should pull back from him, slap him across his cocky jaw, but she couldn't find the strength. Instead she closed her eyes and for one glorious, taboo moment she kissed him back, opening her mouth, feeling the slick penetration of his tongue.

Her skin tingled. Her pulse clamored. Her blood heated.

He wound his fingers through her hair and the rubber band holding it in place broke, allowing the thick tresses to tumble free.

Stop this madness, Tiffany, stop it now. While you still can. But her protests were forgotten as his lips moved to her cheeks and eyes. His body pressed against hers and her nipples tightened expectantly.

Deep inside she began to palpitate, with a quivering need that chased away all her doubts.

"Tiffany," he said on a sigh, and his breath was hot against her skin. He kissed the length of her neck and rimmed the circle of her throat with his tongue.

Her head lolled backward and silently she offered him more. A dozen reasons to push him away entered her mind only to be thrust aside by the greater urge to love and be loved, to feel a man's hands, his lips, his tongue.

His fingers scaled her ribs and his thumbs reached forward, each warm pad pressing against breasts, seeking and finding that taut button beneath her dress, then moving in gentle circles, stirring her blood, stoking the already heated fires of desire that made her skin so hot that perspiration dotted her skin.

He found the front buttons of her dress, easing each pearl fastener through its hole, parting the fabric so that the warm night air caressed her suddenly bare skin. An ache formed deep between her legs and she knew in an instant that she wouldn't stop him; that no matter how far he wanted their lovemaking to progress, she would gladly receive him.

His tongue licked her collarbone and she whispered his name.

"Jay, oh, please—oooh!"

He kissed her through the lace of her bra and she cradled his head against her as his lips found her nipple. Through the fabric he suckled and she could barely keep her balance on the bench. One of his hands reached around her, rubbing her buttock as he teased and kissed her breast.

"Aaaahhh!" A terrified scream pierced the night.

"Christina!" Tiffany sat bolt upright. J.D. released her.

Buttoning her dress and calling herself a moron, she raced to the house, up the back steps and through the door.

"Mommy!" the little girl cried. "Mommeee!"

"I'm coming, sweetheart!" Tiffany flew up the stairs. J.D. was on her heels.

"Daddy! Daddy!"

"I'm here, baby," Tiffany said, running down the hallway and tearing into her daughter's room. "Right here."

Christina was in the middle of her bed, rocking back and forth, tears streaming down her little face. Tiffany scooped her daughter up and held her tightly, kissing her cheeks, holding her buttocks with one arm and her head with the other. "It's all right, Chrissie, Mommy's here. I'll always be here."

Sobbing, Christina clung to her. "I scared."

"I know, honey, I know. But there's nothing to be scared about. I'm here." She dabbed at her daughter's eyes and taking up Chrissie's favorite blanket sat in the rocker near the bookcase, the rocker she'd used when the children were infants. J.D. stood in the doorway, looking as if he wanted to say something, but he held his tongue and a second later Stephen, his hair at odd angles, half staggered into the room.

"Nightmare?" he asked and Tiffany nodded.

"Bad dream!" Christina whispered.

"You gotta do somethin' about it," Stephen said, rubbing his eyes and yawning.

"I'm trying. Shhh."

"Yeah, yeah." Stephen rolled his eyes at his uncle, then returned to his own room.

"Can I do anything?" J.D. asked, his face tense.

She shook her head, but held his gaze as Christina, giving up a tiny sigh, snuggled against her. "We're fine," Tiffany said and ignored the doubts in his eyes. "Just fine." She picked up the well-loved floppy-eared stuffed rabbit and tucked it into her daughter's arms. "Here's Bub." Then she pressed a kiss to her daughter's curly head and kept rocking.

Thankfully J.D. took the hint. "If you need anything—"

"I won't."

"I'll be upstairs." She held her breath as she heard him climb the steps to the third floor. Christina calmed as she always did and her eyelids slowly lowered as the tempo of her breathing steadied. Humming softly, Tiffany continued to rock until she felt her daughter's bones turn to butter.

Gently Tiffany tucked Christina into the bed and tiptoed into the hallway. She left the door ajar and walked toward her own room, pausing for a second at the open door to the third floor.

It was an invitation from her brother-in-law. She let her fingers run alongside the edge of the door and thought long and hard about his silent offer. A part of her longed to dash up the stairs and throw herself into his arms. Another part restrained her. J.D.'s invitation was one she couldn't accept. She'd been a fool to kiss him tonight. Letting him touch her and feeling all those long-buried sensations was tantamount to emotional suicide. With renewed determination and more than a trace of regret, she closed the door and walked to her room.

She could never, never let J.D. get close to her again. It was just too dangerous.

Slowly she unbuttoned her dress and caught a glimpse of herself in the freestanding mirror. Her hair was mussed, her dress wrinkled, her face still flushed. "Oh, Tiffany," she said. "Be smart. For your kids' sake."

She tossed her dress into the hamper and slipped on a cotton T-shirt, then slid between the sheets of her bed and turned off the lamp. Why couldn't she just tell J.D. to take a hike? To leave her and her small family alone?

Because you want him, Tiffany. It's just that simple.

And oh, so complicated.

Once before, she'd given in to temptation and she'd lived to regret it. She shuddered and closed her eyes. It had all started with the accident, the damned accident that had altered the course of her life forever. She'd been driving down from the mountain after a day of skiing. Philip had dozed off in the passenger seat. The kids had been in the back of the sedan, Christina strapped in her toddler seat while Stephen, exhausted and half asleep, was listening to his headphones. It had been nearly nine months ago, but she remembered it as vividly as if the horrible night had just been this past week.

The snow had been blinding as she'd eased down the steep hillside, not realizing that within minutes her entire life would change....

The snow just wouldn't let up. Fat flakes fell onto the windshield before the wipers could scrape them off. Ice had collected on the wiper blades and the steady glare from the headlights of the cars driving up the mountain were giving her a headache.

She'd never liked driving in the snow in western Oregon

where it usually began to melt only to freeze over again, leaving a layer of ice on the pavement.

Road crews were working around the clock and she comforted herself with the fact that the road past Government Camp on Mount Hood had been sanded and plowed and resanded. Yet her studded tires slid a little as she rounded a corner and she looked forward to finding dry, or wet pavement, at the lower elevations.

She was wearing gloves and her ski clothes and the heater was blasting hot air, yet she felt chilly inside. She punched a button on the radio, hoping to catch the weather forecast, but the signal was weak at this altitude, with the craggy peaks of the Cascade Mountains causing interference, so she settled for an old Otis Redding song that crackled and sputtered through the speakers.

Another set of headlights approached. She tried not to stare at the intense beams but she experienced a strange sensation, one that reminded her of a doe transfixed by the glare. *Relax.* The sound of a truck's engine rumbled and its tire chains buzzed over the muffled music.

It's just a truck. Big deal. There are dozens of them on this stretch of road, no matter what the conditions.

She tapped the brakes. They slid just a bit, then grabbed. Good.

To be safe, she eased as far to the right as she dared, but the guard rail was low in spots and the black canyon that gaped beyond her viewpoint worried her.

Honk!

She jumped, her foot slipping on the brake.

The truck's horn blasted again.

Her fingers tightened on the wheel. She pumped the brakes lightly.

Nothing.

Don't panic! But the truck was roaring toward them on

the left and to the right was the gaping darkness of the edge of the cliff.

Honk!

"Philip," she said as the truck's horn blared again. "Philip!"

"Wh-what?" he said around a yawn.

"The truck, oh, God!" At that moment the semi seemed to swerve and come right at them.

"Jesus!" Philip was instantly awake. He grabbed for the wheel.

"Wait!"

She hit the brakes. They locked. The car shimmied.

"Holy Mother Mary!" Philip was wide-awake and swearing, yanking at the steering wheel.

"Don't! Philip!"

The car slid sideways as the truck, only feet away, loomed like the very specter of death. "Tiffany! Crank the wheel! Pump the damned brakes! Get us out of here!"

"I'm trying!"

"Mom?" Stephen's voice cracked with fear.

She managed to turn just enough, but the truck, rolling past and out of control, clipped the rear end of the sedan. It spun wildly. She tried to stop, but hit a patch of ice and suddenly the car slammed through the guardrail and into the abyss.

"Oh my God!" Philip cried.

Tiffany screamed, and Christina let out a wail.

"Oh, no, oh, no, oh, no," Stephen muttered as the car, with a bone-jarring thud, scraped down the side of the mountain and skidded downward. Faster, faster, the wheels spinning, the brakes useless.

"Stop! For God's sake—"

Bam! They smashed into something. Hard. The windshield shattered. Glass sprayed. The car spun around.

"Mommy!"

"I'm here, sweetie."

"For the love of Christ!"

Again they were rolling rapidly forward. Faster and faster.

"Damn it, stop the car!"

"I can't!"

She saw the creek. Silver water slicing through the canyon, "Oh, my God—"

The wheels hit water. Bam! Every bone in Tiffany's body jarred. Ice-cold water ripped through the shattered windshield.

"Get out!" Tiffany yelled.

She scrambled for her seat-belt buckle.

"Mom! Dad!" Stephen's voice was strangled by terror. He was flailing in the back seat. Christina cried. Philip was cursing. Wild, raging water flooded the interior.

"Get out. Everyone get out!" Philip yelled.

Christina was crying and Stephen, too, was screaming.

"Tiffany, for God's sake, get to the shore." Philip was opening his door as she fumbled with her seat belt. The latch refused to give. "I'll get the kids."

"I can't get out!" Stephen's voice was filled with panic. It was black and dark and so damned cold. Water gurgled and swirled, splashing and rushing around them in an icy current.

Tiffany's fingers fumbled with the safety-belt latch.

"Get out! Get out!" Philip was outside the car, attempting to open the back door. "Christina, hang in there! Stephen, try to get out of the car!"

Tiffany was shaking, her fingers numb, but the latch finally gave way and she shouldered open the door only to fall into waist-deep water. Her feet slipped on the rocks, but she clung to the car, fighting the current, praying that they would all get out of this alive. So cold she could barely move, she found the back door and tried to pull it open. It wouldn't budge.

"I can't get out!" Stephen yelled.

"The safety locks!" Philip shouted. Tiffany couldn't see him but heard him splashing in the icy water. Christina was crying weakly.

"Get out the front!" she yelled to her son as the car filled with water. "Hurry!" She felt, rather than saw, Stephen crawl over the front seat to hurtle through the open door. Miraculously she caught his arm.

Sputtering and shivering, he clung to her.

"Christina!" she cried.

"Got her." Philip's voice sounded so far away.

"Okay, hang on to me. Let's try to get to shore," she yelled into Stephen's ear, though she had no idea how wide or deep the creek was. It could be a river, for all she knew.

"This way." Stephen stepped around the car only to be half-dragged underwater.

"Philip!" she cried, but there wasn't an answer. "Philip!" Oh, God, had he drowned? Did he have the baby? "Philip!" Where was he? She strained to listen but heard only the wild rush of the river. "Philip!"

"Dad!"

Her heart stopped. "He's got Christina, don't worry," she said to her son though she was dying inside. Her husband. Her baby. Where were they? Dear God, keep them safe! Oh, please!

"Mom?" Stephen's voice was faint, his teeth chattering and she realized that she was numb all over. Not a good sign.

"Try to get to the shore," she managed.

"Where?"

If she only knew. Frantically she looked around. Blackness everywhere. Only inky, cold, terrifying blackness. They could be in the middle of the creek or close to one bank. Who knew? But they couldn't stay in the freezing water. They'd both die from hypothermia.

Which way?

"M-m-mom, I'm so cold."

"Hang on, Stephen." How long had they been in the water? "Philip!" she cried and strained to hear. Far away there were voices. "Listen!"

She looked up and saw a bobbing light. The freezing water whirled and danced madly around her.

"Hey!" a male voice boomed. "Anyone there?"

"Help! Oh, God, help us!"

"Hang on, we're comin'," the voice assured her and she clung to Stephen and the car, trying to stay conscious, praying that her husband and daughter were safe.

She didn't remember the rescue. It had taken over an hour and both she and Stephen, suffering from hypothermia, had passed out. She awoke in a hospital in Portland to the news that she and both children had survived, but Philip, as a result of his efforts to save Christina, had died on the way to the hospital. No attempts at reviving him had been effective.

Tiffany was barely out of the hospital, hardly able to function from grief and despair, when she had to arrange a funeral. All of Philip's family was at the long, mind-numbing service. She was a widow. Alone with her children.

J.D. sat between his parents and sister-in-law, not so much as touching her or offering any sign of condolence during the funeral. White-faced, drawn and tense, he'd partially shielded Tiffany from the rest of the family.

But it hadn't worked. Philip's father, Carlo, had been

grim and forbidding, his black eyes boring into Tiffany throughout the eulogy. Frances, seated at her husband's side, wouldn't even look in Tiffany's direction, but shunned her and pretended that her daughter-in-law didn't exist.

Philip's ex-wife, Karen, a short blond woman with huge blue eyes, clung to her ex-mother-in-law and sobbed loudly, blowing her nose and sliding furtive glances at the woman who had, eventually, replaced her in her ex-husband's heart. She wailed loudly, while her children, Robert and Thea, were stoic and grim. Philip's older children were both in college, both acting as if they'd rather be anywhere in the world but at the funeral home, both seeming more bored than grief-stricken.

Throughout the service Tiffany held on to both of her children. Christina sat on her lap, and Stephen, pale and wan, was beside her in the pew.

Even without the harsh glares cast in her direction or the cold shoulders meant to shut her away from the rest of the family, Tiffany didn't have to be told that the entire Santini clan blamed her for Philip's death. She'd been the one who'd insisted upon going skiing that day. Philip had only indulged her. And she'd been behind the wheel at the time of the accident.

There had been a gathering of family and friends at the Santini winery in McMinnville after the funeral and gravesite service. Tiffany had never felt so alone in her life. Everyone was coldly polite and the hours went by at an excruciatingly slow pace. She just wanted to be alone, to hide and lick her wounds, to mourn her husband and plan her future; her children's futures.

The words of sympathy echoed in her heart.

"Sorry about your loss."

"A tragedy. Such a tragedy."

"I don't know what Carlo will do without him. And Frances... My, how this has aged her."

"Good luck to you and the children."

But after a few kind words—a courtesy to the Santini family—the mourners let her be, each finding his or her small group at the gathering, each whispering and talking about the accident, sending her looks that bordered on pity but oftentimes were tinged with hate.

She'd put on a brave face for nearly two hours, sipping too much wine and fighting back tears of desperation, when a voice behind her said, "Let's get out of here. I think you've done your time for today."

She whirled to find J.D. with her coat and the kids' jackets. Somehow she managed a thin smile and shook her head. "Thanks, but I have my own car."

"I know." Carefully, he removed an empty wineglass from her hand. "I think I should drive." For once he seemed sincere. Almost kind. "This has been a rough day."

"Amen," she agreed, and didn't bother to argue. She gathered up Christina and Stephen and handed J.D. the car keys. On the ride home, she closed her eyes, grateful for someone's thoughtfulness—even her irreverent brother-in-law's.

At the home she'd shared with Philip in northwest Portland, she managed to get the kids into bed before she felt herself coming undone. "I don't know how to thank you," she said as J.D. lingered in the kitchen.

"Brotherly duty."

"Above and beyond the call, if you ask me." She poured herself another glass of wine, though she was already light-headed. She was a widow. A widow, for goodness' sake. The future, once so certain, seemed suddenly bleak as it stretched endlessly before her. "Join me?"

"I think I've had enough."

"Me, too." But she took a long swallow of last year's Santini Brothers premium Pinot Noir. Feeling dead tired, she kicked off her high heels and leaned over to rub her arch.

"I'll help you to bed."

"You don't have to."

"I know. But don't fight it." He eyed the wine bottle and scowled. "Didn't the doctor prescribe some tranquillizers for you?"

"Haven't taken any."

"Don't. Not until you're sober."

"I am sober," she argued, and defiantly drained her glass.

"Come on, I'll help you upstairs."

"I don't need any help," she lied, determined to appear independent. She'd fall apart when she was alone.

"Fine."

She started for the staircase and nearly stumbled. J.D. caught her and sighed. "Come on, Tiff. I know it's been hard."

His gentle words, so unexpected and sincere, caught her off guard. With a tender smile, he managed to pierce the emotional armor she'd worn since the accident. Tears gathered in her eyes for the first time since the funeral service. "I'm...I'm okay."

"So you've been trying to convince everyone."

"But I am."

"Sure."

She swayed again and he picked her up, swinging her off her feet as deftly as if she weighed nothing. "Come on, Tiff, let's put it to rest." He carried her upstairs and down a long hallway to the bedroom she'd shared with Philip. Once there, he placed her carefully on top of the bed and brushed a strand of hair from her eyes. "It's all right to break down, you know."

Her chin wobbled and tears drizzled from her eyes.

"You were married to the guy."

"I'll miss him."

His jaw hardened. "It's only natural."

She dabbed at her eyes and sighed. "Oh, God," she admitted, "I'm so scared."

He stared down at her for a long moment, then shrugged out of his jacket, tossed it over the back of a chair and lowered himself onto the bed beside her. The old mattress squeaked as if in disapproval. "You'll be all right," he said, wrapping his arms around her and holding her close. His breath whispered across her hair and she let go of the storm of tears that had been building for days. Sobs racked her body as he held her, keeping her safe, whispering soft words of encouragement. She didn't fight him but let him hold her and by the time she fell asleep, emotionally and physically exhausted, the front of his shirt was wet with her tears and smudged by her makeup.

During the night, he'd pulled the covers around them and when she awoke sometime before dawn, her head aching, she turned and found him staring at her with eyes a deep, smoky gray. She didn't say a word. Didn't have to. He kissed her gently. Once. Twice. A third time.

Something inside her stirred. They kissed again—longer this time—and his lips were warm and gentle; his hands, when they touched her, were loving.

He didn't ask.

And she didn't say no.

Yet they took comfort in each other. Loving, kissing, stroking and finding solace in their shared grief.

In the morning, it was over. All the quiet comfort of the

night was gone and guilt, her companion ever since, lodged deep into a very private place in her soul....

J.D. had left and never once called her. Nor had he written or stopped by. She'd moved to Bittersweet, and, until that day just last week when he'd shown up and rented the upstairs room, she hadn't seen him again.

She'd thought what they'd shared was long over. A mistake. A one-night stand.

Now she knew differently.

And it scared the heck out of her.

Chapter Eight

"I'm just telling you she's doing the best she can," J.D. said into the mouthpiece of his telephone. It had been installed on Friday and he'd finally decided to report to his father.

"She's no mother," Carlo insisted, then his voice was softer as he turned away from the phone. "No prune juice... I don't care, Frankie, I won't drink it. Just coffee and toast. We'll have brunch after Mass."

"I think you're wrong." J.D. wasn't afraid to stand up to the old man.

"About Tiffany?" Carlo snorted. "What would you know?"

"She loves her kids."

"Love, shmove. Stephen's already in trouble with the law, isn't he?"

"A little," J.D. lied. There was no reason to bring up the Isaac Wells mess; not until there was concrete evidence as to Stephen's involvement. J.D. intended to take care of the situation—without his father's interference. "She's got problems, but she seems to be handling them."

"Sure." Carlo didn't bother hiding his sarcasm. "What happened, J.D.? Have you fallen under her spell like your brother—may he rest in peace—did?"

If you only knew. "I'm just telling you what I've observed."

"Yeah, and remember, if it wasn't for her, he'd be alive today."

"You don't know that, but let's not get into it again." J.D. wasn't foolish enough to point the finger at Tiffany for Philip's death, but his parents needed someone to blame, someone to punish for the loss of their firstborn.

"You're already standing up for her and you've hardly been there a week yet." Carlo sighed in disgust. "Sending you down there was probably a mistake."

"Probably," J.D. countered, refusing to be baited by the irascible old man. "You know I go by gut instincts."

"Humph. And what does your gut tell you about a new winery?"

"Still working on it, but I'll fax you copies of the most promising," J.D. said, thankful that his father had dropped the subject of Tiffany, if only for the moment. Frances was chattering in the background. "Your mother wants to know if you're keeping up with your physical therapy, if your leg is any better."

"Stronger each day."

"Good. I'll pass the word along. You'll call again?"

"Soon," J.D. promised as he hung up. He was surprised that he'd stood up for Tiffany, that he was changing his mind about her. He rubbed the tension from his shoulders with his right hand.

Tiffany wasn't quite what he'd expected when he'd

driven to Bittersweet. Stronger than he'd suspected, a better mother than he ever would have thought, she gave the outward appearance of being a responsible woman trying to make it in the world. Even if, as his parents were convinced, she'd been a gold-digging girl looking for a father figure a long time ago, she'd grown up, blossomed and done her best with the kids.

"Dammit all, anyway," he growled.

No matter what, she was a problem.

For him.

He wanted her. More than he'd ever wanted a woman. He'd given in once, when she was grieving and alone. She'd reached out and he'd reached back, going too far. He'd felt like a heel ever since, and yet he couldn't stop thinking about her, wanting her, needing her. Taking a room in this house with her just one flight down the stairs had been a mistake he'd probably regret for the rest of his life.

Tiffany Nesbitt Santini was the one woman on this earth whom he should avoid. Being with her was a betrayal of his dead brother. It didn't matter that he and Philip had never been close. Blood was supposed to be thicker than water. Honor and loyalty to a person's family were more important than lust. And yet, where Tiffany was concerned, J.D. was able to toss away his deepest convictions.

Well, he couldn't just turn tail and run. No, he had to face her. Until he'd finished his business down here and could return to Portland.

To what?

An empty apartment.

A domineering father.

A worrywort of a mother.

A job he detested.

"Hell," he ground out, then decided he had to do something—anything to keep his mind off her and his hands occupied. He'd start with the fence. One section of the old boards sagged and that was just the beginning. There were more projects around here to keep him busy. The porch was rotting, the windows losing their seals, and the roof and gutters needed attention. He could keep himself busy for a couple of weeks and maybe do some good for his sister-in-law and her kids. *Just stay away from her, Santini.* He found his shoes and hitched his way down the stairs. His leg still bothered him, but it was healing without the physical therapy that his mother seemed so focused upon.

On the second floor he hesitated outside Christina's room, then poked his head inside the partially open door and saw that the little girl was still sleeping. The bed was rumpled, the one-eyed rabbit on the floor again, but the imp was tucked into a fetal position, her thumb near her lips, as if ready to be sucked at any moment. He smiled to himself and walked the few paces to Stephen's room where he rapped gently on the door, despite the Do Not Disturb sign hanging from its knob.

No response.

He knocked a little more loudly.

"What?" was the groggy response.

J.D. took that as a sign to enter. He twisted the knob and shoved the door open to gaze upon a mother's nightmare. The kid's room was a mess. Clothes, towels, magazines, CDs and guitar picks were strewn all over the floor. A sleeping bag, unrolled, was kicked into the corner and the wastebasket overflowed with candy wrappers and empty fast-food drink cups. Stephen's guitar, with one string broken and curled, was propped against the end of the bed and a set of weights was rolled against a wall housing a low bookcase. "What d'ya want?" Stephen asked, then opened his good eye a crack and spied J.D. His demeanor changed instantly from surly to wary.

"You could lend me a hand." J.D. stepped inside, crunching a corn chip beneath his shoe.

"Doin' what?" Stephen rubbed his face groggily and with an exaggerated groan sat up in the bed.

"Some things to help your mom. A couple of downspouts need to be replaced, the gutters cleaned, the rail of the porch should be shored up, there's a broken step on the back porch, the windows need recaulking—"

"I get the idea." Stephen flopped back on the bed. "Maybe later."

"In half an hour."

"How about three hours?"

"Be ready." J.D. didn't give the kid a chance to worm out of the chores. He found Tiffany in the kitchen, wearing a soft yellow bathrobe and slippers as she poured pancake batter onto a griddle already sizzling with oil. At the sound of his footsteps, she glanced over her shoulder. Hot color washed up her neck and cheeks, and her eyes, gold in the morning light, slid away from him.

"Morning, Jay," she said as if he'd come down her stairs at eight in the morning every day of her life. She plucked a few fresh blueberries from a colander and dropped them onto the heating griddle cakes.

"Hi. I stopped by Stephen's room and tried to nudge him out of bed."

She smiled and cleared her throat as if neither of them were thinking about last night and the kisses they'd shared on the bench outside. Just at a whiff of the memory, his damn crotch tightened.

"How'd that go over?"

"Oh, you know, like the proverbial lead balloon."

"I'll bet. He usually sleeps in on Sunday. No summer

school.'' She smiled and showed the hint of a dimple. ''Stephen's not known for being overly enthusiastic in the morning.''

''Is any teenager?''

She shook her head, the dark strands gleaming in the morning light that streamed through the windows of the nook. ''There's coffee in the pot if you're interested.''

''Thanks.'' He poured himself a cup from the glass carafe and tried not to notice how her hips shifted invitingly beneath the terry cloth. ''I've been thinking, Tiffany.''

''Always a dangerous sign.''

''About Stephen.''

All her muscles tensed and her spine stiffened slightly. ''What about him?''

''We both know he's not involved in Isaac Wells's disappearance.''

''Of course he isn't,'' she snapped testily. ''He's only thirteen, for crying out loud! How could he be involved?''

''He's not. You're right. But my guess is that he knows more than he's saying.''

''Knows what?'' She kept her back to him as she worked, but he knew he had her undivided attention. ''Oh, this is ridiculous. He's just a boy.''

''Then why didn't he come clean weeks ago?''

''What are you saying, Jay?''

''It could be he's protecting someone.''

''Who?'' she asked, looking over her shoulder, her eyes darkening to the shade of amber he found so mesmerizing. In the terry-cloth bathrobe with her hair piled haphazardly on her head and the barest touch of makeup, she was damned near irresistible.

''I thought you might have the answer to that one.''

Sighing, she blew her bangs from her eyes. ''Stephen doesn't confide in me all the time.'' She flipped the pancakes deftly. "You know I think this is all a wild-goose chase on your part and the police's, but I'll ask him."

"Good." He wondered what the kid knew. What was eating at him. Sipping from his cup, J.D. opened one of the windows near the kitchen table and tried to ignore the scent of Tiffany's skin. Ringlets, still wet from her shower, framed her face and straggled invitingly at her nape. Again his groin tightened. His blood stirred as it always did when he thought about Tiffany and what sweet pleasure it was to make love to her. There were so many barriers between them—most of his own making, but barriers that needed to be scaled. "About last night—"

"Last night?" She froze, one hand holding the spatula.

"In the backyard."

"Oh." The back of her neck turned a vibrant shade of red. "I, uh, I don't think we should talk about it." She waved her spatula in the air as if she could physically block the train of conversation.

"Why not?"

"Because... Because... Oh, I don't know." *Because you confuse me. Everything about you makes me challenge my own convictions.* "Let's just chalk it up to bad timing, okay?"

"It was more than that."

Was it? Oh, Jay, part of me wants to believe you, but I just can't. "I don't want to hear this." She scraped the pancakes from her griddle and tossed them expertly onto a platter.

"We can't run away from it."

"Sure we can." She poured more batter onto the griddle and as the pancakes started to cook, turned to face him. "I've got a lot to deal with, Jay. A helluva lot. I don't need or want any man—even you, believe it or not—complicating things."

He smiled and she rolled her eyes, grabbed another handful of berries and tossed them onto the cakes.

"I'm not trying to complicate anything."

"Oh, right." She shook her head and sighed theatrically. "Maybe you can't help it," she said. "Maybe it's a part of your makeup, in your genes." She smiled a little. Goodness, he was handsome, even in the early morning. Unshaven, his black hair a little too long and shaggy to be fashionable, he looked rugged and hard and unbending. A man to avoid at all costs.

"I just thought we should discuss what happened."

"What happened was a mistake. Period. You're my brother-in-law. Nothing more. Even though Philip's dead and your family already despises me. My kids are dealing with the loss of their father in their own ways and I don't think that I have any right, or...or...desire—" He lifted one eyebrow, silently calling her a liar, and she sighed. "Okay, bad choice of words, but you know what I mean. I'm not ready to, well, you know, make things more difficult for anyone. Including myself."

Smothering a smile, he took a sip from his cup, then set it on the counter. "You're kidding yourself, Tiff."

"No way." She turned the pancakes and he came up behind her and slipped his arms around her waist. She wanted to push him away but she couldn't find the strength, or the desire. He dragged her closer, nestling her buttocks between his legs, allowing her to feel that he was already aroused. Deep inside she sensed a dangerous warmth spreading through her bloodstream. "Jay, don't—" she started to protest, then stopped. Because she wanted him. That was the simple and horrid truth.

He nuzzled the back of her neck and she let out a soft moan. "I'm warning you—"

"Good." His arms tightened around her slim waist. "Warn all you want."

"This isn't a good idea."

"The worst," he agreed.

"I mean it, Jay."

"You're gorgeous in the morning. Well, really, you're gorgeous at night, too."

"And you're incorrigible."

"I can only hope." Turning her in his arms, he rested his forehead against hers. Morning sunlight glistened through the windows and the odors of drying herbs and sizzling griddle-cakes mixed with her feminine scents of soap and lavender. His lips found hers and she opened her mouth as easily as a flower to the sun. The bathrobe slid open and his hands slipped around her waist, feeling her bare skin, the weight of her firm breasts unencumbered by a bra.

"Jay," she whispered as he lowered himself to his knees. She closed her eyes and he kissed first the top, then the underside of one breast before leaving a wet kiss on the nipple. "Oooh," she whispered and he took the anxious bud into his mouth. He teased its tip with his tongue and teeth and she leaned against the counter for support. With his hands, he parted the skirt of her robe and his fingers skimmed the insides of her legs. She sagged a bit and he reached higher just as she started.

"The breakfast," she gasped, and looked down at him in horror. "Oh, no, no, no." What had she been thinking, letting him kiss and touch and pet her so thoroughly right in the middle of the kitchen on a bright sunny day? The kids could have come downstairs or Mrs. Ellingsworth could have shown up on the back porch and caught them acting like a couple of hot-blooded teenagers. "For the love of Saint Jude," she whispered, scraping the burning pancakes off the griddle and tossing them into the sink to be devoured by the disposal. "I don't know what got into me," she said, pouring the last of the batter onto the griddle.

"Don't you?" He laughed wickedly and she blushed to the roots of her hair.

"Look, Santini, instead of bothering me—"

"Bothering you? Oh, lady, you don't know how much more I could bother you if I set my mind to it."

Maddening. That was what he was. "Why don't you make yourself useful? Pour orange juice or set the table or something."

"I've got a better idea." He kissed her cheek and she shot him a glare she hoped could cut through steel. "Call me when it's time to eat." Taking his cup of coffee with him, he walked to the back porch, then sauntered to the garage. Pretty high-handed of him, she thought, until she saw him return with a carpenter's belt slung around his waist and a ladder over his shoulder. Within minutes he'd propped the ladder against the side of the house and had climbed to the second story where he started pounding, presumably to secure one of the shutters surrounding one of her bedroom windows—a shutter that had hung at an angle ever since she'd moved in.

She shouldn't trust him, she told herself, as she started frying bacon and added the last of the berries to her pancakes. She always suspected him of having his own agenda and yet the memory of his touch caused her insides to melt.

With a clang of ancient pipes, water from an upstairs faucet began running. Obviously Stephen was up and showering.

Soon both of her children had padded downstairs. Christina was still in her pajamas and dragged her blanket with her. Stephen was wearing distressed jeans and a faded T-shirt. His hair was wet and his expression was sour, which wasn't unusual and often didn't disappear until his second helping of eggs or bowl of cereal.

"Mommy!" Christina ran across the kitchen and flung herself into her mother's waiting arms.

"Good morning, kiddo."

"I'm hungry."

"Well, breakfast is ready." Tiffany helped her daughter into a booster chair. "How about you?" she asked Stephen.

He slumped into one of the wooden chairs that surrounded the table and slid a glance toward the window where the ladder and the toes of J.D.'s boots were visible. "What is it?"

"Blueberry pancakes and bacon. Eggs if you want them."

"No eggs!" Christina cried, shaking her head as Tiffany snagged an oven mitt from the counter and pulled out the platter of pancakes. She slid one onto a plate, drizzled it with blueberry syrup, then pronged a slice of bacon from the frying pan.

"Careful, it's hot," Tiffany said, placing the plate and a small fork onto the place mat in front of Christina. "What about you?" she asked Stephen. "Eggs?"

"Naw. Just pancakes."

As she was fixing a plate for her son, she opened the window over the sink and invited J.D. to join them. Christina grinned as she saw her uncle climb down the ladder, but Stephen's mouth tightened at the corners.

"Are we goin' to the wedding?" he asked when the eggs were cooked and they were all seated around the table. He stared at Tiffany through a fringe of too-long hair.

"No." She didn't bother to elaborate. "I think you'd better go down to the barbershop this week."

"I want to go to the wedding," Christina insisted. "I want to see brides."

Stephen snorted contemptuously. "There's only one."

"So?"

"You don't even know who's getting married."

"Who is it?" the little girl demanded.

"Our grandfather, that's who," Stephen said.

It was on the tip of Tiffany's tongue to argue with her son and tell him that John Cawthorne would never be his grandfather, but she held the hateful words back. Why lie? Who knew what the future would bring? Though she saw no reason to celebrate his marriage to his longtime mistress, she hoped she wasn't so bitter about her lonely childhood that she couldn't someday be civil to the man and his wife.

"Have you considered going?" J.D., seated across the table from her, cut into his stack of pancakes with the edge of his fork.

"Fleetingly."

"But—"

"I'm not ready. Not yet." Using her fork, she shifted her scrambled eggs around on her plate and realized the turn of the conversation was affecting her appetite. "I'm not sure I ever will be."

"I think we should," Stephen said, settling low on his chair.

"Why?"

"Why not? He wants you to."

"I know, but—"

"Are you chicken?"

The light banter fell away. Tiffany's heart squeezed hard. "No," she replied. "It has nothing to do with fear.

I just don't think I should...honor—if that's the right word, or maybe validate would be better—this man's decision.''

"Why not?"

"It's a long story. Goes back to when I was a little girl and he wasn't around.''

"But he wants to be around *now*. Doesn't that count?'' Stephen asked, eyeing her with such scrutiny she wanted to squirm out of his line of vision.

"It counts. A little.''

Stephen reached for the syrup and poured a rich purple river over his stack of pancakes. "I thought you always said it's important to forgive.'' Tiffany's throat constricted. Her son had a point and there was more going on here than the typical teenager-parent argument. Stephen might be trying to tell her that she was lucky to have a father— even a latent, unconventional one like John Cawthorne. After all, Stephen had lost his own dad and was a little like a ship without an anchor, drifting emotionally. He probably needed a positive male role model in his life. Somehow John Cawthorne, who had kept a mistress for years while married to another woman and who had fathered two children out of wedlock, didn't seem the best candidate.

"I'll probably forgive John someday.''

"But you won't call him your father?'' Stephen prompted.

"Being a father is more than a question of biology and genetics.''

"Yeah, sure.'' Stephen shot her a look that called her a liar and a hypocrite as he pronged a forkful of pancakes. "You're always telling me to give people a chance.''

"Is that what you want?'' she asked and her son looked away.

"Dunno," he admitted, then nodded. "I think we should go to the wedding."

"Too late." She felt a sheen of perspiration coat her body.

"I want to go!" Christina said, her face smeared with syrup, her hands a sticky mess.

"Not this time."

"He's our grandfather!" Stephen challenged.

"I know, but—"

"This is something your mom has to deal with in her own way," J.D. interjected and Tiffany felt as torn as she had when she'd first learned of John Cawthorne's wedding.

"Maybe later we can all get to know each other," she said, realizing that her son was somewhat isolated down here. He'd left friends in Portland when they'd moved. The few he'd made here were trouble. She took a long swallow of her coffee and thought about the cousins that he had. Her half sister Katie had a boy, Josh, a few years younger than Stephen and Bliss was going to marry Mason Lafferty, who had a daughter, Dee Dee, from his first marriage. Surely there would be a baby on the horizon. And Katie had three brothers, none of whom were married, but who might link up with women who already had children.

With bone-chilling certainty Tiffany realized that Stephen was reaching out for a family, longing for more than he had, searching for a father figure. *Just as she had when she'd been his age.*

Tears stung her eyes and her hands shook as she set her cup on the table. "We can't go to the wedding today, but—"

"You mean *you* won't go," Stephen interrupted.

"But I'll see that we get together with your... grandfather and his new wife soon."

"Goody!" Christina said, throwing up her hands and

losing a piece of bacon from her fist. It fell to the floor only to be sniffed at disdainfully by a curious Charcoal who had been sunning himself near the window.

J.D. looked like he had more to say, but one glance at Tiffany seemed to tell him that she was having trouble with the discussion, so he quickly changed the subject to fixing up the house with Stephen's help.

"What do you mean?" Stephen asked when J.D. suggested they start with the fence.

"We'll shore it up, replace a few boards and then work on the porch or the windows."

"I don't know how to do anything like that."

J.D.'s eyes glinted. "Then it's time you learned."

Though Stephen acted as if he'd do just about anything to escape from his uncle's proposed list of duties, he finished his breakfast, dropped his plate into the sink and followed J.D. outside. Tiffany, still recovering from her son's interrogation, cleaned the kitchen, then helped Christina take a shower while J.D. and Stephen tackled everything from the gutters to the back porch.

It was almost as if they were a small family.

Be careful, Tiffany, she cautioned herself. *That kind of thinking might land you in trouble. Big trouble. J.D. is your brother-in-law. Not your husband!*

But Christina didn't know it. She seemed to be in heaven hanging around outside, a satellite who orbited around her uncle. Stephen, on the other hand, made no bones about the fact that he felt used and overworked. He grumbled continuously as he and J.D. cleaned the gutters and straightened the fence. He complained that he was supposed to meet friends, that his back hurt, that he was tired, but his uncle would have none of it and ran the boy ragged.

They stopped around one for sandwiches and lemonade,

then went back to fixing the back porch where it sagged. Meanwhile, with the sound of hammers pounding nails ringing through the house, Tiffany changed the beds, did the laundry and caught up on some neglected paperwork.

Christina had protested vehemently against a nap and was starting to get cranky around three-thirty. By that time, Stephen looked exhausted and J.D. finally released him from his duties.

Stephen was on the phone in a second and had made plans before Tiffany could say anything. "We're going swimming," he announced.

"Who?"

"Me and Sam."

"Sam and I," she automatically corrected.

Stephen rolled his eyes while Christina chased a grasshopper through the dry lawn.

"Be back by six for dinner," Tiffany told her son as he grabbed his scarred skateboard and sailed down the sidewalk.

"I'm not hungry."

"You will be," she called after him.

"Yeah, yeah," he said before adjusting his balance and coasting agilely around the corner.

"He's not such a bad kid," J.D. said, watching Stephen vanish past a stand of pine trees and draping an arm familiarly over Tiffany's shoulders. They stood at the edge of her rose garden near one side of the house. Honey bees buzzed around the blooms and their fragrance filled the hot air. Why did it feel so natural for his hand to rest on her shoulder? Why did the scent of his after-shave tickle her nostrils and make her think of tumbling into bed with him?

"Never said he was." She shrugged and slid away from his touch.

"I was kidding, Tiff. You've always stood up for your kids and your family. Even Philip."

"Why wouldn't I?"

His eyes narrowed on the distant horizon, but Tiffany suspected he wasn't watching the jogger and the black Lab running along the sidewalk, or that he noticed a van full of kids and a harried mother drive by. No, his mind was turned inward and he was focused on his own vision, his private viewpoint. "Philip wasn't a saint, you know."

"And you are?" She plucked a dying rose from its thorny stem and an angry bumblebee, buzzing indignantly, flew out of the petals as they dropped to the ground.

J.D.'s laugh was without a drop of mirth. "A saint? Far from it."

"What is it they say about casting stones?" She twisted another dying bloom from the nearest rosebush, then decided to wait until she'd located her gardening shears to finish the task. "I know Philip gambled, Jay." She squinted up at him as the late-afternoon sun was still bright, the day hazy and hot. Perspiration began to collect on her scalp. "And I realize that he cheated on his first wife." Her brother-in-law's eyes registered surprise. "He told me about sneaking around on Karen when Robert and Thea were still toddlers," she admitted. "Granted, he didn't confess until after we were married, but still, he told me."

"Maybe he thought it would be better coming from him rather than hearing it from a stranger."

"Well, he was right. As far as I know, he never betrayed me, and even if he did, what good would it do now to know about it?" she asked, searching his face for any kind of clue as to what he was trying to say. She'd known Philip's flaws as well as anyone. "The fact of the matter is that he died saving Christina's life."

"So he *is* a saint."

"Just a good man. With his share of faults."

J.D., if he was going to argue, didn't get the chance because at that moment Christina finally caught the bug she'd been chasing and let out a horrified squeal. Brown stain covered her fingers. "He's bleeding on me." She dropped the grasshopper as if it had bitten her.

"It's just his spit," J.D. said with a laugh.

"Spit?" Christina was horrified.

"We used to call it tobacco juice," Tiffany said, hauling her daughter into her arms.

"It's icky!" Tears rolled down her eyes.

"Come on, let's clean you up, then get something to eat."

For once her daughter didn't protest and after a bath, a peanut-butter-and-jelly sandwich and glass of milk, she settled down to watch television. Tiffany started dinner by cooking pasta for a salad and mixing the dressing in the blender. J.D. stopped his work for a bottle of cold beer, then continued to work outside, fixing a leaning handrail and several window latches. Exhausted from a long day, Christina dropped off in her chair and rather than rouse her for dinner, Tiffany carried her upstairs and tucked her into bed.

After she'd picked up a few scattered toys in Christina's room, Tiffany finished making the salad and checked the time. Stephen was already half an hour late and she was a little nervous. The kid always pushed her and was forever ten or fifteen minutes late, but a half hour was longer than usual.

"Don't borrow trouble," she told herself as she tossed shrimp, green onions and artichokes into the pasta salad, then turned on the oven to preheat. Stephen would be home soon. After all, he'd mislaid his watch a few weeks back. He'd probably just lost track of time.

Chiding herself for being a worrywort, she glanced up the drive as she walked outside to the corner of the house where J.D., wrench in hand, was fixing a broken outdoor faucet. The handle had fallen apart and he was replacing the worn piece with a new one.

"You don't have to do all this, you know," she said. "It's not part of the rental agreement."

"Just wait till you get my bill."

"Oh, right. And how much will that be?"

His eyes glinted wickedly. "Well, Ms. Santini, we're not talking dollars and cents, you know."

"No?"

"Uh-uh. I was thinking more along the lines of a trade. Tit for tat. I scratch your back, you scratch mine...."

She laughed. "I don't even want to know what you're thinking."

"It's twisted," he teased.

"Mmm. Sounds interesting."

"If you only knew." He winked at her, then turned his attention back to the task at hand. Setting his jaw, he gave a final tug on the wrench and twisted on the faucet. For the first time in months water spewed out of the tap and didn't spray at odd angles from the spigot.

"You're a natural," she said with a laugh.

"If you think this is good, just wait until you see me sink my teeth into a double valve, if there is such a thing."

At the sound of tires crunching on gravel, they both looked toward the street. Tiffany thought Stephen might have found a ride home, but her son wasn't anywhere in sight. She began to worry a little more.

A Dodge pickup that had seen better days rolled into the drive and the man behind the wheel, a lanky stranger, climbed down from the cab. Tall and slow-moving, he crossed the expanse of grass and approached them. "You in charge?" he asked J.D.

"Not usually."

The man, his hair a dark shade of blond, nodded toward the Apartment for Rent sign in the front yard. "I'm lookin' for a place to stay for a few months."

"I'm Tiffany Santini, and this is my brother-in-law, J.D." She offered her hand. "This is my place," she said and noticed J.D.'s mouth tighten a bit.

"Luke Gates."

He shook her hand, then offered his to J.D., who hadn't smiled since the pickup had stopped in the drive. Obviously Jay had reservations about the stranger who looked like he was more comfortable in a saddle than in the bucket seat of a truck.

Tiffany sized him up. His clothes were clean but worn, pride kept his spine straight and his eyes, she thought, had seen more than their share of pain. Crow's-feet fanned from his eyes and calluses on his hands suggested that he wasn't afraid of hard work. "I've got two units available, one in the basement of the main house, the other over the old carriage house. I ask for first and last month's rent, a security deposit, cleaning deposit and references."

"I imagine you do." His smile was slow, and his west Texas drawl nearly imperceptible. "Got both. Let's see the one over the carriage house."

"This way."

J.D.'s limp had nearly disappeared as he followed them around the house, then went back to work cleaning a patch of asphalt on the far side of the garage. He'd already told Tiffany he thought it would be a good place to hang a basketball hoop for Stephen. "A boy needs something to do when he's got time on his hands. He can shoot baskets, hit a tennis ball against a wall, or work out with a punching bag, but you need to give him something to do here, preferably something that he can do alone or with his friends, so that they'll hang out at the house. Assuming that's what you want.''

''I'd rather have them where I can see them than at someone else's place.''

''Good point.''

They'd settled on the hoop.

Luke Gates nodded as he walked into the upper unit of the carriage house, though, Tiffany suspected, he'd decided to rent it before seeing the patina on the hardwood floors, the red brick of the fireplace or the single bedroom. She guessed he'd made up his mind before he'd even parked his truck.

Luke signed the papers in her kitchen, offered her a list of references and paid the rent and deposits with cash. Crisp one-hundred-dollar bills.

This wasn't the first time she'd been given currency up front, since renters who hadn't yet opened local bank accounts sometimes had enough cash on them, but it always made her a little wary. Never would she carry that amount of money in her purse, but Luke acted as if it was natural and he intended to move in that very night.

''So where're you from?'' J.D. asked as they walked outside to the spot where Luke's truck was parked.

''All over.''

''You must've started out somewhere.''

''Yep.''

''But not from around here,'' J.D. prodded.

''Nope. Texas. A little town east of El Paso.'' With an enigmatic smile, he climbed into his truck, ground the gears and backed out of the shady drive.

''I don't trust him,'' J.D. said once the truck had

rounded the corner, leaving a trail of smelly blue exhaust in its wake. They stood on the porch together as the shadows of evening began to stretch across the parched grass.

"You don't trust anyone," she observed, but understood what J.D. was saying; Luke was the kind of man who made people edgy, not so much by what he said as by what he didn't say—a man who didn't give out much information but took in a whole lot.

"Not true." One side of J.D.'s mouth lifted and Tiffany's heart skipped a silly little beat. As easily as if he'd done it a thousand times before, he wrapped his arms around her waist. "But people have to earn my trust and it takes time."

"Does it?"

His face was so close to hers that she noticed the webbing of colors—blue and green—beneath the gray of his eyes. "Yep. A long time." He kissed her then, and her insides melted. His lips were firm and warm. So damned inviting. She and he were becoming familiar—way too familiar—and the feel of him, of his hands locked behind the small of her back, was a sensation she didn't want to give up. Ever.

When he lifted his head, she smiled, sighed, then rested her head against his shoulder. "James Dean Santini, what in the world am I going to do with you?" she asked as the moon began to rise.

"Good question. I was just thinking the same thing about you."

"They say that great minds think alike."

"Do they?" he asked, his voice deep, his gaze so intense that she had to look away, at anything. She chose her watch and felt a frisson of dread. "Stephen's so much later than usual."

"He's a thirteen-year-old boy."

"I know, I know, and he's chronically pushing his curfew back, but not by more than fifteen, maybe twenty minutes."

"He'll show up." J.D. was confident. Always.

"I hope so."

He folded her into his arms again and kissed her temple. "Worrying isn't going to help."

She knew it, but couldn't help the edge of concern that nagged at her. Lately Stephen had been getting into more and more trouble. It wasn't the pack of cigarettes she'd found in his room that bothered her, but this business with Isaac Wells and the fight with Miles Dean the other day. Not to mention his general bad attitude.

"It'll be all right," J.D. promised, as if reading her mind.

"I hope you're right."

Somewhere not too far away church bells tolled, the chimes ringing through the town and echoing off the surrounding hills. Tiffany lifted her head and sighed.

"Something else is bothering you," J.D. said, touching her chin with one finger.

"Hear that?" The melodic bells continued to peal and Tiffany's heart squeezed painfully.

"Late service?"

"Nope." She rubbed her arms as if to ward off a chill. "I think my father just got married."

Chapter Nine

"I've called everywhere," Tiffany said, hanging up the kitchen telephone and leaning heavily against the wall. "He's gone."

"We'll find him," J.D. insisted. "Ask Mrs. Ellingsworth to watch Christina and we'll start looking for him."

"Where?"

"You tell me."

Don't panic. He's fine. He's got to be. With trembling fingers she dialed Ellie's number and tried to remain calm as the telephone rang. When the older woman answered, Tiffany explained what was going on.

"I'll be up in a second," Ellie said without hesitation. "Now don't you worry."

If only that was possible. These days, worry seemed to be Tiffany's middle name.

True to her word, Ellie was at the back door within minutes and bustling them both outside. "You know how boys are, never can keep track of time. My Charlie, he was the worst. Gave me every gray hair on my head, I swear.'' But the concern in her eyes betrayed her. She, too, was upset.

''It's so unlike Stephen to be this late,'' Tiffany said, once they were in J.D.'s Jeep and driving through the narrow streets and alleys of Bittersweet. Dusk had given way to the deeper shades of evening and a few streetlamps had begun to glow.

''Relax.'' J.D. patted her knee as he shifted down. ''Let's start with the obvious. Tell me where his friends live.''

''Okay. Let's think. He said he was with Sam—Sam Prescott—but when I called over there, no one answered.''

''Where does Sam live?''

''On the outskirts of town, to the north, near the water tower.''

J.D. maneuvered his Jeep through town, past the park and shopping mall to a residential district. The Prescotts resided in a log cabin that had been in the family for generations. The house was dark, the porch light burning when Tiffany hurried up the front path to the door. She rapped firmly on the old oak panels, then jabbed at the doorbell, but though the buzzer went off inside, no one answered.

''Something's really wrong,'' she said, spying Sam's ten-speed chained to a post supporting the roof of the porch and his skateboard left near the steps. ''If Sam were with Stephen he'd be on his bike or skateboard.''

''You think.''

''I know.'' Though the evening was warm, she felt a chill deep in her soul and rubbed her arms where goose bumps had taken hold. Where was Stephen? Thoughts of injury, kidnapping or worse skated through her mind. She noticed the uneaten bowl of cat food and two rolled newspapers left on the front porch, as if no one had been home for a couple of days. "It's possible the Prescotts are out of town," she admitted.

J.D.'s expression hardened as he, too, noticed the signs of inactivity at the house. "Looks that way, doesn't it?"

"So Stephen lied," she said, disheartened. Ever since Philip's death, her son had become more secretive, and he'd started lying about the time of Isaac Wells's disappearance. "I think we should go over to the Deans' house. They live in a mobile home about two miles up the road."

J.D. didn't waste any time. He drove unerringly to the Dean property and pulled into a weed-choked drive. Two disabled cars sat rusting by a vegetable garden surrounded by a high chicken-wire fence to keep out the deer. Besides the mobile home, there were a shed and a lean-to barn by which a skinny horse stood, flicking flies with his tail and trying to find any blade of grass in the small paddock.

Tiffany was out of the Jeep before it stopped. She hurried up a couple of weathered steps, nearly banged her head on a hanging pot overflowing with dying geraniums and pounded on the door. Vera Dean, Miles and Laddy's mother, opened it a second later. She was tall and thin, with a fading beauty that matched her worn-off lipstick, short, shaggy blond hair and tanned skin stretched taut over high cheekbones. She looked as tired as a plow horse after a day in the fields, and her smile, friendly at first, fell as she recognized Tiffany.

"Hi, Vera. I'm sorry to stop by unannounced, but I'm looking for Stephen," Tiffany said. "He's missing and I thought he might have come here."

"After the fight he had with Miles?" Vera shook her head and reached into the pocket of her jeans for a leather case that held a pack of cigarettes. "No way."

"You're sure?"

"Absolutely."

Tiffany wasn't convinced the woman was telling the truth. "Could I talk to Miles?"

Vera unclasped the case and stared at J.D., looking him up and down as he stood on the step behind Tiffany. "Miles isn't here."

Warning bells clanged in her mind. Both boys, known to get into trouble together, were missing. "Do you know where he is?"

"Miles?" She let out a throaty laugh. "Nope. That boy's just like his old man. Never around when you need him. But I'll let him know you dropped by." She shook out a long, slim cigarette and held it between two fingers. "Anything else?"

"No. Just please have Miles call me when he gets in."

"Will do." She shut the door and Tiffany walked back to the car, convinced that the boy would never get the message.

"Friendly," J.D. observed sarcastically.

"She doesn't like me. Or Stephen."

"Any particular reason?"

"Not that I know of, but I don't take it personally. She doesn't get along with many people. Her husband, Ray, is a guy who hires on at local ranches and he's been in and out of jail since he was nineteen. Right now he's out, but no one thinks it'll last."

"You know a lot for a newcomer to Bittersweet."

"It's a small town. Everyone has his nose in everyone else's business. I hear it all day long—down at the insurance office or when I'm having coffee down at Millie's or, if all else fails, from my renters."

They drove toward town as the stars winked in the dark sky. Tiffany leaned her arm out the open window and tried to imagine where her son had gone. Was he with Miles, and more importantly, was he safe? Oh, dear God, she prayed, please, let him be all right.

"I have an idea," J.D. ventured as he slid her a glance.

"About Stephen?"

"Mmm." He drove through town, but didn't head toward her house. "Remember this morning at breakfast? Stephen seemed pretty determined to go to the Cawthorne wedding."

She felt her shoulders sag as she remembered the conversation about her father. "It was just talk."

"Was it?" J.D. asked as they passed the post office.

"It's his new thing—try to argue Mom into a corner."

"Or he could have been serious."

"Why?"

J.D. lifted a shoulder. "Curiosity. Or a need to connect with his mother's family. Who knows?"

Tiffany didn't want to believe that Stephen would openly defy her. Not this way. "He…he wouldn't have gone to the wedding. No way. Same goes for the reception."

"A few days ago you were certain he knew nothing about Isaac Wells's disappearance. Now you're not so sure."

"He must be somewhere else." She didn't want to believe that her boy would lie so blatantly—especially about this—and yet, she couldn't overlook any possibility. Staring out the bug-spattered windshield, she realized that J.D. wasn't listening to her arguments anyway. He was driving out of town in the direction of Cawthorne Acres, John's ranch. The thought hit her like the proverbial ton of bricks. "You're not really going to take me to the wedding reception, are you?"

He lifted a dark brow. "Seems as if you were invited."

"I know, but—"

"We'll just see if anyone's seen Stephen."

"No!" She was emphatic.

"Got any better ideas?"

She wanted to come up with something—anything other than her estranged father's wedding—but she couldn't. Her stomach twisted into tight little knots. "All right, we'll check," she finally conceded because she couldn't think of another place Stephen would have gone. "Discreetly," she said, hating the thought. "We'll inquire discreetly. I don't want to cause a stir." Then she looked down at her attire. Jeans and a short-sleeved blouse. Everyone else would be dressed to the nines for the wedding. Not that it mattered. She'd suffer any kind of humility; just as long as Stephen was okay.

"There won't be a stir," J.D. assured her as he slowed at the lane leading to John Cawthorne's place. The gate was open and the curved sign that spanned the lane read Cawthorne Acres. A black ribbon of asphalt sliced between moon-washed fields of cut hay. In the pasture on one side of the road a few bales had yet to be hauled to the barns. They stood like unmoving, rectangular sentinels in the dry stubble. On the other side of the lane, long-legged foals romped and bucked around a small herd of serene older horses. Silvery moonlight played upon their white markings, making them appear ghostlike.

At the end of the lane, the ranch house and grounds were ablaze with lights.

Tiffany's stomach tightened and her fingers curled into fists of anxiety as she saw dozens of cars parked in the lot between the house and barns. More vehicles had been directed into one of the fields while still others were parked along one side of the lane.

Dear God, what am I doing here? she thought as J.D. eased his Jeep behind a sports car nearly a hundred yards from the house. *You're only here to find your son. Nothing more. Remember that.*

"It's now or never," J.D. said and Tiffany steeled herself. She climbed out of the Cherokee and was hit by the strains of "The Anniversary Waltz" being played by a small dance band. The notes carried on a breeze tinged with the scents of cut grass and honeysuckle. A faint odor of cigarette smoke wafted through the summer air and the hum of conversation grew louder as they approached the single-story house.

Millions of tiny white lights decorated the trees and fence line, as if it were the Christmas holidays instead of the beginning of August.

Guests, dressed in everything from silk and diamonds to denim and rhinestones, wandered the grounds. But no Stephen. "This is insane," Tiffany muttered under her breath as she followed a path that led behind the house. Rounding the corner by the back porch, she nearly slammed into a woman walking in the other direction.

"You decided to come after all!" Bliss, dressed in a shimmery silver-blue dress, smiled widely. Her blond hair was pulled into a French braid and her eyes sparkled as brightly as the thousands of tiny bulbs. Beside her was a tall man with light brown eyes and sun-streaked blond hair. His hand was placed firmly in the middle of Bliss's back.

"I don't know if you've met Mason," Bliss said. "My fiancé, Mason Lafferty. This is Tiffany Santini, my half sister."

Somehow, despite the worry congealing her insides, Tiffany managed to make the appropriate noises as well as introduce J.D. as her brother-in-law and explain why they'd shown up. "We decided to come here because I'm worried sick about Stephen and he isn't at any of his friends' houses. No one knows where he is but he was

interested in coming to the wedding today and I thought...
I mean, J.D. thought he might have shown up here.''

Bliss's smile had slowly given way to a frown of concern. Tiny lines of anxiety etched her forehead. ''I wish I could help out, but I don't remember seeing him,'' she said, looking to Mason for support.

''Don't ask me, I've never met him.'' Mason glanced around the crowd that had collected around the rim of a temporary dance floor in the backyard. ''There are a lot of kids here, though.''

''It's true.'' Bliss's eyes clouded with genuine worry. ''There were a few boys about Stephen's age at the ceremony, and more here.'' Her gaze swept the area. ''But it's easy to get lost in this place.''

Tiffany's stomach, already tense, tightened another notch. ''You don't mind if we look around?''

''Of course not. Dad will be thrilled that you're here,'' Bliss said.

''Not if he found out I came here because I lost his grandson.'' Why did her tongue still trip over the word?

Bliss nodded. ''But you should let him know. He does care about you and your kids. I know that sounds weird, considering all that's gone on and how he dealt with you in the past, but I've seen firsthand the pain he's been going through, the struggles. He would want to help find Stephen and he'd be mad as a hornet if we didn't let him know Stephen was missing.''

Tiffany's heart was drumming, her pride dissipating by the minute. ''I'll take all the help I can get,'' she said fervently. When J.D. had suggested coming to this party, she'd been reticent, but a part of her had hoped that she would locate her rebellious son, stay long enough not to offend anyone, then hightail it back to her house. Now, all she wanted was to find Stephen.

"He's not here," she whispered to J.D.

"We don't know that yet."

Again, Tiffany searched the faces of the people talking in small clusters. She recognized a few of the townspeople, and several of the kids, but she didn't see any sign of her son. Music filtered through the throng. On the dance floor Brynnie, dressed in a lacy creamy-white gown that showed off her ample cleavage, smiled radiantly up at her new husband. Her flame-colored hair was pinned in curls to her crown and decorated with tiny rosebuds and sprigs of baby's breath. Her face was flushed, her eyes bright, merriment fairly oozing from her expression.

For a second Tiffany forgot her worries and watched as John Cawthorne twirled his bride around the makeshift floor, dancing as if he were a man twenty years younger, a man who didn't fear another heart attack or facing the Grim Reaper. Dressed in a gray tuxedo, he swirled and dipped, causing Brynnie to laugh out loud.

They stared into each other's eyes as if they were high-school sweethearts about to embark upon a new adventure instead of two older people who had kept up a clandestine love affair for years; a man and woman who had brought an illegitimate daughter into the world and let another man claim that child as his own. Katie had grown up thinking Hal Kinkaid was her father. Neither her mother nor her biological father had discouraged the lie—until a few months ago.

John was an adulterer, a cheat and a liar. Brynnie was a loose woman who had married a string of men before finally claiming the love of her life as her husband. There had been lies, neglect, dishonor and betrayal; but tonight, under a kind, pearlescent moon, with romantic music filling the air and champagne flowing from a silver fountain

Brynnie and John looked for all the world like a couple in love.

Like they belonged together.

Tiffany's heart tore. She would never be a part of her father's life. It had been his choice when she was a child, it was hers as an adult. Her throat was hot, her eyes burned a little as she turned to J.D. "I don't see Stephen."

"Neither do I, but I'm going to start asking some questions. Why don't you walk around, see if there is anyone here he might hang out with?"

"Okay," she said and started working her way through the crowd. She smiled at people she met, managed a few words to those she knew, but her eyes were forever moving, hunting, seeking a glimpse of her child. She paused beneath the branches of a large locust tree in the backyard and silently prayed that Stephen was all right.

"The bride has requested a snowball dance," the bandleader said over the microphone before the melody of "The Blue Danube" filled the air. Tiffany was vaguely aware of John and Brynnie dancing as she wended her way through the guests gathered around the dance floor. She saw several boys she recognized but didn't know their names and when she questioned one lanky, pimply-faced kid, he said he hadn't seen Stephen since the end of the regular school year. *This is a wild-goose chase. He isn't here! Dear God, where is he?*

"Switch," the bandleader instructed and Brynnie and John broke up to pull two unsuspecting people onto the floor. Brynnie nabbed her eldest son, Jarrod, who eased his mother around the parquet as if he'd done it all his life, while John took hold of Bliss's hand and led her to the middle of the temporary dance floor. Tiffany, though she fought the urge, couldn't help but watch her father and half sister, smiling, laughing, gliding easily in front of the crowd. To her absolute horror, she experienced a little nudge of envy.

Don't do this, she warned herself as she edged closer to the dancers.

Bliss looked like she belonged on the dance floor. She was in perfect step, smiling and laughing, tossing back her head, her cheeks tinged a deep pink, her eyes glimmering as she danced with her father.

As if they've done it a hundred times before.

They probably had. Not that it mattered. Tiffany didn't care. The past was long gone and right now, her only purpose was to find Stephen. That was why she was here. Nervously she scanned the crowd. Oh, this was getting her nowhere.

"Switch."

She barely heard the bandleader's command as she started toward the back door of the house. There was a chance, though slim, that Stephen, if he had come here, was inside.

"Dance with me." Strong fingers surrounded her arm.

Oh, no.

Her heart sank as she whirled around and faced the man who had sired her. Reflexively, she jerked her arm away. She was about to tell John Cawthorne to leave her alone, just as he had for most of her life, when she realized that over fifty pairs of curious eyes were trained her way. This was her chance. If ever she wanted to pay him back, to mortify him for all those years of neglect, she could simply stomp away and show her utter disdain for a selfish son of a bitch who'd never so much as sent her a birthday gift or a card at Christmas. She could not only personally belittle him but publicly embarrass him at his own wedding reception. If she had the guts.

"I—I—"

"Come on, Tiffany. You're here. Let's get to know each other." His hint of a smile belied the inner torment she saw in his eyes.

"But—" She blushed and bit back all the angry words that wanted to leap to her tongue. What satisfaction would she get out of ruining his day or his bride's party? "Okay," she finally acquiesced. "Why not?"

Brynnie was already dancing with one of her twin sons, Nathan or Trevor McBaine, Tiffany didn't know which. Jarrod had found Patty Lafferty, Mason's willowy sister, and Bliss was molded to her fiancé. Stiffly Tiffany took the floor, feeling self-conscious and out of place. Unlike Bliss, she hadn't been trained in dance, but she'd grown up with music, through all the years her mother had taught piano. Rose Nesbitt would die, would absolutely have a heart attack, if she suspected that Tiffany was turning coat and waltzing with the enemy.

"I'm glad you came," John said as he maneuvered her past Bliss and Mason. "I really didn't expect you to."

"It—it wasn't planned."

"Doesn't matter." He grinned down at her and she felt like a heel, not that she had any right to her ridiculous emotions. She couldn't forget how he'd ignored her growing up, neglected her for over thirty lonely years.

"I came because I'm looking for Stephen."

"He didn't come with you?"

She shook her head, stepped on his toe and wished the damned song would end. "He's missing. Been gone a couple of hours. J.D. thought he might have come here."

She felt her father tense, his muscles stiffen, his hand tighten around hers. "But I saw him earlier."

"Here?"

"Yes." He looked instantly confused. "I mean, I think I did. It was either here or at the wedding. I know because

I recognized him and spoke with him. I asked about you, but he was evasive.''

There was no way to avoid the truth, no reason for Tiffany to lie. ''He, uh, attended behind my back. Lied about it. Said he was going swimming with a friend.''

''I see,'' her father said and a wounded look crossed his eyes. ''Well, I guess I can't blame you for how you feel.'' He sighed audibly and his shoulders slumped a little. ''What is it they say, 'Time heals all wounds'?''

''Or wounds all heels,'' she said automatically, then wished she could call the words back when she noticed his lips flattening over his teeth.

''Well, for what it's worth, I'm glad you're here, Tiffany, no matter what the reason. Don't worry about Stephen. He's here somewhere, I'm sure of it. Enjoy the reception.''

''Switch,'' the bandleader called out just as the tempo of the music changed. Her father released her. She turned and walked quickly off the dance floor just as she recognized the first strains of ''And I Love Her,'' an old Beatles tune.

She ran smack-dab into J.D. ''Found him,'' he said, cocking his head in the direction of the stables. A few boys had gathered in the shadows, perched on the fence rail like birds on a telephone wire. ''Stephen's over there,'' he said, and when Tiffany started to bolt toward the group, J.D. held her hand. ''Let him be, Tiff. I already talked to him and gave him the lecture of his life about scaring you the way he did. He knows you're going to tear into him, so wait a few minutes. Let what I said sink into his brain and allow him to sweat about what you'll do to him. Then you can go for it.''

Her knees went weak with relief. ''I'm just glad he's okay.''

"But he did lie and sneak around."

"I know. I'll deal with it. Believe me."

"Later." J.D. manacled her wrist in his strong fingers and pulled her back to the dance floor. "Right now, let's indulge ourselves."

She shook her head vehemently. "I think I disgraced myself enough for one night."

"Not yet," he said, propelling her to a space on the rapidly-shrinking floor. "There are hours and hours yet for you to really make a fool of yourself."

She giggled despite herself. "Flatterer." With a smile, she added, "Hey, don't I get a say in this? Aren't I the one who's supposed to be looking for a new partner?"

"You found him," he replied and his expression was so intense that her breath got lost somewhere in her lungs. For a heartbeat the sounds of the reception faded, the lights and music blurred and she fought against the feeling that they were alone and intimate. He tugged on her hand, pulled her tightly into his embrace and sighed against her hair. "Isn't this better?"

"Much," she admitted, though she didn't want to think about the consequences of pressing her body to his, of swaying to the music in the evening-dark night. Other couples danced around them. John had found his youngest daughter and Katie, in peach silk, was beaming up at him as she danced. Brynnie had, presumably, chosen the second of her twins to dance with, though Tiffany wasn't sure. For all she knew, Brynnie could have been dancing with the same brother. Mason and Bliss had found new partners but their gazes sought each other continuously.

For a few wonderful minutes, Tiffany closed her eyes, rested her head against J.D.'s chest and lost herself in the feel of his body, so long and lean and possessive. The scent of his after-shave filled her nostrils and she heard the beating of his heart, comforting and steady.

Why was it that being in his arms felt so right when she knew deep in her heart it was wrong? Why did his touch thrill her as no one else's had? There had been men who had tried to date her when she'd moved to Bittersweet. A widowed rancher with a hundred-acre spread bordering Cougar Creek and three half-grown daughters had shown interest, and a divorced insurance adjuster who lived in Medford had called a few times. She hadn't responded to either. She'd been grieving, trying to get over the guilt surrounding the accident that had taken Philip's life, while attempting to keep her small family intact. She hadn't had time for a relationship of any kind; but with J.D. her silly heart wanted to make an exception. The touch of his splayed fingers against the small of her back was erotic, even through her blouse; the sensation of his breath fanning her hair made her tingle.

What was wrong with her? This was J. D. Santini, for crying out loud. Her brother-in-law. A man she was no more sure of than sand shifting beneath her feet.

"Okay, let's switch again," the bandleader said, and reluctantly J.D. released her.

"You go ahead and dance," she said, slipping away from him and breaking off the magic that she felt existed between them, "but I'm going to have a talk with my son." She couldn't be swayed by the seduction of the night, nor let her mind wander into the dangerous territory of thinking J.D. was anything but her brother-in-law.

But he wasn't about to be left behind. He caught up with her as she rounded the house and wended her way through the parked cars toward the barn. Four boys sat on the top rail of the fence and the smell of cigarette smoke burned in the air.

Stephen was at one end of the group and he watched her approach with openly suspicious eyes.

"We need to go home and talk," she said without making any small talk or allowing her son time for introductions.

"Why?"

She motioned toward the other boys. "You want to go into it here? In front of your friends?"

In the paddock a horse snorted loudly, then plodded away. The boy sitting next to Stephen on the rail, a kid Tiffany didn't recognize, slid farther along the fence, putting some distance between his body and Stephen's, as if in so doing he would avoid some of the fallout from her wrath.

Stephen wasn't going to be cowed in front of his friends. His eyebrows drew together and he glared at his mother as if she were the problem. "I came here because I wanted to," he said boldly. "You wouldn't bring me."

"So you lied."

"You're the one who always says family's so important."

Stephen's eyes flashed with challenge and in that slice of a second, Tiffany witnessed the man he would become.

"You're changing the subject."

"John Cawthorne's my grandpa."

"He's a stranger."

"And he'll always be one if we don't get to know him."

Where did all this logic come from? And why did he care about a grandfather who for years had pretended he didn't exist? Fuming, she tried to understand her son, who, until the past year, had tried to please her. Now, it seemed, he drew strength, even enjoyed, defying her.

"It's time to go home, Stephen. Whatever it is you

wanted to accomplish by breaking the rules, it's over. Come on.''

He hesitated and Tiffany nearly stepped forward, grabbed him by his rebellious thirteen-year-old arm and yanked him off the fence, but just as she found the inner strength not to give in to the impulse, J.D.'s fingers tightened over her wrist, restraining her from further humiliating her son in front of his newfound friends.

Grudgingly Stephen hopped to the ground and started striding toward the lane where the Jeep was parked.

''Tiffany!'' Katie, holding her skirt in one hand was waving frantically as she weaved in and out of the haphazardly parked cars. ''You're not leaving already, are you?''

''I think it's time.''

''But we never even got to talk— Oh, hi,'' she said to Stephen. ''I'm Josh's mom, but you know that, don't you?'' She turned her thousand-watt smile on J.D. ''Don't tell me, you're Philip's brother.''

''J. D. Santini.'' He extended his hand and Katie shook it in both of hers.

''Glad to meet you. But please, don't leave yet. The party's just beginning. I'm just thrilled that you decided to show up. I know it means a lot to John and to my mom. They have this wild notion that we can all become one of those big blended-patchwork kind of families.''

Tiffany hazarded a glance at her son. Was that what he wanted? A large family, complete with aunts, uncles, cousins and grandparents? How could she blame him? Hadn't she, at his age, longed for the very same thing? ''Maybe, in time, it'll all work out,'' she offered and didn't add, *But I wouldn't hold my breath.*

''Sure.'' Katie seemed convinced. ''It won't be easy, but, hey—'' She shrugged. ''Why wouldn't it work?

We're all adults—well, most of us,'' she added, winking at Stephen. "I'm looking for Josh right now. I don't suppose you've seen him?"

"He was, uh, playing in the hayloft with some of the younger kids," Stephen said, obviously uncomfortable, as if he'd broken some code of honor by telling a parent where to find her son.

Katie rolled her eyes. "He's probably ruined his new slacks and jacket. I just bought them for this deal and I was hoping that he wouldn't grow out of the blazer before he wore it again—say, for Bliss's wedding—but now it's probably ruined. Oh, well, such is the life of a single mother."

Tiffany thawed a little. Katie's warmth and enthusiasm were downright infectious. Besides, she and Katie had so much in common. Not only were they John Cawthorne's illegitimate daughters, but they were both struggling as single parents and working women.

"We really do have to go," Tiffany said. It wasn't a lie. Mrs. Ellingsworth had been pressed into duty to watch Christina, and Tiffany wanted to take Stephen home and set down the rules.

"Then call me for lunch someday," Katie replied.

"I will." Tiffany didn't know if she was ready to embrace this ready-made family, but one lunch wouldn't matter. As Katie headed for the barn, Tiffany asked Stephen, "Didn't you bring your skateboard?"

"Oh, yeah. I'll get it." He jogged over to a shiny Dodge pickup, reached into the back and withdrew his wheels. "I, uh, got a ride out here from the wedding," he explained when he rejoined them.

"You went to the ceremony?"

"Uh-huh." He lifted a shoulder.

"Who gave you a lift out here?" She bristled, as she

didn't recognize the truck. She hoped he wasn't foolish enough to ride with strangers.

"Trevor McBaine."

One of Katie's twin brothers. Part of the extended family. Perfect, she thought with more than a hint of sarcasm.

"He's got a kickin' truck."

"That he has," Tiffany said tightly. She didn't know whether to throttle her son or hug him close and beg him not to pull any more stunts like this.

They climbed into J.D.'s Jeep and didn't say a word all the way home. J.D. stared through the windshield as he drove and Tiffany, rather than blast her boy, fiddled with the controls for the radio until she found a station that was clear.

The atmosphere inside the Jeep was tense, and the ride, only twenty minutes long, seemed to take forever. Before the truck had stopped completely in the driveway, Stephen had unbuckled his seat belt and was out the door and across the lawn. He slammed up the back steps and Tiffany told herself to give him time to cool off. But she couldn't. She was too angry herself.

J.D. cut the engine. Tiffany unclasped her seat belt and reached for the handle of her door, but J.D. caught hold of her shoulder, restraining her. "Give him time to think things over before you rip into him."

"I think he needs to know what he put me through."

"I know," J.D. said with an exaggerated patience that made Tiffany's blood boil. "I don't have a doubt that you want to tell him exactly how you feel, but wait until you've both had time to think about it."

Irritated, she retorted, "Is this the voice of experience talking?"

"It is."

"Oh, right," she said. "Since when did you become a parent?"

His nostrils flared and his eyes flashed. "I was talking from the kid's point of view—a troubled kid. I've been there."

"Forgive me for thinking like a mother, okay? But I think it's more important to be a parent than a friend." She jerked her arm away from him. "If I remember correctly you were the one who pointed out that I was having trouble with my son."

"You are," he agreed, his face set.

"Well, it's my problem, okay? I'll handle it how I see best." Her eyes held his for a rapidly-accelerating heartbeat. "It's not your responsibility to step into Philip's shoes, you know. It's not your fault that he died."

He eyed her for a second and she felt as if the interior of the Jeep had shrunk, become far too intimate. "Funny," he said in a soft voice. "That's exactly what I was going to tell you."

Her chest tightened and she looked away. "Your parents blame me."

He didn't argue. "They're having trouble with all of this."

"Did your father send you down here to spy on me?" she asked—the question that had been on her mind from the moment she'd found him on her front porch springing to her lips.

"He was worried about the kids."

"Was he?" Anger shot through her. "You know, Jay, of all the things I would have expected from you, it wouldn't be that you'd end up as some kind of gopher...or...or what do they call spies these days? Moles? I can't believe you'd come down here to be a mole, or whatever you want to call it, for your father."

"I'm not."

"Then why are you down here?" she demanded, poking a finger at his chest. "Why are you in a room in my house? Why didn't your father send someone else—someone with more experience—down here to check out possible vineyard sites? You know, this whole thing has been bogus from the start!"

"Have you ever thought that I might be here because I couldn't stay away?"

"From what? Me?" She shook her head and reached for the handle of the door again. "Oh, come on, Jay, it's been months since Philip died. *Months.* If you really cared, you would have— Ooh!" He pulled her close and kissed her so hard she couldn't breathe for a second, couldn't think. Strong arms wrapped around her, preventing her escape.

Fire screamed through her blood. Desire shot through her insides, turning her liquid. Oh, why was it always like this with him? He groaned as his kiss deepened and erotic images flashed through her mind.

"Tiffany," he said and his voice cracked a bit. He lifted his head and she saw in his eyes a raw pain she didn't understand. "I do care, Tiffany," he admitted, though he seemed to hate the words. His arms, strong and warm, were still wrapped around her. "I care too much. Way too much."

Her heart pounded for a small second. Oh, God, how she wanted to believe him, to drown in his words, to trust in the concern in his eyes; but she couldn't. This was J. D. Santini, her brother-in-law, a man who felt some kind of obligation, a duty to his dead brother's memory and widow. "Then don't, Jay," she said, tamping down that stupid little romantic part of her heart that cried out to give him a chance. "Just don't care. I…we… The kids and I are doing fine.'' She kept her voice devoid of emotion. ''We don't need you.''

The lie hovered between them for a second. He stared deep into her eyes as if in so doing he could search her soul. She wanted to kiss him, to hold him, to tell him that she loved him— Dear God, she loved him?

That thought scared her to the bone, turning her blood to ice. Of all the men in the world, she couldn't fall in love with J. D. Santini.

Never.

Before he could guess the turn of her thoughts, she fumbled for the door latch, scrambled out of her seat and raced across the lawn as fast as if Lucifer himself were on her heels. She only hoped that she could run away from the awful truth. She couldn't love J. D. Santini. *Wouldn't!*

Behind her she heard the Jeep's engine fire again. With a screech of tires, J.D. backed out of the drive. Tiffany didn't turn around, just dashed up the two steps of the porch and propelled herself through the front door. He was leaving. Good. The more distance between his body and hers, the better. But it was only temporary. He'd signed a lease for six months.

Six months!

Inside, she slammed the door shut and sagged against the wall. She was perspiring and gasping for breath, her mind spinning in restless, unending circles. She'd never make it. Never. She couldn't face living in the same house with him for the next two days, let alone half a year.

She couldn't see J.D. again. Not now. Not ever.

Unfortunately, she didn't have a choice.

Chapter Ten

"**W**rite up an offer. Five-percent less than the owners are asking. Make it contingent on the soil analysis and water report." J.D. eyed the surrounding acres of the Zalinski farm and told himself that he wasn't making a hasty decision, that these three hundred acres were the right piece of property, that he wasn't grasping at straws just to leave Bittersweet and Tiffany in his dust.

It had been days since the wedding and he'd barely seen her since. The tension between them was stretched to the breaking point; it was time to leave.

Max Crenshaw tugged at his tie and grinned widely. Beads of sweat slid down from his bald pate, over his fleshy cheeks and along his neck to disappear beneath his collar. "This is a good choice," he said with a wink. "And the sellers are motivated. The offer shouldn't be a problem."

"Good." J.D. liked what he saw. The farm consisted of

a stone house, barn and outbuildings set in rolling hills with a creek that zigzagged through the fields. Pine and oak trees offered shade around the buildings as well as fringed the neat acres now planted in grass. A few head of cattle grazed on dry stubble while sheep and goats occupied pens closer to the barn, and a tractor with a trailer hitched behind was parked on the knoll of one grassy field. The exposure and drainage looked right, the soil was known to produce high-quality grapes for Santini Brothers' Sémillon, a white Bordeaux wine. The Cabernet Sauvignon and Merlots would be perfect for a new blend of red wine his father wanted to try. As far as J.D. could see, this place would be perfect.

And he could leave.

Before he got too entangled in Tiffany's life.

Before his heart was involved.

"I'll stop by your office later today and sign the offer, then fax a copy to my father in Portland," J.D. told the Realtor. "He'll want to see all the information you've got on this place. If there is any problem with water rights or the property being sublet or rented, he'll need to know about it."

"Shouldn't be a concern. The Zalinskis have already moved and the acres are being used by a cousin who lives near Ashland, but he knows that they're trying to sell. He'll move his animals and equipment on the spot. Not a problem," Max said with a congenial nod. J.D. could almost see the wheels turning in the real-estate agent's mind as he mentally calculated his commission on this place. "I've done some digging with the title company and I think we're all right. Aside from a small mortgage with a local bank, the property is free and clear. But I'll get a title report and see that all the paperwork is done."

"Fair enough." J.D. slid into Max's car and told himself

that this was the first step. Soon he'd be able to extricate himself from this little town and return to Portland where he could start working for his father in earnest.

The thought made his jaw clench. He'd never been one who pursued his own happiness, or worried much about it. He considered life a challenge, one with rewards as well as disappointments, and he'd prided himself on being his own man, not his father's flunky as Philip had been.

But he'd changed. Absently J.D. rubbed his thigh, the old pain from his accident returning with a twinge of conscience.

Max turned the car around in the dry grass by the garage and headed down the long, winding lane to the main road. He was still going on and on about the location of the property, resale value and such, but J.D. wasn't paying much attention because as they drove toward town, the dry acres of Isaac Wells's ranch came into view. "Let's stop here," he said suddenly and Max shot him a glance.

"But you're already making an offer on the Zalinski place."

"I know, I know. I just want to check something out."

Always one to please, Max turned into the drive and cut the engine.

"I'll be right back," J.D. assured him and ignored the No Trespassing sign posted on the gate. He climbed over the graying slats and hopped to the ground on the other side. His leg pained him a little, but he jogged around the side of the small house with grimy windows, overgrown garden and weed-choked lawn. Behind the house was a woodshed and farther back, a huge barn. A padlock kept the door in place, but one window was open a crack and J.D. looked into the gloomy interior to see four automobiles parked inside. The concrete floor was swept clean and the smell of oil filled his nostrils. Tarps had been thrown over the vehicles and from the accumulation of dust, he concluded that none of the cars had been moved in months.

The barn was surprisingly neat and tidy, as if Isaac had prided himself on the old car collection. Tools, all neatly placed on racks, covered one wall; shelves filled with books, wax, cleaning supplies and small replacement parts filled another. Hubcaps and old license plates were hung higher on the empty wall space, as if Isaac had spent a lot of time out here.

Odd.

Why would a man just up and leave?

Had he been forced? Had there been foul play? Or had he just left voluntarily for reasons known only to himself?

It just didn't make any sense.

But Stephen had some idea of what was going on. J.D. was willing to bet on it. He just had to find out what the boy knew. J.D. owed it to the kid. To Philip. To Tiffany. His jaw clenched as he started back towards Max's car.

Tiffany. How the devil was he going to erase her from his mind? He could leave Bittersweet; that part was easy. But he had a deep worry that he'd be taking her with him—in his head, and, dammit, in his heart.

He kicked at a dirt clod, sent it reeling against the barn and told himself it didn't matter. He just had to get the hell out.

"That Dean boy was over here again," Mrs. Ellingsworth said as Tiffany tossed her jacket over the back of one of the kitchen chairs. The scents of cinnamon, vanilla and nuts filled the room.

"Mommy!" Christina, standing on a chair near the sink, raised her flour-smudged hands.

"Hi, sweetie." Tiffany dropped a kiss onto Christina's

crown and touched the tip of her daughter's tiny nose with her finger. "What're you up to?"

"Ellie and me is making cookies."

"I see that," Tiffany said, and held her tongue rather than corrected her daughter's grammar. "What kind?"

"Peanut butter and jelly."

"Just peanut butter," Ellie said. "When this batch is done, we were planning to go out and get a hamburger, then go to the library for storytime, then stop at the park on the way home and play in the fountain."

"And feed the ducks!" Christina said.

"And feed the ducks." Ellie chuckled deep in her throat and winked at the little girl she'd affectionately dubbed, "the granddaughter I'll never have."

"Can you come, too?" Christina asked her mother.

"I hope so. I'll try to meet you there," Tiffany promised, and gave her daughter a hug.

"You bring Unca Jay."

"Him, too?"

"Yep." Christina nodded her head sharply as if she called all the shots. "I like him."

Ellie lifted a knowing brow. "So do I," she said.

Me, too, Tiffany thought, but kept her feelings to herself. J. D. Santini was a pain. A sexy, intelligent, stubborn, pain in the backside. And she was falling in love with him.

As Christina turned back to the ball of dough on a flour-dusted cutting board, Tiffany dragged her thoughts away from her brother-in-law. "You said that one of the Dean boys was here. I assume it was Miles."

"Whichever one is the older." Ellie wiped her hands on the oversize apron that covered her clothes. "I never could keep those two straight."

"Miles is a few years older than Laddy."

"Then he's the one. He came around here right after

Stephen got through with summer school, I think. You know, I usually get along with kids—all kids, no matter how old they are. But that one, he makes me uncomfortable, let me tell you. Shifty-eyed, like he couldn't tell the truth if his life depended on it.'' Ellie picked up a spatula and wagged it under Tiffany's nose. ''That father of his is a no-account, I'm afraid. He's been in and out of prison for as long as I can remember.''

''I know,'' Tiffany said, fighting a headache that was pounding behind her eyes. ''It's not Miles's fault that he's got Ray Dean for a dad.''

''No, but it's not your fault, either, and now he seems to be your problem all of a sudden.''

Tiffany couldn't argue that point.

''Anyway, the two of them, Stephen and Miles, left a little while ago, but they're supposed to be back by six.''

''Good.'' She told herself not to be nervous. So Stephen was hanging out with Miles again. It wasn't the end of the world. Or was it? When Stephen and Miles were together there was always trouble brewing.

The timer dinged and Ellie put on an oven mitt before removing a batch of cookies. ''Okay, pumpkin, you and I, we've got ourselves a date.'' She untied her apron and helped Christina from her chair. Aside from the one cookie sheet and Christina's messy cutting board, the kitchen was clean.

''I finally managed to say a few words to the new tenant,'' Ellie commented as she reached for her purse. ''Handsome devil.''

''Is he?'' Tiffany wasn't going to rise to that bait. From the minute Ellie had moved in, she'd been playing matchmaker.

''Almost as good-looking as that brother-in-law of yours.''

Tiffany cocked an eyebrow at the friendly older woman. "Almost?"

"That J.D.'s got something, honey, and don't tell me you haven't noticed. On top of that, he's lots more outgoing than Luke." She looked through the window to the carriage house and wiggled a finger at the upper story. "Luke's been in the place for what—several days now? Gee, almost a week, I guess—I can't keep track—but I haven't hardly seen him."

"Maybe he's avoiding you," Tiffany suggested with a smile.

"Don't be teasing, now. I think you might be on to something there. He's not avoiding me, per se, but everyone in general. A real recluse. Probably has some deep, dark secret from his past."

"Probably," Tiffany said, swallowing a smile. Sometimes the older woman's imagination ran away with her. In Tiffany's opinion it was because of all the spy and mystery novels Ellie devoured.

"Ah, well." The older woman sighed and turned her attention away from the window. She took Christina's small hand in her wrinkled one. "We'll be back in a few hours. Right, Chrissie?"

"Right!" Another strong nod of affirmation. "Bye, Mommy." Christina held up her arms to be hugged and Tiffany swung her off her feet.

"Be a good girl for Ellie, won't you?"

"I will."

"She always is," Ellie insisted, but Tiffany rolled her eyes.

As they left, Tiffany finished washing and drying the last of the cookie sheets, then went upstairs to change. Pausing at the open door leading to the third floor, she ran a hand down the woodwork and wondered about her brother-in-law. Since their last argument on the night of John Cawthorne's wedding, she and J.D. had avoided each other and kept to themselves.

Grudgingly she had taken his advice and tried to reason with Stephen, but her son seemed to be slipping away from her. She knew that it was only natural. As the years progressed Stephen would start withdrawing from her, but she wasn't ready for it, nor could she turn a blind eye to his rebellion. The strain in the house had been nearly palpable and everyone was feeling the pressure.

Even Christina had sensed the stress and been grouchy from the tension in the air. The little girl was finally getting over a summer cold that had caused her to sniffle and cough for three days. But she hadn't woken up screaming. During the past week Christina had slept through the night.

That was the good news.

J.D. was the bad.

James Dean Santini. The enigma. She'd tried to avoid him, but it had proved impossible with him living upstairs. Every night she'd thought about him, only one floor away, as she'd lain in her bed.

There weren't enough cold showers in the world to keep her mind from replaying in sensual detail the few kisses they had shared, the intimate caresses. *You're just lonely,* she'd told herself over and over again. *And it's been a long time since you've been touched or held by a man. What you're feeling is normal. It's just too damned bad you're feeling it about J. D. Santini.*

She walked into her bedroom and kicked her shoes into the closet. Aside from the tense atmosphere at home, she'd suffered an incredibly long day at the office. The fax machine had refused to work, the new insurance rates from the company had caused a dozen customers to call in with complaints or ideas about how to lower their premiums, she'd helped two clients fill out accident reports and, to top it all, the computers had decided to take the day off.

She pulled on a pair of shorts and a V-necked T-shirt, then snapped her hair into a ponytail.

Barefoot, she padded to Stephen's room and eyed his clutter. Empty pop cans and dishes littered the room. His bed was unmade and there were magazines, comic books and video-game cartridges scattered across the floor.

Whether he liked it or not, the kid would have to clean up the mess. She only hoped it wouldn't take a fire hose and an exterminator to get the room clean again. The phrase "A man's home is his castle" flitted through her mind, and she thought a more apt description would be "A boy's room is a garbage dump."

At the sound of an engine, she crossed to the window, her naive heart soaring at the thought that she would see J.D. again. Instead she spied Luke Gates's pickup pulling into the drive. Ellie was right. He was an interesting but mysterious man. He was quiet, kept to himself and hadn't caused any problems so far. Crossing her fingers, she hoped against hope that he'd turn out to be a perfect tenant, because she needed the money to stay in the black.

Now, if she could just lease the other unit in the basement, she could probably make ends meet. Probably.

Rubbing the kinks from her neck, she walked downstairs and hit the landing just as the front door burst open. Stephen, his face red with exertion, his eyebrows drawn into a single harsh line, his young jaw set, strode into the house.

"Hi."

He nearly jumped out of his skin. "Mom. Gosh, I didn't see you."

She hurried down the last few steps and started for the kitchen. "Didn't mean to scare you," she said. "Christina and Ellie made cookies. You want some?"

He hesitated, then shrugged. "Sure."

"Ellie said you were with Miles."

Every muscle in his body tensed. "So?" He snagged a couple of cookies from the cooling rack.

"Where'd you go?"

Tossing his hair out of his eyes, he shrugged. "We just hung out at the river."

"But you didn't swim." His hair and clothes were bone-dry and there was a hint of smoke tinging the air surrounding him.

"Nope."

She knew prodding him any further would get her nowhere, so she changed tactics. "How's summer school?"

"Bo-ring." He opened the refrigerator and pulled out a jug of milk.

"You doing all right?"

"Yeah. Why?" Grabbing a glass from the cupboard, he averted his eyes and paid attention to pouring the milk.

"Just checking," she said. She reached for a cookie and took a bite. "It's a mother's job, you know."

"Crummy job, if ya ask me."

"Oh, I don't know. I kind of like it." She smiled and tousled his hair.

Rolling his eyes, he said, "It sucks."

"Let's not talk like that."

"Fine. I'm going to a movie tonight." There was only one theater in Bittersweet and the movies it showed could sometimes be rented at the video store.

"Are you?" she asked. "You were grounded, remember?"

"Until today."

She couldn't argue the point. He'd done his time for his disappearing act. "Okay, but first clean your room."

He seemed about to argue, but wisely held his tongue

and washed down whatever words he was about to utter with a big gulp of milk.

"Who're you going with?" she asked, hoping he hadn't made plans with Miles Dean.

"Sam."

She didn't bother hiding her relief. "Okay. So who's driving?"

"Sam's older brother, Seth. Is that okay?"

She decided to trust him. Seth was almost twenty and worked at one of the mills around town. He seemed to be a straight arrow. "Just come home right after the movie, okay?"

"Yeah. No problem."

She only hoped so. It hadn't been that long ago that the police had been questioning him about Isaac Wells's disappearance, though she hadn't heard a word since the interrogation at the police station. She had tried to convince herself that the police had found other leads, other suspects, but she still shuddered every time the phone rang, fearing that the long arm of the law was about to reach out and grab her son.

But that was crazy. She believed Stephen. Surely if he knew more about the old man's disappearance, he would confide in her. Or would he?

Trust him, Tiffany. He's your son.

Jarrod Smith looked as frustrated as a barking dog who'd treed a raccoon and couldn't get anyone's attention. He paced back and forth in his office and gave J.D. a quick update on the Isaac Wells case. "The police have had several leads, none of which amounted to anything. Originally, they thought some of Isaac's relatives or friends were involved. They were convinced the old man had been the victim of foul play—murder, kidnapping, you name it.

But nothing seems to fit.'' He offered J.D. a sheepish look. "I hate to say it, but it beats me what happened to Isaac. It almost looks as if he just got up and walked away.''

"Why would he do that?'' J.D. asked.

"That's the question that keeps everyone coming back to square one—that he must've been forced to leave or lost his marbles. Every day in this business, you hear about old men and women snapping and just wandering off.'' He rubbed the bridge of his nose as if to clear his head. "But I've talked to a lot of people who knew Isaac better than I did. A lot. None of them think he was suffering from some kind of dementia or paranoia or schizophrenia, or anything else. Supposedly the old guy was sharp as a tack. Spent his time running that ranch and babying the classic cars in his barn. Other than that, he kept to himself.'' Jarrod settled on the corner of his desk, one leg swinging in agitation. "I even thought that he might have staged the whole thing in hopes of somehow getting the life-insurance money. I thought whoever was the beneficiary of his policies might be in on the con, but nope. All he had in life insurance was enough to bury him. So if he left, he walked away from a ranch worth about a hundred and fifty, maybe two hundred thousand dollars—though it was mortgaged for quite a bit—and his old cars, which he supposedly loved more than his half-breed bloodhound that died a month or so before he disappeared.''

Jarrod picked up his coffee mug, saw that it was empty and scowled. With a thump, he set the mug onto the desk. "How about a beer?'' he asked. "I'll buy.''

J.D. nodded. "Sounds good.'' He liked Smith, who seemed to be a straight shooter. Everyone he'd met in this small town was starting to appeal to him—which was odd. He'd never thought he would like anything to do with a tiny burg and the small minds he always assumed would occupy it. He'd been wrong. Not that he would ever live here. No way. He was making tracks as soon as possible.

Once they were outside the office building, Jarrod showed him a shortcut through a couple of back alleys that he'd used for years. "An escape route when I was a kid," he explained. "Believe me, I had my own share of trouble back then, but not half as much as my brothers. Trevor and Nathan gave my mother more gray hairs than she'd ever like to admit." The late-afternoon sun was still warm but a cool breeze shot between the buildings.

They walked through a back door to the Wooden Nickel Saloon and slid into a booth. The interior of the restaurant/ bar was decorated with Western memorabilia—everything from two-handled saws, wagon wheels and saddles, to lanterns, mining picks and the heads of stuffed animals, their glassy eyes surveying the premises from high above the bar. Embedded in the thick, clear plastic of each tabletop were genuine plug nickels surrounded by glitter that, J.D. assumed, was supposed to represent fool's gold.

They ordered a pitcher of beer distributed by a Portland microbrewery that J.D., as a VP of Santini Brothers Vineyards and Winery, had personally inspected.

The bar was nearly empty, with only a few stools occupied and one pool table in use. Above the barkeep, mounted on its own angled platform, was a television tuned in to an all-sports network where the scores of the previous day's baseball games were being flashed. Over the click of billiard balls, the clink of glasses and the whisper of conversation, country-and-western music drifted from hidden speakers. J.D. didn't recognize the song or the singer and really didn't give a damn. The music just added to the backwoods, rural America atmosphere that was beginning to appeal to him.

A buxom blond waitress clad in tight jeans, boots,

checkered shirt and cowboy hat deposited a frosty pitcher of beer and a bowl of some kind of party mix, then poured two glasses. "Anything else?" Her smile was genuine; her green eyes actually held a spark of interest.

"Naw, Nora. This is fine. Thanks."

"Just let me know if you want something." She winked at Jarrod, then sauntered back to the bar.

Jarrod took a long swallow, let out a deep breath and set his glass on the table as Nora swung over to another table, deftly scooping up her tip as she swiped away rings made by the half-full glasses. "Went to school with her older sister, April," he explained, glancing at Nora's backside as she leaned over the table. "I dated April for a few months, took her to my senior prom. Nora was just a little kid at the time."

"All grown up now," J.D. observed as Nora, smiling at several customers, hurried back to the bar.

"Yep." Jarrod glanced over his shoulder and watched as she wiped the bar with a thick white towel, then cleared his throat and turned back to J.D. "If you're asking what Stephen knows about Wells's disappearance, I really can't tell you. You'd be better off getting the facts from him, but I doubt that he's involved. He might have some ideas—kids are always telling tales—and he probably swiped the old man's keys as a prank that nearly blew up in his face, but no one—not me or the police—really suspects that he did anything. They're just interested in what he's heard. The strong-arm tactics down at the station were just to scare him into telling them what he knows."

J.D. should have felt relieved, but he didn't. He still suspected that Stephen was holding back, hiding something important, though what, he couldn't imagine.

As he and Jarrod finished the beer they talked about the baseball season, the past NBA draft and everything and nothing. J.D. learned that Smith had been with the police before breaking out on his own and becoming a private investigator.

When Jarrod asked about him, J.D. mentioned that he was a lawyer, who, until recently, had been involved in personal-injury cases.

"So when Philip was killed, the old man pressed me into service," he continued. "I didn't jump on it at first, but after an accident on my motorcycle, when I had a few weeks to think about things, I decided to join the family business, at least temporarily." He drained his glass. "Philip's death made it clear that life's too short not to try some new experiences."

Jarrod studied the two inches of beer in his glass. "I heard you were making an offer on the Zalinski place."

J.D. tensed. "Just this morning."

"You know what they say about gossip traveling faster than the speed of light in a small town."

"One of the reasons I like the city."

Jarrod shrugged. "It's not so bad here. Sure, there're a lot of people sticking their noses in everyone else's business, but it works both ways. If you're ever in trouble, everyone in town's willing to pitch in and help you."

"Except in Isaac Wells's case."

Jarrod sighed. "Have to admit," he agreed, "that one's got me stumped." He leaned back in the booth. "So how're you and your sister-in-law getting along?"

The muscles of J.D.'s shoulders immediately tightened. His jaw clenched and he braced himself as if he were expecting a physical blow. "Well enough." Where had this come from and where was it going? J.D. wondered. Smith didn't seem the kind to pry into another man's personal life.

"She's a beautiful woman."

J.D. nodded.

"Had a few tough breaks, what with her old man skipping out on her mother and then losing a husband at her age."

"She's holding up." J.D.'s fingers gripped his glass as if his life depended upon it.

"She's strong. Well, all of John Cawthorne's daughters are. Must be in their genes. Take my sister, Katie. Tough as nails. Growing up with three brothers, she had to be." His gaze clouded for a minute. "She's had her share of troubles, too, and managed to get by. Nothing that happened broke her." He said it almost in wonder. "She's an amazing woman. In fact, Katie's one of the most upbeat people you'll ever want to meet. But she's pushy as all get-out. When she wants something, watch out, she'll just steamroll her way through." Jarrod chuckled, then sobered as he poured a half glass of beer from the pitcher.

"As for Tiffany, she's different from Katie. Quieter. More thoughtful." He rubbed the edge of his jaw. "It can't be easy trying to raise two kids so far apart in age, especially when the older one seems hell-bent on rebelling. Yep, Tiffany Santini is a helluva woman."

J.D. narrowed his gaze on Jarrod. "Is there a reason you're telling me this?"

"Just reminding you what a lucky guy you are to be related to her."

"Seems as if you're related, as well."

Smith grinned. "I know. When John married my mother, I ended up with two stepsisters. I guess I'm lucky, too."

"So it would seem," J.D. said, finishing his drink.

Jarrod reached into his wallet and dropped some bills onto the table. "This one's mine," he added when J.D. pulled out his money clip.

Rather than argue, J.D. tucked the clip back into his pocket. "Fair enough, Smith, but the next time it's on me."

Jarrod didn't argue.

"So I thought, if you're not too busy, we—you and Bliss and I—could meet for lunch tomorrow," Katie suggested from the other end of the telephone line.

A cold sweat had collected between Tiffany's shoulder blades. "I guess that would be all right," she heard herself saying. Katie was trying so hard to get the three of them together. Too hard. But it was inevitable they would meet at some point in time, and Stephen had already let her know that he wanted to belong to a larger family. "How about one-thirty? Doris will be back by then."

"Great! I'll set it up with Bliss and we'll meet you at the Blue Moon Café. They've got outdoor tables."

"I'll see you then," Tiffany promised and hung up. Great. She was going to have to deal with her sisters whether she wanted to or not.

She heard the front door open.

"Tiffany?" J.D.'s voice rang through the house. Tiffany braced herself. The tension between them had been so thick she was certain it could have been sliced with a butcher knife.

"In here." She was in the hallway when he met her.

"Where are the kids?"

"Out for a couple of hours or so. Christina's with Mrs. Ellingsworth and Stephen's with some friends at the movies—"

"Great."

Great? Why didn't she think so?

"It's time we took a little time off and celebrated."

Something in his voice gave it away. She felt a cold,

dark emptiness as she said, "A celebration. Why? No, don't tell me. Let me guess. It's because you're leaving."

He paused, his gray eyes holding hers for an intimate second. "It's what you've wanted since the moment I walked in your front door."

Oh, dear God. No. The thought of the house without him caused a new dread to fill her heart. "But—but your lease is for six months."

"I know." He rubbed the back of his neck in an attempt to ease the knots of tension in his muscles. "But I'll keep the apartment because I'll be back."

Her stupid heart soared at the thought. "When?"

"Off and on, probably a couple of days a month."

"That's all?"

A smile slid from one side of his mouth to the other. "Don't tell me you'll miss me."

She managed a cold smile. "In your dreams, Santini."

"Always."

She froze and something in his eyes beckoned her, touched that part of her soul she'd tried to keep hidden. "Come on, Tiff," he said, his voice low. "There's something I'd like to show you."

"What?"

His flinty eyes sparked as if with a very private secret. "The reason I can leave sooner than expected."

"Oh," she whispered and felt as if she'd been kicked in the gut. "Sure."

"Isn't that what you wanted?"

"Yes. No." Confusion tore at her. She'd told herself a million times over that if only J.D. would go back to Portland, or L.A. or Timbuktu, for that matter, her life would be better, but now, faced with the fact that he would be gone, she felt none of the elation she'd hoped for. "I, uh, don't know."

His eyes searched her face, as if hunting for a hidden message, a silent clue to her feelings. For a second she thought he would kiss her. Instead he pulled on her hand. "Come on, Tiff."

She couldn't resist.

Before she could come up with one bit of argument she was inside his Jeep, sitting close to him and staring out the windshield as the main streets of town faded behind and they were on a winding country road, slowing for a tractor pulling a mower, whipping around a truck towing a horse trailer, and avoiding squirrels that dashed frantically across the strip of asphalt that carved through the hills.

"Ever heard of the Zalinski place?" J.D. asked. The windows of the Jeep were open and the hot breeze that filtered in ruffled his hair and tugged at her ponytail.

"I've met Myra Zalinski at the agency. They moved."

"But they hadn't sold their farm. Until today."

"*You* bought it?"

"Actually, Santini Brothers did." He drove past Isaac Wells's property and Tiffany felt a chill as cold as death when she wondered what had happened to the old man. Where was he? And what, if anything, did Stephen know about his disappearance? *Nothing. He knows nothing! Remember that, Tiffany. Trust your son.*

A little farther up the road J.D. turned into a winding drive that was little more than two graveled ruts. Tall weeds grew along the sides of the lane and between the tire tracks, scraping the bottom of the Jeep. A few cattle stood in the surrounding fields and a creek, little more than a trickling stream in the late summer, wound its way into a tiny valley where the house sat, its windows shut tight, the curtains drawn.

"What made you choose this place?"

"Size, price, proximity to the freeway, the general appearance of the land, and a gut feeling." He slid her a knowing glance as he parked the Jeep near an ancient oak tree with spreading branches. "It's not a done deal yet," he said, "but it looks like it should fly." His mouth drew tight at the corners and he drummed his fingers on the steering wheel. "Just what Dad was looking for."

She didn't know what to say. Part of her wanted to tell him adios so that she could get back to living her life the way she wanted, without Santini eyes watching her every move and judging her. Another part had decided that she liked having him around, that he wasn't cut from the same cloth as his father, that he really did care about his niece and nephew. Yet another part—one she didn't scrutinize too closely—wanted him to stay because she was fool enough to love him. An ache had already begun to settle around her heart and she tried desperately to ignore it.

"So you think you can grow grapes down here," she said, trying to sound lighthearted, while a part of her was withering inside.

"Not just grapes. The *best* grapes."

"Oh, right." She couldn't even summon a laugh. He was leaving. *Leaving.* A cold wind swept through her soul and she suddenly felt empty and desolate inside.

"Well, Santini Brothers won't be the first winery. There are quite a few vineyards between Bittersweet, Ashland and Jacksonville. We'll just have to see if we can make our mark."

"And grab your share of the market."

"If Carlo has his way."

"He always does, doesn't he?" she said, and for a second he hesitated, as if he wanted to tell her something that hovered on the tip of his tongue. Clearing his throat, he looked away and lifted a shoulder. "Most of the time. Come on. I'll show you around."

He reached into the back seat and pulled out a backpack that he slung over one shoulder before getting out of his Jeep. "For the celebration," he explained as they walked to the house, a stone cottage that was nestled in a grove of trees. A swing set that had seen better days was rusting by the side of the house and an herb garden, now going to seed, had encroached upon a flagstone patio that over-looked the creek.

"It's beautiful—well, it will be." Forcing her thoughts away from the heart-wrenching fact that she'd have to patch her life back together without him, Tiffany tried to show some interest in her father-in-law's next project. She looked past the obvious need for repairs to the house and grounds. On the far side of the cottage, away from the shade, a vegetable garden with an arbor flanked an orchard of fruit trees and a small raspberry patch. A breezeway separating the garage from the house was trimmed with lattice that stretched into a grape arbor.

"The first season's harvest," J.D. joked, lifting one of the hundreds of clusters of tiny green grapes. He grabbed her hand, linking their fingers and causing a silly little thrill to climb up her arm.

Don't think about it, she told herself. *For once, enjoy the moment. He'll be gone soon and then where will you be? Alone. Again. Hasn't every man who ever was a part of your life left? First your father, then your husband, now J.D.* Her throat turned to cotton and a pain, needle sharp and hot, ripped through her heart.

She told herself that she was being a ninny, that he didn't care for her, had never cared for her, and any feel-ings she was harboring for him were just silly, romantic whimsies.

Remember, Tiffany, you can't love this man. You just can't!

But she did. The simple, unalterable and painful fact was that she loved him. Wrong or right. *For better or worse.* Cringing inside at the turn of her thoughts, she was just a step behind him as he showed her around the grounds, pointing out reasons this farm was better than the others he'd seen.

The sun dipped below the horizon and the few clouds hanging low over the western hills blazed brilliant orange and magenta as J.D. followed a path from the house to the barn. Swallows were nesting in the rafters and screeched their disapproval of anyone in the vicinity. A few frogs began to croak and in the distance a coyote sent up a lonely howl.

"It's peaceful out here," she said. "Different from the city."

"Just a tad." The barn door was on rollers and he shoved it open. It creaked and groaned, as if protesting their entrance before finally giving way.

"Needs a little oil," she observed.

"A lot of oil. The whole place needs work. Obviously, but not more than I expected. Both the house and this barn are over a hundred years old and even though they've been updated, the wiring's shot, plumbing needs to be redone and the house reroofed. But with some time, money and effort I think the cottage could be restored and turned into a gift shop and this place could be converted into a wine-tasting room." He motioned to the musty interior with its time-darkened beams, wide stalls and hayloft. High overhead a round window let in the last shafts of daylight and an owl, disturbed, fluttered in the rafters.

J.D.'s eyes narrowed thoughtfully, as if he were already imagining what the converted farm would look like. He led her through a back door where the pasture dropped off steeply into a natural bowl. "This could be tiered and landscaped into a natural amphitheater that could be rented for parties, or summer concerts or weddings."

"Just like the vineyard where you and I met," she said automatically, then felt like a fool for mentioning something so personal.

"The same idea." He shoved his hands into his pockets. "Didn't think you remembered."

"How could I forget?"

He eyed her for a second, as if trying to read her mind. A small smile toyed at his lips. "You were catering the wedding and trying your best to look grown-up."

"And you were doing your best I-don't-give-a-damn-about-anything impression."

"Did it work?"

"Oh, yeah. Big time. Everyone who saw you thought you were the reason we'd hired security guards."

He lifted one eyebrow. "That was a long time ago."

"A lifetime," she admitted, a trifle breathlessly. It was happening again, this feeling of closeness and intimacy that she wished didn't exist.

"You weren't married yet."

"Neither were you," she retorted.

"Never have been."

"Why not?" she asked, but before he could answer, she added, "And don't give me the line about not finding the right woman, Santini, because I wouldn't believe it."

He hesitated for a second and when his gaze returned to hers it was dark, intense. The wind seemed to have died and it was so quiet she heard the sound of her heartbeat in her ears. "Maybe I found her, but she was promised to someone else."

Her breath caught in her throat.

"In fact, she was engaged to my brother."

Oh, God. There it was. So many times since Philip's death she'd wondered. Had the one night she'd spent with J.D. been, as she'd told herself, just two people trying to console each other in their grief? Or had it been more? This was dangerous territory, very dangerous, and yet she couldn't resist stepping over the imaginary line she'd drawn in her mind. "For me," she said, swallowing against a lump in her throat, "commitments aren't to be broken."

"I know."

"I...I loved your brother."

His jaw tightened almost imperceptibly.

"I know your family thought I married him for his part of the Santini estate, or for the fact that I never knew my own father and was searching for a replacement, but the truth is I fell in love with Philip. It might not have been the wild passion people expect to find, and it certainly changed and became...more difficult as the years went by, but I loved him nonetheless."

J.D. snorted. "So did I." His lips flattened into a thin, self-deprecating line. "Why do you think I stayed away for so long?"

"I...I didn't know."

"Why do you think I'm leaving now?"

"Oh, God, don't say it—"

"Because I can't stand the thought that I want my brother's wife." His expression was grave. "I saw your marriage falling apart," he admitted. "I know that Philip became...less enchanted and I beat myself up because a part of me wanted it to fail."

"No. Please, Jay." Somewhere deep in her being there was a rendering, painful and filled with remorse. Her heart was pounding so loudly he could surely hear its erratic cadence. "I…I don't think we should be talking like this," she said in a voice she barely recognized as her own.

"You asked."

"But…" Somehow it seemed wrong, such a betrayal of Philip's memory. "It's just that what happened between you and me was…was…"

"Not supposed to," he finished for her, his jaw tight, his nostrils flaring slightly. A muscle worked in the corner of his jaw and his hands balled into fists of frustration as he gazed upon the still waters of the pond and saw past its clear depths to the bottom of his own soul, his private hell. "I know. Believe me, I know."

"I had no intention—"

"Neither did I," he said crisply, as if to dismiss the subject. They walked down the natural bowl in the hill to the pond and a thicket of cottonwood, pine and oak that guarded one bank. The sky was turning a deep shade of lavender and a soft breeze raced across the pond.

Guilt, never far away, nudged even closer. She'd been faithful to Philip, never so much as touched another man. Her heart had been with her husband. Always. Except for a few lonely moments when she'd thought of J.D., of his kiss, or what might have been. But she'd never said a word, never lifted the phone to call him, never uttered his name in the middle of the night when Philip, off on business or a gambling junket, hadn't been around. She rubbed her arms to ward off a chill before she realized how warm the evening was.

A hawk flew overhead, lazily circling in the dusky sky, but Tiffany hardly noticed because of the man beside her. *Rebel. Black sheep. Hellion.* Names she'd heard Philip call his younger brother. Foolish names that weren't true.

"On to better things," he said, as if he'd chased the

ghosts of his past away. From the backpack he withdrew a bottle of wine. "I thought we should christen this place."

"And how did you want to do that?" she asked, her stupid heart racing at the prospect.

"I'll show you." He pulled a jackknife from the pocket of his jeans and flipped out the corkscrew. "Santini Brothers' award-winning private reserve." With an exaggerated flourish, he uncorked the bottle. "Want to sniff the cork?"

"I'll trust you," she said, then saw the stiffening of his spine. "I mean—"

"I know what you meant." He set the bottle on a flat rock near the edge of the pond to let it breathe, but he was tense, his muscles flexed. "And the fact of the matter is you don't trust me." He looked at her with eyes that flashed a silver gray. "You never have."

"I think that goes both ways, Jay. From the moment you laid eyes on me you went out of your way to let me know that I wasn't good enough to marry your brother."

"It wasn't a matter of being good enough."

"No?" She didn't believe him. "Then what?"

"I thought you were too young for Philip."

"It really wasn't any of your business, was it?" she demanded, stepping closer to him, elevating her chin and skewering him with a stare meant to melt steel.

He didn't so much as flinch. "I guess I made it my business."

"But you had no right," she said, all the years of pent-up frustration surfacing. "Just like you have no right to come down here and force yourself into my life."

"Is that what I'm doing?"

"Yes! You seem to think that you…you can do anything you please and damn the consequences."

"Not true, Tiffany. If it were, then things would be different between us."

"Would they? How? Oooh!"

He grabbed her. Strong arms surrounded her and his mouth, hard and unyielding, pressed firmly over hers. Her breasts were crushed against his chest and she couldn't breathe, could barely think as he pushed the tip of his tongue to the seam of her lips.

A thrill swept through her and she opened her mouth willingly. A thousand reasons to push him away slid into her mind. A thousand-and-one reasons to hold him close chased them away. His tongue explored her mouth, touching, tasting, tickling, and her knees turned liquid.

Large, callused hands massaged her back, moving sensuously over the light cotton of her T-shirt. Fingers dipped beneath the waistband of her shorts and heat invaded her blood.

Her resistance fled.

Common sense failed her.

His weight pulled them to the ground and he trembled as he kissed the patch of skin exposed by the neckline of her shirt. Her fingers tangled in his hair and she refused to pay attention to any lingering doubts still clouding her mind. She didn't protest when he lifted her T-shirt over her head, didn't offer any objections as he kissed the top of each breast so sensually that she ached for more.

She pulled his shirt over his head, mussing his hair, then touched the thick mat of hair covering his chest. She traced the indentations of his muscles and she felt his abdomen contract when she toyed with the rim of his navel.

"You're asking for trouble," he whispered.

"I know. I just hope I'm going to get it."

"Oh, yeah, lady." He unhooked her bra and stripped it away. "Oh, yeah." His breath was hot and seductive, his fingers pure magic as they skimmed over her.

She arched upward as he kissed and licked her breast,

teasing and toying as she writhed beneath him. Like a slumbering animal, desire awoke, stretching and yawning deep inside her, aching to be filled.

"Jay," she whispered, his name floating on the evening breeze.

"Right here, love," he assured her as his fingers found her zipper and it opened with a hiss. She sucked in her abdomen as her shorts were pulled over her hips and she was suddenly naked, aside for the scrap of lace between her legs.

"You are beautiful," he said, kissing her belly button, his breath and tongue tantalizingly close to the apex of her thighs. "So beautiful." Lowering himself, he pulled on her panties with his teeth, deftly removing them before inching back up her legs with his mouth.

Her throat was as dry as a desert, her blood on fire. She arched as he discovered her most intimate recesses and caught her buttocks in his hands.

"Jay, oh, Jay," she moaned, her eyes closed, her body glistening with perspiration.

Somehow he kicked off his jeans and parted her legs with his knees. "Stop me now," he said through gritted teeth and she shook her head.

"Don't ever stop."

"You don't know what you're asking," he said, but lost control. Arms surrounding her, he thrust deep, fusing his body with hers only to retract and push forward again. Tiffany moved with him, her body catching his rhythm, her mind closed to all thoughts but the powerful pulsing need that he alone could fill.

She dug her fingers into the muscles of his upper arms, pressed her heels into his calves. Hot desire swirled through her. Her breath was suddenly far too shallow, her lungs too tight. The world tilted on its axis and somewhere in the heavens a star burst into a billion sparks of light.

He cried out with a sound as primitive as the night, and Tiffany lost herself, body and soul, in J.D. Santini—the one man who had no right to her heart.

Chapter Eleven

"So who's the new renter?" Katie asked as she dunked a french fry in her tiny cup of catsup and bit off the end. The three half sisters were seated at an outside table in the garden of the restaurant, a large umbrella offering shade from the summer heat, flower boxes spilling blooms in profusion.

"You don't miss much, do you?" Tiffany asked, not entirely comfortable with Bliss and Katie, who seemed to have hit it off already.

"I'm a reporter, remember?" Katie grinned and dabbed at her lips. Perspiration dotted her smooth forehead.

"His name is Luke Gates. He's from a small town in west Texas. Other than that, I don't know much about him. He pretty much keeps to himself."

Katie wrinkled her nose as if she smelled a story. "I wonder what he's doing here?"

"You're always looking for a mystery," Bliss said.

"Not a mystery. A scoop. There's a difference." She took a sip of iced tea and settled back in her chair. The umbrella wasn't big enough to shade the entire table and Katie had to squint a bit, even though she was wearing wire-rimmed sunglasses. "I'd really like to crack the Isaac Wells case, let me tell you. Now, *there's* a mystery and a scoop."

Tiffany froze. The topic was too sensitive.

Bliss cleared her throat. "I wish it were over, too."

Katie thought aloud. "The old man, for no apparent reason, just up and vanishes. Some people, including the police, think he might have met with foul play. They have suspects, but they're reaching for straws. I've been trying to come up with a reason why anyone would do the old guy in. He wasn't very friendly and made his share of enemies, but none who would want to kill or kidnap him. And if he was kidnapped, why no contract or ransom demands? Gosh, I don't get it."

"No one does," Tiffany said and picked up her glass of cola. Beads of sweat slid down the outside of the glass and she swirled the melting ice cubes. She thought of her son and knew in her heart that he wasn't involved. He was only thirteen, for crying out loud, and yet she was worried. Worried sick.

"So, Tiffany," Katie said, holding one hand over her glasses to shade her eyes, "what's the deal with you and J.D.?"

Tiffany was taking a sip from her drink and nearly choked. "What deal?"

"You tell me. I saw you at the wedding reception, dancing with him. The man's in love with you."

"Love?" Tiffany shook her head despite the soaring of her heart. If only she could believe that J.D. really cared. "He's just here on business."

Bliss and Katie shared a knowing look. "Right."

"It's true. He's buying a farm for his father's new vineyard and winery."

"I know all about the Zalinski farm being sold," Katie said. "And I've heard the rumors about the Santini Brothers Winery expanding to southern Oregon, but that doesn't explain why the guy couldn't keep his hands off you last Sunday."

Tiffany felt heat steal up the back of her neck. She remembered all too vividly J.D.'s lovemaking, but she didn't want to attach any emotions to it. Not yet. "J.D. and I are—"

"Don't say it." Katie shook her head. "If you tell me you're just good friends, I think I'll scream."

"That might be overreacting a tad," Bliss said.

"I know what I saw."

"It's Tiffany's business." Bliss sighed and smiled at her older sister. "When Katie gets an idea in her head—"

"This isn't an idea. This is gut instinct."

"Fine. Whatever you want to call it," Bliss said with infinite patience. "But I've learned you've kind of got a one-track mind."

"A reporter is nothing if not dogged."

"Some people might think of it as stubborn or muleheaded." Bliss winked at Tiffany and Katie rolled her eyes as she fanned herself with one hand.

"For the first time I get why sisters complain about each other." Katie swept her bangs out of her eyes. "And I thought brothers were bad."

"I just think you should give Tiffany some breathing space."

"It's all right," Tiffany said, even though she felt decidedly uncomfortable. "My feelings for J.D.... Well, they're complicated."

''That's always what people say when they don't want to admit they're in love.''

Love? In *love?* Was it so obvious? ''Is that the voice of experience talking?'' Tiffany asked and Katie nodded.

''Maybe.''

''I've got kids,'' Tiffany said, opening up more than she expected. ''It's not so easy getting…involved again.''

''Tell me about it.'' Katie laughed.

''How do they feel about their uncle?'' Bliss asked.

''Christina adores J.D. Since he's moved in she's always chattering on and on about him. She's experienced some bad dreams since Philip's death, but they've just about stopped.'' Tiffany ignored the rest of her lunch—a chicken salad—and leaned back in her chair. ''I'm taking Christina to the park this evening. The local theater is putting on a kids' play, and she wants J.D. to go with us.''

''Is he?''

Tiffany shook her head. She hadn't even asked him. ''This is a mother-daughter bonding thing,'' she said.

''It sounds wonderful,'' Bliss said and for the first time Tiffany realized that the woman she'd always thought of as ''the princess'' wanted children.

''And Stephen?'' Katie ventured. ''How does he feel about J.D.?''

''Good question.'' Tiffany didn't understand why she felt she could confide in these two women who, though her half sisters, were still strangers to her. But, for the first time in her life, she didn't overanalyze the situation. It felt good to talk things over. ''He's…he's more difficult. He did see J.D. as a threat at first. You know, he thought, after the accident and Philip's death, that he had to be the man of the house, but then he's still a kid.'' She lifted her shoulders. ''As I said, it's complicated.''

''Look, there's something I want to ask each of you,''

Bliss said and nervously took a gulp of her iced tea. "I know this is odd, considering all that's happened, but I want you to think about it anyway. You both know that Mason and I are getting married. It's going to be a small wedding down here and I thought it would be nice if the two of you would stand up for me."

Oh, God. Tiffany didn't know what to say. Yes, she felt closer to these two women than she'd expected, but she wasn't convinced that it would last. One confidence shared over lunch wasn't a commitment of friendship or sister-hood. Or was it?

"Well, sure." Katie's eyes sparkled at the thought. "Why not?"

A thousand reasons why not! Tiffany looked away. "I...I don't know."

"I don't need an answer immediately," Bliss said. "And I understand why you might have reservations. As I said before, you need your own space, but I would love it if you would do this for me."

"Don't you have friends who would want to be in your wedding?"

"I suppose. But now I've got two sisters. Well, half sisters. And even though I'm not crazy about what Dad did and I hate to think of how my mother must have felt, I think it's time to move on, not dwell on the past, and look to the future. I always wanted sisters...or brothers, for that matter...and now that I know about you two, well, it only seemed right."

"John didn't put you up to this?" Tiffany asked, still not trusting the man who had sired her.

"He doesn't even know about it. Neither does Mason. This is all my decision."

"Well, count me in." Katie finished her drink in one long swallow.

Tiffany felt cornered. If she didn't agree, she'd appear headstrong and one-sided, when the truth was she didn't know how she felt about her half sisters. Some of her anger had dissipated over the past few weeks. But, on the other hand, if she jumped on this bandwagon she might not be able to jump off, and she didn't want to appear weak. "I'll think about it," she said, but then remembered her own wedding day—how she would have loved to have sisters in attendance, or even a father to give her away.

"Do. Just let me know in a couple of weeks."

"I will," Tiffany promised. Could she do it? Accept this olive branch that Bliss was offering?

"Good."

"It'll be a blast!" Katie predicted.

The waitress came with the check and before the others picked it up, Bliss snagged the bill. "This one's on Dad."

"What?" Tiffany's head snapped up.

"He insisted."

"No way. I can pay my share," Tiffany said. She wasn't about to take any charity from John Cawthorne. No way. No how.

"Fine with me." Katie tossed her napkin onto the table. "I've got to run anyway."

"But—"

"Let him pick up the damned tab," Katie said as she slung the strap of her purse over her shoulder. "The way I figure it, it's the least he can do."

Bliss nodded. "You don't have to love him, Tiffany. You don't even have to like him. But let him buy you lunch."

"Fine." Tiffany wasn't sure she liked the idea, but she had more important things to worry about. J.D. and Stephen were at the top of the list.

At the small table in his room, J.D. reread for the thousandth time the deed and the note his brother had signed.

The contract was ironclad. Aside from a few thousand dollars' equity, Santini Brothers owned this apartment house lock, stock and barrel. And unless Carlo could be convinced to sell the place, Tiffany couldn't do anything about it.

So much for her independence.

So what are you going to do about it? he asked himself and felt remorse tear at his soul. He'd made love to her. His brother's wife. True, Philip was dead, Tiffany was a free woman, and yet J.D. didn't feel right about what had happened.

Yeah, but you planned her seduction. You took her and the bottle of wine to the Zalinski place for the express purpose of making love to her.

His jaw tightened and he saw his reflection in the window. Alone in the house, his bags packed, he had time to think, time for recriminations, time to realize that, like it or not, he was in love with his brother's widow. "Hell," he ground out and reached for the telephone. The room was hot. Stuffy. The heat of late afternoon setting in after a long day. He punched out a number he knew by heart, waited until his father had answered and said, "Hi. It's me, Dad."

"Jay. How's it going?"

"I want out." No reason to beat around the bush.

His father's silence was condemning. "You're kidding."

"No joke."

"You've hardly been in the job six months."

"I know, but it's not working."

"Why?"

"A dozen reasons. I should never have taken the job in the first place." He waited a second and softened his voice. "I'm not Philip, Dad."

"You're telling me." Was there a hint of disgust in the old man's voice? J.D. really didn't care. He couldn't be a part of Santini Brothers as long as his father insisted on pulling everyone's strings.

"Listen, Dad, I'm driving to Portland tomorrow. I'm selling my stock, my boat, my bike and my condo and I'm paying off Philip's debts to the company."

"But why—"

"Tiffany needs this place. Her kids need it. I want her to own it free and clear."

"I'm not trying to push my grandkids out of a home," Carlo said. "I just want them closer."

"Forget it. This is their home. Now, I'm paying off the debt and you're accepting it, or we're going to court."

"Always the lawyer."

"Always." J.D. wasn't taking no for an answer.

"You don't have to do this."

"Of course I do, Dad."

"She's got her claws into you."

"Big time."

Carlo sighed. "I don't know what's going on down there, son, but if that woman's turned your head around—"

"What? You'll what?" J.D. demanded. "Find a way to tie her up financially even more than she is? Strap her so that she'll be forced to move closer to you and Mom?"

"Would it be so bad?"

"Yeah, Dad, I think it would. She's her own woman. Independent and tough. She's dealing with her own problems and seeming to get by without any of our interference. The least you could do—*we* could do—is have a little faith."

"But—"

"Draw up the necessary papers. I'll see you tomorrow.

Goodbye.'' J.D. clicked off and half expected his father to call back and the phone to jangle insistently. Thankfully it didn't. J.D. opened the window a crack to let in the evening breeze that was turning the leaves of the tree next to the house. Along with a breath of cool air came the sound of voices, young voices, drifting up from somewhere near the carriage house.

"I mean it, Santini, if you breathe a word of this to anyone, you're dead meat."

J.D. looked into the yard and saw Stephen and another boy, one who looked a little older than he, standing on the asphalt beneath the new basketball hoop.

"I'm not sayin' nothing to no one."

"You'd better not. We had a deal."

"I know, Miles."

So the scruffy-looking kid with the two-toned blond hair and bad complexion was the infamous Miles Dean. He didn't look all that intimidating; in fact, truth to tell, he seemed more frightened than tough.

"Yeah, well, you already screwed up once."

"It...it was an accident."

"You were hiding the keys from me, you little freak. If you woulda given 'em to me like you said you would, then the cops wouldn't have found 'em."

"If you wouldn't have started hitting me, the cops never would have come."

Miles's eyes slitted and he took a step toward Stephen. "Just don't do it again. Stick to the story. You know what'll happen if you mess up again."

J.D. had heard enough. He was on his feet, hopped over his duffel bag that was packed near the door, and was down the two flights of stairs in an instant. He flung himself out the back door and across the lawn before the two boys knew what was happening. At the sight of him, Miles started walking away.

"Not so fast," J.D. said, reaching the older boy and taking hold of his arm.

"Let go of me."

"Not yet." J.D. wasn't going to be intimidated.

"Leave him alone," Stephen ordered, his eyes wide.

"Not just yet." But J.D. abandoned his grip and placed both hands on his hips. "I overheard part of your conversation."

There was stunned silence. Mosquitoes whined around them as the heat of the day began to recede.

"You shouldn't threaten people," J.D. said.

"Crap!" Miles muttered.

"Now why don't you tell me what's going on. What do you know about Isaac Wells's disappearance?"

"I don't know nothin'," Miles spat out.

"No? Then why all the scare tactics while you tried to intimidate Stephen here?" He hooked a thumb at his nephew, who was as pale as death and sweating like he'd just run a marathon.

"I don't know what you're talkin' about!" Miles sneered.

"No? Then let's find out. We'll go down to the police station together. Call your mother, see what she has to say."

"You can't."

"Just watch me."

"No, don't!" Stephen insisted.

"Why not?"

"Because—because—" Stephen looked to Miles for support, and in that instant, Miles jerked his arm free and ran. Like a fox being chased by hounds, he vaulted the fence and took off through the neighboring yards. J.D. had half a notion to run after him, but decided the kid wouldn't get far on foot.

"You shouldn't have done that," Stephen said. "This has nothing to do with you."

"Of course it does," J.D. countered, turning to face his nephew. "Because you're involved."

"So?"

J.D. eyed the boy. "I care."

Stephen snorted. "You're not my dad."

Needle-sharp pain seared J.D.'s brain.

"Just because Chrissie thinks you're hot stuff, doesn't mean I have to." Stephen was on a roll and all his fears came tumbling out. "I've seen you and Mom, you know. Seen you together, and Christina's just a little kid. What does she know, huh? She was messed up when Dad died, started having all those nightmares and now…now, just 'cause you're here, that seems to be over, but they'll come back. Just as soon as you leave." His eyes flashed a blue challenge and J.D. inwardly cringed. The kid might be right. Christina had seemed to attach to him and if he left—no, *when* he left, which was going to be tomorrow morning—the little girl would be disappointed.

Or devastated. Maybe worse than she was when you arrived down here, Santini. Boy, have you made a mess of things. The worst part of it was that, he, too, would feel the pain of separation, he'd started to think not only of Christina as his little girl, but of Stephen as his son.

"I'm your uncle, Stephen. I care."

"Yeah, right."

"It's true."

Stephen's jaw worked. He stood his ground, his fists clenched, his nostrils flared, more bravado than conviction straightening his spine.

"Now, why don't you tell me about Isaac Wells."

"Nothin' to tell."

J.D. caught his arm. "Just start at the beginning. And this time, no lies."

"Let go of me!" Stephen said, immediately defensive.

J.D. released his grip. "I just don't want you to run off like your friend."

"Miles Dean isn't my friend."

That was one for the good guys.

"That's a start. Tell me about Isaac Wells and his car keys."

"I can't." Stephen shook his head and his skin turned the color of chalk.

"Sure you can."

"Oh, gosh," Stephen said, chewing on his lower lip anxiously. "You—you don't understand."

"Try me."

Stephen blinked rapidly. "Miles will kill me."

"He's not going to kill anyone."

"You don't know him. Or...or his dad."

"Ray Dean?" J.D.'s ears pricked up. "What about him?"

"He's back in town and he's...mean."

"Either talk to me or to the police." J.D. felt sorry for the kid. Obviously he was in big trouble, wedged between the proverbial rock and a hard place, but J.D. couldn't help him if he didn't know the truth.

"I *can't.*"

"Why not?"

Stephen hesitated. He rubbed one elbow with his other hand and nearly jumped out of his skin when Charcoal galloped out from under the porch. "Oh, God."

"Whatever it is, it can't be that bad."

Stephen looked over his shoulder and his eyes were

wide with fear. "You don't understand. If I say anything to you, or to the police...they'll hurt Mom and Chrissie."

J.D. saw red. "Who?" he demanded. "Who'll hurt them?"

"No one." The poor kid's voice cracked on the lie as he tried to backtrack, but J.D. grabbed his shoulders and shook him.

"Listen to me, Stephen. No matter what you're involved in, no matter what happened, I'm going to help you. You got that?" When the boy didn't answer, but just looked at the ground, J.D. shook him again. *"You got that?"*

"Yeah." Stephen nodded.

"Okay. So what's going on? Who's threatening to hurt your mother and sister?"

Stephen swallowed hard. His lips were chalk white. "It's Miles," he said. "Miles and his dad."

"So Ray's involved."

"No...yes... Oh, man..." Stephen shoved his hair from his eyes. "He's...he's been in jail before and he...he's the one who wanted Mr. Wells's keys."

"Why?" he asked, turning the information over in his head.

Stephen shook his head. "I dunno. He heard I stole the keys once and drove one of the cars. Miles told him and then Miles dared me to do it again and bring him the car and keys, but I didn't. I messed up, stole the keys but didn't get the car and...and... Well...I decided I couldn't be a part of whatever it was, so I didn't turn over the keys. I thought I'd get rid of 'em, but then Mr. Wells disappeared and..."

"And what?" J.D. demanded. The kid couldn't clam up on him now.

"I...I just hid 'em. Miles got real mad. Beat me up. Told me he and his dad were going to hurt Mom and

Chrissie if I didn't give 'em the keys, and then the police came and…and I got in big trouble.''

J.D. held Stephen at arm's length and looked him straight in the eye. He felt a connection with this boy, his brother's son, who was so much like him. ''Well, Stephen,'' he said, his jaw rock-hard, ''I think it's time to get you out.''

Carrying a sleeping Christina, Tiffany tried to open the back door, but it was locked.

''What in the world?'' she wondered, balancing her daughter as she fumbled in her purse, fishing for her keys. Stephen should have been home hours ago and J.D. was normally around at this time in the evening. She glanced around the driveway and noticed that his Jeep wasn't in its usual spot.

Good.

Then she wouldn't have to deal with him.

A part of her ached to be with him, to relive the lovemaking they'd shared, and yet she still needed time to think, to sort things out.

Christina yawned and opened her eyes.

''We're home, sweetie,'' Tiffany said as she found the key and managed to unlock the door. ''Stephen?'' she called, but no one answered. ''Great.'' She glanced at the table and saw no note, but didn't panic. Not yet.

''Let's get you upstairs and into bed,'' she told her daughter, and for once the little girl didn't protest. Within twenty minutes Christina was washed and tucked into her bed, snoring softly and sucking her thumb as Tiffany turned out the lights.

The house seemed empty without her son.

And without J.D.

She walked outside where evening had settled and down

the flight of steps to Mrs. Ellingsworth's apartment. The door opened after the first rap of her knuckles against the panels. Curlers were wound through the older woman's gray hair and her face, devoid of any makeup, appeared older than usual. "Sorry to bother you, but I was looking for Stephen."

"Isn't he here?" Ellie frowned thoughtfully.

"Not that I can tell."

"Well, he was. He and that other boy—you know the one I mean, the hooligan—well, he looks like one—"

"Miles Dean." Tiffany's heart nearly stopped. There was more trouble simmering in the summer night. She could feel it.

"The older Dean boy, if that's the one," Ellie said, nodding. "Never can keep those two straight. Anyway, he and Stephen were here earlier. I saw them through the kitchen window." She pointed to the window in question. Though her unit was on the lowest level of the house, it still got natural light as the lot sloped sharply on the north side.

Tiffany tried to forestall an inevitable feeling of dread. "Thanks."

"Don't mention it. Oh—" She snapped her fingers. "Did you ask J.D. where Stephen went?"

"He's not here, either."

"Isn't he? Funny, I thought I heard his Jeep earlier. Oh, well." They chatted for a few minutes more, then said good-night. Tiffany, lost in thought and worry, walked up the steps and was rounding the corner to the backyard when she caught sight of Luke Gates locking the door to his upper-story unit of the carriage house.

He offered her a slight smile. "Evenin'."

"Hi, Luke," she said and then asked, "Have you seen Stephen anywhere?"

Luke gave a curt nod. "Earlier. With J.D. and that scruffy-lookin' friend of his."

"Miles?" What did J.D. have to do with it? Worry set her teeth on edge.

"Don't know his name." Luke flashed her a crooked smile. "I just caught a glimpse of them earlier, then heard a truck or some kind of rig pull out. Thought it was probably J.D.'s Jeep."

"Thanks."

"Anytime."

As Luke climbed into his old truck, Tiffany headed back to the house. What was going on? She felt a dread, as cold as a north wind, cut through her soul as she walked up the stairs, checked on a sleeping Christina, then made her way to Stephen's room.

It was cleaner than usual, thanks to his efforts during the period when he'd been grounded, but she found no hint in the scattered CDs and magazines as to where he'd gone. *He's probably with J.D. He'll be all right,* Tiffany tried to convince herself as she ran her finger over the top shelf of his bookcase and noticed the little car he'd fashioned from wood and entered a race with years ago when Philip had been alive. *But Miles Dean is involved and that spells trouble. Trouble with a capital* T.

Having found no clues to Stephen's whereabouts, she left his room and hesitated in the hallway. The door to the third floor had been left open, was slightly ajar. Beckoning. Though she felt a sense of guilt for invading J.D.'s privacy, she mounted the stairs to the loft tucked under the eaves.

She took one step into his room, turned on the lights and tensed when she saw his duffel bag, fully packed, standing ready near the door. He was leaving. Just like that. After they'd made love.

Though she'd known it would happen, had tried to prepare herself, a part of her withered in pain. Why had she expected anything different? He was just a man, and like most of the men in her life, he was leaving her.

Don't dwell on it. Buck up.

But the dull ache around her heart only increased. She walked to the window to look through the branches of the night-darkened tree when she noticed his briefcase, open, and a document spread upon the table.

Don't look at it.

But she saw her name—and Philip's—on the contract.

The contract?

With trembling fingers she picked up the pages and read each of the pages. Slowly, as she sifted through the legalese, she understood the reason why J. D. Santini had come to Bittersweet. It wasn't just to buy a winery. It wasn't to see his niece and nephew. It wasn't to check on her. No, the reason he'd shown his face down here and rented an apartment from her was because he was checking out his father's investment in this house, this Victorian manor she'd called home. Her heaven.

Only it wasn't hers.

Santini Brothers owned the lion's share of it. Philip had signed away most of what she had assumed was her equity. Nothing much was left.

And it had been J.D.'s job to come and give her the news. Only he'd chickened out.

Tears burned behind her eyes. Betrayal raged through her soul. How had she trusted him? Believed in him? Made love to him?

Because you're a fool for that man. You always have been and you always will be.

Her knees turned to jelly and she sagged against the table. The first tears began to rain from her eyes and she heard the sound of an engine. Swallowing hard, she looked out the window and braced herself as J.D.'s Jeep came into view. Her fingers curled over the damning papers and she forced her leaden legs to move. It was time to have it out, once and for all.

Chapter Twelve

"Who do you think you are?" Tiffany flew across the dry grass like an avenging angel. Her eyes were as bright as twenty-four-karat gold, her face flushed, her beautiful lips compressed into a furious pout, her black hair streaming behind her. In one hand she had papers, legal papers, clutched into a wad.

J.D.'s stomach tightened. Every muscle in his body tensed as he climbed out of the Jeep. He knew why she was furious. Stephen didn't.

"Mom—"

"Go into the house, Stephen," she ordered.

"But—"

"You heard me!" So angry she was shaking, she stopped at the Jeep's fender. Her eyes, luminous and burning with wrath, focused on J.D. "Your uncle and I have something important to discuss."

"We took care of it," Stephen said.

"You what?" Her perfectly arched eyebrows drew together.

"At the police station—"

"She's not talking about the Isaac Wells case," J.D. clarified.

Tiffany stumbled backward a step. "Isaac Wells? Police?" She looked at her son for the first time. "What are you talking about?"

"What are *you* talking about?" Stephen asked.

"I think we'd all better sit down." J.D. reached for Tiffany's arm because she looked as if she might fall over, but she recoiled as if the mere thought of his touch sickened her.

"Just tell me what's going on."

"Stephen had a long talk with Sergeant Pearson down at the police station."

"Oh, God—" Her voice failed her. She blinked and clasped a hand to her chest. The papers—the damning deed and note—fluttered to the ground, suddenly forgotten.

"It's all right, Mom," Stephen said.

"All right?"

"Stephen explained what's happening. Why he's been acting the way he has, what the deal was with old Isaac's keys," J.D. told her as he reached down for the note and deed. Folding them together, he added, "I'd venture to guess that right about now, Ray Dean and his son Miles are being questioned."

"Ray Dean?" she repeated. "What's he got to do with anything?" She licked her lips. "I knew he had been released but…is he involved in this?"

"It looks that way."

"Oh, Lord." Her legs seemed to wobble again.

J.D. reached for her arm and this time she didn't back away. He helped her into the kitchen and noticed how homey the room appeared with its hanging pots, fragrant herbs, and children's artwork on display. He'd miss this place, he realized, feeling a pang of regret. He'd miss the house, the kids and Tiffany. God, how he'd miss her.

"Tell your mother everything you told the police and me," J.D. said, once Tiffany and Stephen were seated at the table. He poured her a glass of water, which she ignored, and he wished there was something, anything he could do to erase her pain. Though she was relieved that her son was only a minor player in the drama unfolding around Isaac Wells's disappearance, he was involved nonetheless.

"So…so Miles told me if I didn't do what he said and get him the keys and the car, his old man would hurt you, Mom. You and Chrissie." Tears filled Stephen's eyes and he looked more boy than man at the moment. Tiffany couldn't bear to see his pain. "I thought I should try to protect you."

"Oh, honey, you didn't have to—"

"Yeah, Mom, I did. Dad wasn't around, so who was going to take care of you?"

Her heart swelled and she got up from her chair, pulled her son to his feet and embraced him. Tears ran down her face and she felt his frightened sobs against her shoulder. "You don't ever have to worry about taking care of me, Stephen. I'm the one who does the taking-care-of around here. It's my job. It's what I want to do." She stared at J.D. over her son's shoulder. "I'm in charge, honey," she whispered, kissing Stephen's temple and feeling the scratch of new whiskers against her chin.

"I don't think you'll have to worry," J.D. said. Leaning against the counter, his long legs stretched in front of him, his hands at his sides supporting his weight against the counter's edge, he looked damnably sexy, but Tiffany told herself she was immune. Never again would he get to her. "The police have zeroed in on the Deans. No one knows for sure what's happening with Isaac Wells yet, but it's only a matter of time. I called Jarrod Smith and he's working on the case independently. My guess is that the old man will turn up in a few days.''

"You think Ray Dean's held him hostage?"

"Possibly."

"But you're not sure?"

"Not yet." He pushed himself upright. "The important thing is Stephen is out of it. His testimony will lead the police in the right direction. Pearson called his juvenile counselor and in light of the situation—that he was coerced, but then came clean—the local authorities will talk to a judge and expunge any charges, no matter how minor, against Stephen.''

Tiffany's heart lightened. "That's the best news I've heard in weeks."

"J.D. did it," Stephen said with something akin to awe for his uncle in his voice. "He's the one that insisted I get a break because of all this."

"Is that right?" She looked at the man before her with new eyes.

"I have taken my share of criminal law," he admitted, "though it was a long time ago."

"I guess I owe you a debt of thanks."

"Do you?" He pulled the wrinkled documents from his pocket and she stiffened. The note.

"Listen, honey, why don't you go up to your room?" Tiffany said to her son. "Uncle Jay and I have something to discuss."

"What?" Stephen demanded, looking from one to the other. "What?"

"It's personal," Tiffany said. "I'll explain later."

Stephen hesitated, but J.D. nodded. "Go on up. This'll only take a minute or two."

Not certain, Stephen started for the swinging doors. He paused just as he reached them, then studied the floor for a few seconds. "Does this have anything to do with me?"

"No!" they said in unison.

Stephen managed a thin smile. "Good. I thought maybe I was in trouble again." He disappeared through the doors and Tiffany heard his footsteps on the stairs. A few seconds later he'd tuned up his guitar and notes were wafting through the floorboards.

"I should tell him not to wake Christina," she said, but decided it wasn't the time. Instead, she turned and faced the man she loved, the man who had taught her that it was all right to be done with grieving, the man who had used her so callously.

"What's going on?" she demanded.

"It's simple. I came to Bittersweet to tell you that you don't own the house, that Santini Brothers do. They bought Philip out to cover his gambling debts."

Pain burned through her soul.

"So I'm tossed out? Me and the children?"

"Nope." He tore the deed and note in half, then half again. "It's forgiven."

"What?"

"The debt. It's been taken care of."

"How?"

"My father's had a change of heart," he said, still shredding the documents and letting the small confetti-like pieces fall to the floor.

"You paid him."

He didn't answer.

"You didn't have to, you know. I would have taken care of it." She should have been offended but found the gesture somehow comforting. Maybe their relationship wasn't for naught. "I'll pay you back."

"Don't worry about it."

"I said I'll pay you."

"Drop it, Tiffany. You and the kids, you're part of the family."

"Don't lie to me, Jay. It belittles us both. I never have nor will I ever be part of the Santini clan. That was your father's choice. Not mine."

His jaw worked. "I said, things have changed."

She didn't believe him, but changed the subject to the worry that had been gnawing at her for the past hour. "You're leaving, aren't you?" Her voice was barely a whisper.

"In the morning."

"Nice, Jay." She couldn't hide her disappointment. How would she live without him? These past few weeks had been glorious torments, a kind of bittersweet pleasure that she would miss. As she would miss him. She looked at him and wondered if she'd ever be blessed with his smile again, ever feel his lips on hers, ever quiver at his touch. *Oh, foolish, foolish woman. Pull yourself together. He doesn't care about you. Never has. Never will. Your love for him is a joke.*

"And when were you going to tell me about the deed?" she demanded, chasing away her painful thought of love or the lack of it. "Or were you going to wait until Carlo decided to evict me?"

"That's not happening." He was firm.

"Isn't it? Then why all the secrecy? Why didn't you tell me the truth?" she demanded, walking closer to him, stopping only when the toes of her sandals brushed the tips of his boots.

His jaw slid to the side and he stared at her with an intensity that stole the breath from her lungs. "Why?" he countered. "You want the truth?"

"Absolutely."

His mouth tightened at the corners and his eyes took on the color of midnight. "Because, lady, from the moment I set my eyes on you again, I knew that I was lost."

"'Lost'?" What was he saying? The room was suddenly hot. Way too hot.

"That's right, Tiffany." He pushed his head forward, bending so that his nose was a hair's breadth from hers, so close that his clean male scent enveloped her. "The second you climbed out of your car the first day I was here, it was all over for me."

"I—I don't understand."

"I'm trying to tell you that I fell in love with you, dammit."

"In love with me?" Could she believe it? No way. Her insipid heart took flight.

"That's right."

For a heartbeat there was silence. Hot, condemning silence. She swallowed hard. *Love? J.D. loved her?*

"I don't know what to say."

He straightened and a look of weary defeat gathered in his eyes. "You don't have to say anything, Tiff." Shaking his head he started past her, but she reached out and grabbed the crook of his elbow.

"Wait."

Beneath her fingers, his muscles tensed. He looked at her over one muscular shoulder with eyes that reflected a pain that tore at his very soul. "For what?"

"Me," she whispered, swallowing the lump forming in her throat. "Wait for me."

He closed his eyes.

"I love you, too, Jay." Tears spilled over at the admission. "I...I have for a long, long time."

For a second he didn't move and then his eyes flew

open, he grabbed her and kissed her hard on the lips. Her arms wound around his neck and his circled her waist. They clung to each other as if they'd been separated for years, star-crossed lovers who had at last rediscovered each other.

When finally his head lifted from hers, he cracked a smile. "So?"

"So marry me, Santini," she said with a low chuckle. "Make an honest woman of me."

"I don't know if that's possible."

Tossing her head back, she giggled. "Try me."

"All right. You're on. We'll drive to Portland tomorrow, find a justice of the peace and be married in the afternoon."

"No way. I did the quickie marriage before. This time we're going all out. My son's going to give me away. My daughter's going to be the flower girl and my sisters..." She surprised herself. "My sisters will be there."

"What about your father?"

A cloud crossed Tiffany's mind and her heart squeezed in the same painful manner it had for all of her lonely life, but she decided it was time for a new beginning. Time to bury all her pain. "He'll be invited. To be a guest, nothing more. If he shows up, fine."

"And if he doesn't?"

"His loss."

J.D. placed a kiss on her forehead. "Are you sure about this?" he asked.

"As sure as of anything I've ever done."

"We still could lose the house. Dad might not approve."

"Then we'll move, won't we?" She felt lightheaded, freed of the blackness that had shrouded her for so long. "But what about your job?"

"Already quit." He regarded her with twinkling eyes. "You know, I think there're some ambulances down here just dying to be chased."

"No doubt."

"Besides which, I'm not destitute, you know."

"No?"

"No. But we do have one more obstacle to overcome."

"What's that?"

"I want to adopt the kids."

"But you're already their uncle."

"I know." A dimple showed in his cheek. "But when they're ready, I want them to think of me as their father."

"Do you think that'll happen?" she asked skeptically.

He twirled her off her feet. "Haven't I been telling you all along that anything's possible?"

"That you have, J.D.," she admitted.

"Then, for once, Tiff, trust me."

"I do," she promised, and he kissed her as if he would never stop.

Epilogue

Two weeks later Tiffany twirled in front of the mirror. The blue silk dress swirled around her like a cloud. "It's beautiful," she said, turning to face her half sisters.

"Yep. Looks great." Katie, dressed in an identical gown, agreed.

"Good." Bliss flopped into a chair at the dressmaker's shop where she had ordered not only her wedding dress but the two bridesmaid's gowns, as well.

Tiffany felt a sense of family. She and J.D. were going to marry, her half sisters and she were discovering each other, and her kids, finally, had settled down. Under J.D.'s influence, Stephen seemed to be trying to walk the straight and narrow and Christina was on cloud nine.

"Okay," Bliss said, "let's get out of here. I'll buy you both a soda."

"I think we deserve gin and tonics after this ordeal,"

Katie teased as she peeled off her dress and handed it, along with the marked hem to Betty, the shop owner.

"Well, how about a glass of Chablis instead?"

"You're on!"

They changed and walked outside where the afternoon sun was glistening overhead. The streets of Bittersweet were shaded on this edge of town, the traffic slow.

"I can't believe that both of you are getting married," Katie said with a sigh as they walked to Bliss's Mustang convertible which was parked in the shade of a giant oak tree. The top was down and Bliss's dog, Oscar, a golden mutt of about twenty pounds, gave out an excited yip and, at Bliss's command, hopped into the back seat.

"You'll be next," Bliss predicted as she slid behind the wheel. Katie climbed into the back and petted the dog while Tiffany took her place in the passenger seat.

"No way. I've got too much to do before I get married."

"Such as?" With a flick of her wrist Bliss turned on the ignition. The sporty car roared to life.

"Such as finding out the story behind Ray Dean and Isaac Wells."

"Can't you leave it to the police?" Tiffany asked as Bliss pulled out of the parking lot.

"And miss the scoop of a lifetime? No way."

Wind breezed through their hair as they drove. Tiffany leaned back and smiled. Life was definitely improving.

"So, what've you learned about your newest tenant?" Katie asked.

"Luke? Not much. He keeps to himself."

"I wonder why?"

"Why don't you ask him?" Tiffany asked.

"I just might." Katie laughed, the sound tinkling and

light over the growl of the engine, and Tiffany smiled as her house came into view. In a grand gesture, as an early wedding gift, her father-in-law had given her the title to the house. He had refused payment from J.D. and was desperately trying to wheedle his son back into the Santini Brothers fold. But J.D. was determined to hang his shingle in Bittersweet.

"Mommy!" Christina flew out the front door as Bliss pulled into the drive. J.D. was on her heels. His limp had all but disappeared, and his eyes glittered mischievously. Oscar hopped out of the car and washed the little girl's face with his long tongue. Christina giggled with delight.

As Tiffany climbed from her seat, J.D. held the door open for her. "Glad you're home."

"Are you? Gee, and I thought you loved baby-sitting," she teased.

"I do."

At that moment Luke Gates's dilapidated pickup pulled into the drive. He parked and slowly stretched his way out of the cab. "Here's your chance," Bliss said to Katie in a stage whisper, and the younger woman grinned widely.

"You're right." She climbed out of the car. "You know me," Katie said, straightening. "I'm not one to pass up an opportunity."

"What's this all about?" J.D. asked.

"It's a long story." Tiffany smiled as J.D. wrapped his arms around her and Katie crossed the lawn toward the tall Texan. "But don't be surprised if you read about it in the *Review*."

"Uh-oh. Katie's on to a hot story," J.D. guessed.

"She only hopes," Bliss said and Tiffany sighed contentedly, glad to be a part of this scattered, but loving, family.

Someday she might even forgive her father.
Someday.
For now, her focus was on loving J.D.

* * * * *

Don't miss Katie's story in
A FAMILY KIND OF WEDDING
by Lisa Jackson, coming in October 1999,
only from Silhouette Special Edition®.

Dear Reader,

I hope you enjoyed reading about Tiffany and J.D. Santini and their special family. The next book, *A Family Kind of Wedding*, is the story of Katie Kinkaid, Tiffany and Bliss's half-sister, and Luke Gates, the mysterious man who has come to Bittersweet, Oregon, with an agenda of his own, an agenda that involves Katie and her son, Josh.

What Luke doesn't expect is to face a dynamo of a woman whose curiosity and natural love of life leave him questioning his own values and motives. He's not the type to fall in love with restless, redheaded Katie, but then Katie has convinced herself she will never find the right man for her—especially not someone with a clouded past. She has too much to do what with her newfound half-sisters and Bittersweet's mystery of the century begging to be unravelled.

But fate has a way of intervening and along with trying to put her newfound family together, Katie has to deal with Luke and look herself in the mirror. How can this drifter, this man whose own dreams are so detrimental to her own, be the love of her life?

Happy Reading!
Lisa Jackson

♥™ SILHOUETTE
SPECIAL EDITION®
AVAILABLE FROM 20TH AUGUST

FATHER-TO-BE Laurie Paige

That's My Baby!

One night of passion with Hunter McLean was all it took for Celia Campbell to fall pregnant with his child. But was marrying for the baby's sake really the best solution for this unlikely couple?

THE PRESIDENT'S DAUGHTER Annette Broadrick

Nick Logan had been assigned to *protect* the President's daughter—not fall in love with her. Lovely Ashley Sullivan seemed to return his feelings. But Nick was torn between duty and desire…

PRINCE CHARMING, M.D. Susan Mallery

Prescription: Marriage

Nurse Dana Rowan had to admit surgeon Trevor MacAllister was gorgeous. But she swore to her colleagues she was immune to his charms. After all, only a fool would fall for the same man twice!

MEANT FOR EACH OTHER Ginna Gray

For Leah Albright, Dr Mike McCall was a life-saver because he'd helped prevent her brother's death. But were her feelings for Mike more than just gratitude? And was she ready to trust him with her family secret?

BABY STARTS THE WEDDING MARCH Amy Frazier

Dallas Parker and Julia Richardson had been friends since childhood. And when Julia couldn't face telling her parents she was pregnant— and single!—Dallas offered to pretend to be the baby's father.

UNTIL YOU Janis Reams Hudson

Strait-laced Anna Collins was not well pleased to be playing hostess to irritatingly attractive stranger Gavin Marshall. But she had no choice, Gavin held the clue to her missing brother's whereabouts…

Available at most branches of WH Smith, Tesco, Asda, Martins, RS McCall, Forbuoys, Borders, Easons, Volume One/James Thin and most good paperback bookshops

9908

AVAILABLE FROM 20TH AUGUST

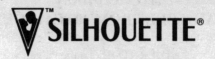

Intrigue
Danger, deception and desire

NEVER LET HER GO Gayle Wilson
A FATHER FOR HER BABY B. J. Daniels
REMEMBER ME, COWBOY Caroline Burnes
TWILIGHT PHANTASIES Maggie Shayne

Desire
Provocative, sensual love stories

A KNIGHT IN RUSTY ARMOUR Dixie Browning
THE BRIDE MEANS BUSINESS Anne Marie Winston
THIRTY-DAY FIANCÉ Leanne Banks
WILL AND THE HEADSTRONG FEMALE Marie Ferrarella
THE RE-ENLISTED GROOM Amy J. Fetzer
MIRANDA'S OUTLAW Katherine Garbera

Sensation
A thrilling mix of passion, adventure and drama

GABRIEL HAWK'S LADY Beverly Barton
SECONDHAND DAD Kayla Daniels
UNDERCOVER LOVER Kylie Brant
ROYAL'S CHILD Sharon Sala

9908

FREE!

4 Books

and a surprise gift!

We would like to take this opportunity to thank you for reading this Silhouette® book by offering you the chance to take FOUR more specially selected titles from the Special Edition™ series absolutely FREE! We're also making this offer to introduce you to the benefits of the Reader Service™—

- ★ FREE home delivery
- ★ FREE gifts and competitions
- ★ FREE monthly Newsletter
- ★ Books available before they're in the shops
- ★ Exclusive Reader Service discounts

Accepting these FREE books and gift places you under no obligation to buy; you may cancel at any time, even after receiving your free shipment. Simply complete your details below and return the entire page to the address below. *You don't even need a stamp!*

YES! Please send me 4 free Special Edition books and a surprise gift. I understand that unless you hear from me, I will receive 6 superb new titles every month for just £2.70 each, postage and packing free. I am under no obligation to purchase any books and may cancel my subscription at any time. The free books and gift will be mine to keep in any case.

E9EB

Ms/Mrs/Miss/Mr ....Initials ....
BLOCK CAPITALS PLEASE

Surname ....

Address ....

....

....Postcode ....

Send this whole page to:
THE READER SERVICE, FREEPOST CN81, CROYDON, CR9 3WZ
(Eire readers please send coupon to: P.O. Box 4546, KILCOCK, COUNTY KILDARE)

E1781

Sometimes bringing up baby
can bring surprises —and
showers of love! For the cutest
and cuddliest heroes and
heroines, choose the Special
Edition™ book marked

That's my
baby!